SHADOW OF THE FALLEN

Francis-Ray Jinks

CONTENTS

SHADOW OF THE FALLEN

CHAPTER 12

What do you say when you have used up all of the words?

You love somebody. You love each other. You come together, you marry. You are excited, entertained, devoted. You are at ease with one another. Too much at ease.

Their marriage had needed to develop, it had needed to be for something. Something other than each other, something other than each individual. They had needed a child. Suzanne was not going to go down that path. There was no momentum, no growth.

What do you say when you have used up all of the words? Their marriage had finally ended because he did not have the answer.

James Arthur sat alone in a diner seven miles East of Las Vegas. Tinted, floor to ceiling windows looked out onto the parking lot and the turn off to the highway. He had finished his breakfast and was nursing a second coffee. His work lay out there and he had little desire to begin. He thought of Suzanne and of the break-up. The divorce was seven months past and it no longer hurt. In a strange way, he liked to think about it, to try to make sense of it all. There had been little pain by the time of the divorce.

For the last two years they had been gliding down towards it. Married seven years, and at the end there was not enough to hold them together. There was enough love, he loved her now as then and she truly loved him though even now she did not believe it. She would have to go through a few relationships, he thought, she would have to put a few years on before she realised that she too, could not love more.

Suzanne was beautiful. Perfect skin, perfect face, perfect hair and a body that was to die for. She had worked very hard at keeping it that way. There had been no need. She could have grown fat and saggy and it would not have mattered to him which was the sort of thing that you said but, deep down, he knew the truth of it. He had never loved her for her appearance. It had led to the initial attraction and had been something of a bonus but he did not love it, he loved her. He had loved who she was and if only she had realised it too then they would be together still. Intellectually, she knew but, inside, she could not believe that anybody could really, really love her for herself. And there lay the reason for their separation, there and in two to twenty other things.

What do you say when you have used up all of the words? A thousand - ten thousand times he had said, "I love you." And at the end, and now, he still needed to say it but how can you say it after seven years when you have tried all of the other words? You want - need - to say it again but to say it in a new way, in a fresh way. To say it with all of the excitement and enthusiasm that you feel bubbling within you but also with truth and simplicity. I love you. There is no simpler way. There is no more adequate way.

He sipped the last, bitter dregs from his cup. An improbably long Silver Bullet '07 pulled off the highway and disappeared from his line of vision to the right. Unusually, it had three or four satellite dishes bolted onto its roof.

College had been good. He had never had any dates worth mentioning in high school and then suddenly in college he was surrounded by gorgeous, wonderful women a steady supply of whom would give him the blessing of their company. In bed too not that he had ever worked particularly hard at it. Mostly he had just let them talk themselves into it. To that day he was not sure why. He sensed that they saw him as a safe bet - or even pair of hands. A little freedom, a little walk on the sexual side and there he was. Last of all there had been Suzanne. College had been very good.

His safeness was one of the two to twenty reasons for their separation. No real ambition. He was not lazy, he worked as hard as any man but, in retrospect, there was nothing out there to really go that extra mile for. Life was very pleasant, work was something that you did to pay where you had to. A goodish degree from a reasonable University whilst he met some wonderful women and had a very pleasant time thank you. A degree in design realisation whatever the hell that was. He knew, of course, but secretly suspected that he did not. Not really. In reality, he was lacking in that simple quality of real direction. He might have spent years before he discovered that basic truth, as it was ten minutes with Grizelda the witch-queen had set him right on that.

Grizelda, also known as Gretchen the mother-in-law. Thankfully now an outlaw. He had never been good enough for Grizelda's little princess and perhaps she was right. That was another of the two to twenty. She had had nothing personally against him or his type. Some of her best friends might be gardeners or dog-walkers but one would hardly invite them to court the princess. James Going-nowhere-and-enjoying-the-ride Arthur was not a suitable match for her daughter. Still it had happened and he was not angry not after the first three or four years anyway.

Suzanne might have truly believed in her own beauty and value if she had ever stopped listening to her mother or, ironically, if she had listened enough to hear and believe in her mother's good opinion of her worth.

Still, he thought, we've all passed a lot of water since then. He waved his cup at the waitress who pointedly ignored him. She had the attitude of a woman who was not going to get up as early and as unwillingly as she had without making everybody in her path pay for it. It was the sort of pettiness which could have easily annoyed him had he not been too mature for that level of petulance. Besides, she had a big zit coming.

A man and a woman appeared to his right presumably from the silver bullet. The man reached the diner door first and held it open for the woman. He gave her a perfunctory smile as she passed, she ignored him. Married and under the cosh, thought

James. He and Suzanne had never managed to hate with quite that intensity, shame really. You can not beat a bit of real emotional passion. That was one of the two and twenty. Vertical toilet seats were in there too somewhere. The couple began to order a breakfast to go or rather the man began to order while the woman waited for him to get it wrong. James smiled wryly to himself, visualising a serious blow from a very large, foam hammer to his own head. Such cynicism in one so young and with such little sincerity.

The waitress began ostentatiously to write out his ticket. He was going to give her a big tip, he decided, just so that she could feel bad about ignoring him. That was his kind of vindictiveness: mess with her head but leave his own hands clean. The mental hammer began to reform in all its multi-foamed glory.

The couple sat down on the table between him and the door. They were not married he realised, suddenly. They had chosen a table and sat without a word in every imitation of the minimal or non-communication that only marriage or enforced confinement can achieve but their eyes were all wrong. There was something odd about the way that they failed to look at one another. Not that they were *not* looking at each other. Such avoidance was one of the finest flowerings of marital discord. No, it was something else. He was sure of it. In all of his sitting back and smelling the roses he had developed a keen sense of human observation. They could be brother and sister. Except that they did not look anything like it. She was auburn-haired, very pretty. He was tall, broad. Blonde haired and grey eyed and with a huge set of shoulders on him. He looked the type to have played college football. A running back for certain not the slippery, nimble type more the "You in my way. You not in my way." type. Good teeth, all in all the sort that's a real catch. Probably as thick as a two by -- er -- two. And why in hell am I looking at him? James mused. Peripherally, he knew that he was mere yards from one of the most gorgeous women in a life full of glorious women and yet he could not look at her. Christ, I must be on the turn, he thought without any real conviction.

For the briefest moment he had a mental image of how he must have looked to the couple as they sat at their table. James Arthur - ordinary face not unpleasant but neither did it bring words such as granite and sculpted to mind. Only his large, brown eyes and thick eyelashes managed to be striking about it. Brown was too non-descript a word for his liking. He preferred to think of them as a kind of chocolate - perhaps that was the source of his appeal to all those lonely college girls. Thickish, ordinary coloured hair. Ordinary body not fat, not thin more sort of ... ordinary. Decent clothes given a little straightening and tightening which he would undertake a minute before meeting the client and undo a minute afterwards, if he remembered.

The waitress sulked past him letting his ticket free-fall a foot or so above his table. Mesmerised, he watched it drop wondering how it was that a piece of paper could manage to float with such undiluted contempt. He began to search his pockets for money. Oh well, the life of a machine parts salesman beckons. James Arthur reaches thirty and turns gay, he smiled, Grizelda would have loved that. No mucky men lusting after her princess' purity. Not that he should mock - there are many wondrous things in life and a mother's love for her daughter has to be right up there. Right up there with the smell of wood shavings and that first mouthful of ice-cold water.

James Arthur, the repressed gay. That had to be it, why else would he sleep with so many women? Well six or seven was not too many. Maybe nine or ten not that it was a competition. Not that it mattered. Oh Suzanne, he thought with regret as he stood. I was put on this earth to love you, if only you had believed. So what now? Simply find the other one that I was put on this earth to love. I wonder what shape she might come in? Female would be decidedly good. Female would be good.

I love you. He stood transfixed, his eyes drawn irresistibly and inexplicably to those of the woman. She stared back at him completely uninhibited. It was one of those rare and powerful moments when amongst all of the social protocols two people really look at each other. No fear, no shame, connection. "Christ...," he heard himself mutter. She was gorgeous, drop dead, kick in the head gorgeous. Her hair was fine, beautifully cut - some haircuts are just stuck on to the head hers definitely framed her face. Rounded cheekbones, the lines of her jaw were finely drawn, a slightly elf-like chin. Her eyes were a warm, if unflinching, hazel. Despite the bulk of her coat and the fact that he was too busy feasting on her face to notice it anything more than peripherally he noted that her body was all where it ought to be and in the requisite quantities. None of the above mattered a jot, he thought, other than to take the breath away. It was her eyes and what lay beyond them. She smiled. He sat again - too heavily – forcing his chair back several inches. Her companion slipped out of his vision to the left. It was how she looked at him. Somehow, he knew that she saw everything in him and liked it. Here was somebody with whom there would be no communication difficulties here was someone who was completely open to him as he was to her. "Christ...." What on earth could he say when so much was being communicated? He began to lever his legs from beneath the table. He had to get over there.

"Drop it." The man had returned carrying two paper bags which, presumably, contained their breakfast. James managed to tear his gaze away from the woman but the man had not spoken to him. His words and whole attention were directed at the woman. James looked back at the woman who had already risen. To his utter amazement she was already leaving. He struggled to follow, his body feeling as if he was wearing it for a friend. By the time that he had cleared the table and felt confident enough in his direction to look up, the man was half out of the door and she followed drawn on invisible threads. She smiled,

"Just enjoy the moment," she said in a distinct but not unpleasant New York accent. And she was gone. He froze in complete incomprehension, how could she let it go like that? In all of life there could only ever be one or two moments when two humans could truly connect as they had and, even given that they were complete strangers, he could not understand how she could just walk away from it. From what might be. He began to walk forward pushing the door open. Outside, he came to an abrupt halt as the Silver Bullet revved past him. The first window that he saw was empty, she watched him from the second. She watched him as he watched her. A few seconds before the link was broken. He saw her regret, her sadness and knew with a certainty that he would come to doubt but which in that instant was absolute, that she was in that vehicle against her wishes.

The back set of wheels pulled on to the highway and the silver bullet disappeared eastward behind the diner.

"Hey you!" Bemused, he turned. The diner chef had followed him out. Panting, sweating and carrying a ten-inch cleaving knife. James' expression must have asked the question. "The bill, you fuck!"

"Sorry," he muttered and searched his pockets. The waitress stood in the doorway chewing non-existent gum, sneering. He handed a twenty over. "Sorry I forgot myself. Keep it all."

"Yeah," he snatched the money ungraciously, "and you'd better not forget it." He turned and walked the rolling walk of the truly hugely thighed back into the diner. The waitress turned with him as he entered and, James thought, if the world is to make any sort of sense, she said something to him that began with the words : "The noyve ..."

Screw it, thought James. For a moment he had glimpsed heaven and what was he left with? The back view of a fat, sweaty chef. Reality, that was what he was left with. Disconsolately, he walked back to his car. He climbed in started the engine and searched in the glove compartment for a mint. Back to reality.

Kaleph Machine Parts. West to Vegas. Not a bad job - considering. He had just fallen into it after Suzanne and it had taken him away from the West Coast to where he needed to be, away from Suzanne. The pay was crap but steady, not that he had anything to spend it on. He popped the mint into his mouth and switched the air - conditioning on. It was such a specialist field that the manufacturers did not really have anybody else to go to for the machine parts. If their needs changed Kaleph changed the specifications. There was no real hard sell. He was more of a courtesy caller than a salesman. He pulled the car out to the edge of the highway. It was just the job for James Going-nowhere Arthur. West to Vegas. He pulled out onto the Eastbound lane and floored the accelerator. How else would he ever know?

Part 1 The Godless Angel

CHAPTER 1

24 Selkirk Road,
Winnipeg,
Manitoba,
Canada,
The Earth.

Name: David Andrew Armitage
Age: 15 Years.
Occupation: Jerk.

The boy underlined the last word three times, screwed the sheet of paper up into a ball and threw it at the waste paper basket by the door. The projectile hit the basket's rim spun furiously above it and came to rest several inches behind it. David decided against picking it up and putting it in the basket. He leaned forward, resting his elbows on the desktop and stared out of his bedroom window at the Huskinson's back yard. Jerk.

Three or four years ago, writing his address as he had would have given it a ritualistic magic. It would have been as if it had said, "This is where I am - I'm here. I matter." But, with the wisdom of age fifteen, it merely said, "Jerk." Three or four years ago he might have mattered. He had believed then that all things were possible and that he could be whatever he wanted to be little realising that jerkdom lay ahead.

He ran his forefinger over the familiar outline of his Voyager model and wondered why it was that things never happened as he intended them to. How many times had he dreamed of the first time that he would talk to Terri Egan? How many little jokes had he rehearsed? Profound remarks? Countless times he had pictured himself rescuing her from the unwelcome advances of Roy Scotton and his leering cronies or from a drug-crazed, grenade-throwing terrorist and in the dreams he would always do the right thing. He would be so damned heroic. Heroic and - Hey! – Seriously calm. Not a fluster to be seen. Even his being wounded in the act of rescuing her would have been a thing of complete indifference to him (preferably a flesh wound to his right leg so that she could support him as they walked off into the sunset).

What would constitute a flesh wound? Blood but no pain? That would do - bloodied but not flustered. All right, so he was being a little far-fetched but then it was his daydream so it might as well be an idealised one. It was not as if he had been unprepared for the reality of their first meeting either. He had realised that it was far more likely to have been through bumping into each other in the corridor and he would have been ready for that too. "It's Terri isn't it?" he would say, smiling, "I've noticed you." Flattering, David thought, but not too corny and she would smile back taking his hand then together they would wander off into the sunset. The drug-crazed grenade-throwing terrorist would come later.

That was how it would be, that was how it should have been.

So today had been the day. Corridor C - on the way to biology - the place. David had been following her at a discrete distance - close enough to watch her but not so close that he could be seen to be watching her - and she had dropped her books.

He had swooped with all the speed and charitable intent of a hawk. He had needed to too, Terri's best friend, Josie, had got to most of the books before he could but, thankfully, not to all. He had risen triumphantly with her biology textbook ("Dissection for fun" Mickey called it) and one of the dark red maths notation books. Then it had happened, that first meeting of eyes, their first words to one another and what did he say? Which of the thousands of carefully honed first lines did he say? It was the moment that he had been preparing for for half a year and what did he say?

"There you go." he had said.

"Thanks." she had replied without looking up from her disarrayed books and they had carried on down the corridor. He had briefly considered a rapier-like,"That's OK." but his cheeks had begun to redden with the mother of all blushes. Fluster. Fluster. Fluster. The two girls had not even sneaked a look at him and giggled. Not even Josie - Josie Caffyn who giggled when Mr Ashburn could not get the class window to open first time. Josie Caffyn, the giggle-girl, five feet two and as silly as they came but then they got to be like that - dwarves.

Terri had not even noticed him and he could not blame her. "There you go." - jerk. It was just not fair. If he had had time then he would have chosen the best and most appropriate line rather than just the first thing that came into his mind. If her best friend had been Sara Dewes - six-foot and still growing - then he would have had more books to pick up and hence more time to think. As it was, what chance had he had against a dwarf?

Of all days, it would have to have happened today. If it had been a normal day then he could have followed it up tomorrow, perhaps he could make some sort of joke about her droppings. Perhaps not but at least he could have followed it up. A thing which was no longer possible, not with it being a Friday and with David and his family going on vacation on the Saturday. The memory of it hit him again, sickening him. He had stood alone in the middle of the corridor, a multitude of happier, worthier students flowing past him. He had felt like crawling to the wall and progressing from there. Seriously flustered. Unutterably flustered. Nobody had noticed him though, nobody ever did. This was it then. There was no point in going on. His life was not worth carrying on with. He considered how painless a method of suicide holding his breath would be before settling on an altogether more satisfactory alternative. He would commit suicide by eating unbearable amounts of chocolate.

David removed his glasses, wiped them with his cloth and placed them on the desktop. He stood, ruggedly thrusting his chair back and made towards the door. In the doorway he paused, checking that nobody could see him, then picked up the paper ball and placed it in the waste paper basket. For a moment David stood in the hallway to glower at its wallpaper and, more particularly, its pattern of faded psychedelic commas. The wallpaper had been there for as long as he could remember and it still stank.

Wearily, he thudded down the stairs.

David was a tall youth with corn-blonde hair, blue eyes and broad, well-formed shoulders. Shoulders whose development was matched neither by his back nor chest. He often thought of himself, contemptuously, as looking like an undernourished cardboard cut-out, which was fairly exaggerated, fairly cruel and not unfairly warranted. Thin or no, he was quite a handsome youth if he would but realise it. However, whenever he looked into a mirror he saw himself only in terms of what was not exactly hideous or what might be worse. It had not occurred to him that Terri Egan or other girls might be interested in him other than for his drug-crazed terrorist despatching capacities.

David had a few good friends whom he liked and was liked by. Quality rather quantity and though he could not number his friends in fifties, hundreds or even tens, he could count upon those that he did have. Their relative sparsity lay simply in the fact that he had no great need for more friends than he had. It was not that there were any great obstacles to his making friends - excepting his highly developed ability to merge with the wall, a talent which was so well perfected that never before had so many said so frequently, "Oh, were you there too?" of another. It would have gotten to him if he had let it and he did.

The stairway led into their lounge. David sprawled over one of its chairs and thumbed the "On" button of the television remote control. An ear-to-ear-teeth salesman flickered into life before him. He pressed the mute button.

From where he sprawled, David could see his mother bathing Paul through the open doorway of the bathroom. His mother was a great believer in openness within the family and in not locking the bathroom door (apart from when she was in there). She noticed David watching. "You could help me wash him if you want," she suggested, soapy water running up her arm.

"No - - it's all right, I think you can be trusted." He flicked channels for a while watching silent arguments, advertisements and conversations several of which appeared to be quite interesting but he knew that it would only spoil their appeal if he was to let the images speak. He watched, wondered why.

Baby Paul was hoisted out of the bath and onto a towel. Paul Armitage. P.A. and D.A. - parents could be so thoughtless. David had grown quite fond of his brother in the year and half since he had first been told if his impending arrival. At first, though, he had hated him with a quite vitriolic and, latterly, inexplicable passion. His hatred had long since lapsed though he could still remember the moment when he had first been let into his parent's "great joy". Of how his cheeks had burned and his mind had become a confusion of suppressed rage and frenetic possibilities. So, fourteen years after his birth, his parents were going to have a third child, he had thought and beneath all of his short-lived jealousies, the question that he had wanted to ask was: "Well what was wrong with me?" Followed, fairly distantly, by "Aren't you two too old to still be doing that sort of thing?"

A great deal had changed in David's life during that time: his elder sister, Susan, had left home for college in so doing, again radically altering his role within the family. He had been given more responsibility, less attention and, despite his initial dislike of the change, he had found that he preferred things to be so. No, David decided, when all things were considered, Paul was all right. He had not thought that he would miss Susan either but he had. Paul said Bysy-bysys before going to bed. Actually, it was his mother who had said "Bysy-bysy" and who had waggled Paul's chubby left upper appendage while Paul had stared disinterestedly at him. David, feeling bitter and world weary that night had waggled his right upper appendage and said, "Nighty-nighty floppy-dropples."

An almost interesting programme came on, David thumbed the sound button then instantly began to think back over his encounter with Terri and to worry, bloodily at his inadequacies.

Shortly, his mother returned having put Paul to bed. She paused at the foot of the stairs concern furrowing her brow. "Are you all right, David?" she asked, "- You seem to be worried over something."

"No." He shrugged, gave a weak smile and shook his head. Separately each gesture would have conveyed its own distinct meaning; undertaken simultaneously they simply confirmed his mother in her worries and made David feel giddy.

"It's just that - -" I'm being ripped apart inside, "well - I don't know what to do with myself."

"Have you packed everything?"

"I've packed everything and I'm not looking at another school book until we get back." She smiled and made towards the bathroom.

"Never mind then, you'll be busy enough tomorrow then."

"Sure- I know."

He had lied partly because he could not tell his mother about Terri but also because it had become such an instinctive part of their relationship since the advent of Paul - not the lying but the wish to reassure. It seemed to him that most of their contact would consist of her signalling concern or interest followed by him reassuring her as to the all-rightness of everything in his life and then her, duty having been discharged, returning to the more pressing demands that Paul made of her. In one, implied, detail he was wrong; his mother was rarely satisfied after their inconsequential talks together. She knew that her elder son had needs but Paul always seemed to be needing her and-having been fifteen herself, blasphemous though the notion would be to David - she was wary of being too overbearing during such a difficult time in his development. Paul was a good boy, even tempered, very like her much loved elder son had been as a baby, the problem was more hers' now. He was the child of "tired loins" - she had read it once somewhere. Read it and lived it.

"Are you looking forward to tomorrow?" she asked, her voice sounding metallic and lost because of the bathroom's acoustics.

"Yes." David replied. "- Yes." In recent years particularly, he had put aside many of his childhood pleasures but Lake Nipigen had still retained its appeal. He would enjoy seeing his Uncle Manny again and the fishing, the quiet.

His mother walked out of the bathroom a towel and bottle of Snoopy bubble bath under her arm. "I'm looking forward to it," she said smiling slightly." I think the change will do us all good."

"Mmm," agreed David swapping channels.

CHAPTER 2

He hovered for an instant then swooped gathering pace and upthrust as he bore down on the pale, brown soil then up, altering the angle of his wings so that he soared upward using the speed of his descent to gain height. Quickly, he reached the peak of his ascent and spread his wings more fully, grasping the air and letting himself glide, gradually losing height until he reached another updraft.

A building appeared before him. It looked something like a windmill though derelict and, instinctively, he began to flap his wings, pushing down on the air until he had gained enough height to land upon the beams that jutted out from its upper, stone, limit and which would serve as a balcony. He landed perfectly, using the building's slight updraft so that when he closed his wings his feet had little more than a few inches to fall onto the wood. He paused for a few minutes on the platform letting the wind tease at his feathers but not yet reaching out to its seductive pull. It was not necessary to fly. He was high enough and the wind blew strong enough to keep him mindful of flight itself but, most importantly, he knew that he could fly if he wanted to and that if he was to fall from his perch, he would merely rise again. He knew that he could fly, that he had that power over all men.

What the hell, why waste it? He stepped off the balcony, fell for several feet before his wings righted themselves – and soared.

"Come on David."

"Mmm?" He woke slowly, reluctantly. "What time is it?" he asked but his mother had already gone. Bleary-eyed he looked towards his alarm clock then clumsily picked it up from his bedside table and held it before his eyes until they had adapted to his waking.

Half past five. He swore to himself and sank beneath his blankets. For a few moments he tried to sleep again and to return to his delicious dream but it was a wasted effort. He knew that he could not sleep on and, besides, the images that flickered beyond his consciousness were not of flight.

Nevertheless, he concentrated on the dream remembering every detail, every second of it. The dream was far too precious to let any part of it go. He wanted to remember what it was to fly and to cherish every exhilarating sensation.

His mother's head appeared from behind the door. "Come on, David," she repeated with an anxious look and disappeared again. David hauled himself out of bed and surrendered to the urgent necessity of a yawn. Lake Nipigen today, he thought and was cheered by the prospect before remembering his meeting with Terri and the slight pleasure that he had felt took on the consistency and weight of leaden worry in his stomach. Yet, even so, he no longer felt as bad about it as he had - it was not as if he had made a fool of himself - and, realising this, he quickly put it to the back of his mind.

Midway through cleaning his teeth he remembered the dream that he had had and smiled to himself as he recounted the details of it. The flying dreams were always the best, and the rarest, which only served to make them ever more precious. It was as if he experienced something within the dreams that he could not experience elsewhere. Perhaps it was a feeling of power or of a unique freedom, whichever it was, it was too close to both for him to be able to differentiate.

David had tried to tell his best friend - Mickey the Hammer - about the dream once. He had begun by relating the incidental details - the scene, what had happened and then, as fully as he could, he had tried to describe the indescribable: the exhilaration and sheer joy of flight. Mickey, who had initially been quite intrigued by the prospect of hearing about his friend's favourite adolescent dream, had listened with an expression of growing distaste. "Jesus, David!" he had declared when David had finished. "I thought you were going to tell me about a wet dream or something."

Mickey had that sort of mind but then with such a fine nickname it was perhaps a form of natural justice that he should have other detractions. His nickname was in part a subtle play on his surname (Spinnane) but was predominantly drawn from his infamous tendency to bang his head against walls in an effort to impress girls. As a girl-friend-getting ploy it was one hundred percent unsuccessful but it had the mark of true inventiveness about it much as his forehead had.

Mickey's nickname was one thing that David envied him. He had often wanted to have a truly distinctive nickname of his own. Neither "Armo" nor even "Army" which he was sometimes called by Roy Scotton and his like were quite what he wanted of a nickname. Now "Colossus-by-whose-stride-the-world-doth-quake" would have been much more like it or even "Drug-crazed-grenade-throwing-terrorist-squitcher" would have been better. At least it would have said something positive about him rather than merely implying that there was something suspect about his armpits.

Yet it was not to be, he realised as he washed prior to getting dressed. If he was to make any progress with Terri then he would have to make more of an impact, he would have to be more outstanding. His failure with Terri and his lack of a nickname were in direct consequence of the anonymity that he had perfected. When he returned from Lake Nipigen he would have to do something about it. Perhaps he could build upon the very minor impression that he had already made. Perhaps he could stop washing his armpits.

Breakfast was an uncomfortable experience. It began with his father lapsing into an insincere all-boys-together act trying, without success, to draw some enthusiasm on David's part. It was not that David was not enthusiastic -Lake Nipigen was fine – but he did not particularly want to theorise about it, not at six in the morning, and his father's false good humour inevitably drove him into non-committal grunting. The meal finished with his father telling Paul about how "Grrrreat" it was going to be, much as he had told David and Susan before him for fifteen plus years. Lake Nipigen would very probably be grrreat but the fun that his father promised would not occur - not with his father anyway.

The holidays always began with his father's generation of dubious enthusiasm. It was his way of demonstrating his commitment to the holiday, to his wife, to himself and, like the enthusiasm, it was a false commitment. By Monday he would be phoning his office again. However, to give him his due, he would be around for a fair amount of the time during the holiday - certainly more than he ever was during the rest of the year.

Dishes were washed, dried. The amorphous tar (allegedly food) which Paul had left was washed down the waste disposal. Cases were checked though his mother did it without her previous anxiety; keys were given to Mrs Cox their elderly neighbour - in order that she might water their plants, conduct satanic rituals, that sort of thing, and the cab had arrived.

Mrs Cox waited while they loaded cases and bodies into the cab before waving and returning to her apartment. No doubt she was in a hurry to get to her telephone to arrange some covenanting, thought David and smiled at himself.

Their journey to the station was, for the most part, a silent one. Had they been friends rather than relatives then they would have felt obliged to talk to one another throughout the drive, David noted and thought that there was some great truism to be drawn from the observation. He briefly considered mulling over it until he came up with a suitable version of it, something which could go into the F.S. Clitheroe Book of Quotations but decided against it as nobody ever read those books except the fourteen-year old David Armitages of the world.

They arrived at the railroad station twenty minutes before their train was due to leave, as per normal. His father said that he could chose a book to read on the journey and ("Golly, gee thanks paw") that he would pay for it. David chose a small paperback which had some of H.P. Lovecraft's stories in it and a regrettably gaudy cover that drew a patronising smile from his father.

While they waited, David began to read pausing only in his absorption of the book when the train arrived and they were allowed onto it.

The Armitages virtually had a compartment to themselves, sharing it only with an oldish, pear-shaped man who smiled deferentially at the two adults and pulled a face at Paul. In the face of such provocation, Paul quickly fell asleep.

After a time David became aware of his mother's presence as though she were staring at him but he refused to look up afraid of what he might discover. The thing that he feared seeing was his mother's disappointment with his immersion in the book. What she might have preferred was for him to be looking out of the window agog with delight at the moving landscape and the novelty of being on a train. He refused to look up, after all, he was fifteen and besides she would be able to share that childish delight with Paul in a few years or with his father then. It was no longer his responsibility. "Unhappy is he to whom the memories of childhood bring only fear - - " he read.

" - - and in that lair of the deep ones we shall dwell amidst wonder and glory for ever." David slowly closed the book disappointed that there was no more to read. He glanced at the blurb on its back cover then studied it more carefully reading each synopsis with a knowing, familiar pleasure. That's only half the story, he thought to himself and slipped the book into his bag. Looking up, he was surprised to find that the pear-shaped man was no longer there and by the sight of his father, head-bent, engrossed in a book. It was a rare yet not in itself a surprising sight. What had surprised him was the realisation of how alike he and his father must have looked. David was fair where his father was dark and - eyes apart - David little resembled him. _ _ _

Except for the occasional action or posture, except for the odd moment.

David's mother was looking dully out of the window. Paul lay asleep on her lap. "When did that man get off," asked David, "the one who got one with us?"

"At the first stop." She replied smiling.

"Oh." said David, it seemed appropriate. He looked out of the window, squinted. "We're nearly there." He stated when he was sure of the landmarks.

"Just a few more minutes." his mother agreed.

David did not particularly resemble her either. She was auburn, dark eyed and with quite delicate features unlike his father, unlike

David. Of his two parents his father's eyes were all that he had obviously inherited and while they had the colour, myopia and sleepy look of his father, the remainder of their faces were entirely dissimilar. His father had a moon-shaped face and subdued bone structure whereas David's face had a broad, well-defined bone structure. If it were not for the glasses he could be quite handsome - or so he kept telling himself. The problem was, that on such matters, he did not consider the source to be trustworthy.

His father stopped reading a moment or so before the train pulled into the station and began to build up to enthusiastic again. David too felt a kindred anticipation, certainly he could feel his stomach churning and a tightness coming to his throat.

The train pulled noisily into the station. With a stretching of cramped muscles they climbed out of their compartment. David's feet reacted unsteadily to the solidity of the platform.

Uncle Manny was waiting for them. Uncle Manny - his mother's brother, the fair, bright-eyed carpenter whom, of all his relatives, David most resembled and respected. He smiled his familiar, droopy-moustached smile, shook his brother-in-law's hand, kissed his sister and refrained from making any trite comment on the changed appearance of either David or Paul. Their cases were quickly transferred to his station wagon while the two elder men talked about the journey. That was stage one of their conversation. Stage two was how their respective jobs were going and stage three would be either basketball or snooker. By Sunday afternoon (stage five or thereabouts) they would have reached the point wherein their conversation was no longer premeditated and was genuinely amiable.

The journey from the station to Uncle Manny's house was a familiar and welcome one to David. The land and the road were intimately known to him but not so much so that he had stopped seeing them. There was still something worthwhile and exciting about the journey. It was too much like renewing friendships to be otherwise.

Uncle Manny and his father had progressed to each other's, declining, break building by the time that the house came into view. It lay at the end of a rutted, unkempt trail with the woods that fringed Lake Nipigen at its back. On their last visit, a year before, David had been surprised and disappointed by the disparity between the actual and remembered size of the house. It was not to be so this year, the place seemed small but familiar and that was what mattered.

Aunt Elaine met them at the door with the obligatory hug and kiss then ushered them into the house where they had a drink of sweet, hot coffee before the "men", David included, fetched the bags in. David returned a third time to find his uncle carrying the last bag. "That's all there is," he said pre-empting David's question. "Shut the door though will you?" David moved to obey only to be stopped by his Uncle's cry.

"Hey David!" He turned, eager to oblige. His uncle smiled. "How are you? - I don't know that I asked you."

"Fine." David replied automatically then asked with a haste that was equally automatic, "Will we be going fishing tomorrow?"

"Sure - you'll have to put up with us for today though. You're Aunt will be wanting to hear all about you brother's toilet training and the like." He went on into the house leaving David with a smile and a greater inclination to tolerate the baby talk than he would have previously. David closed the station wagon's door and paused to look around. He loved this place and knew it well though he could not think of it as home. He almost belonged there - not quite but it was a special place and almost was close. Slowly, contentedly he walked back into the house.

CHAPTER 3

“Gerflumgugen." Or words to that effect. "Gump." David awoke slowly and without particular permanency. Sunday morning - church and a heavy lunch - - they could wait for a time. He cuddled into the hollow that his weight had made in the bed.

Dully, he recalled the details of the previous night from amongst the blur of talk and sleepiness which had, initially, presented itself. He remembered how, when their conversation had turned to Paul, he had shown an enthusiasm and knowledge which had, secretly, pleased his mother but which, he felt, was quite unbecoming for a young man. He smiled at the stupidity of the notion, surprised that it should occur to him in the enlightened times that he believed himself to live in. All those fat-gutted macho attitudes could go hang. Paul was his brother and there was nothing wrong with his having an interest in him or even in his caring for the melon-headed dwarf. Having said which, he was not going to start discussing nappy-rash with Roy Scotton - after all, he might take it personally. David smiled to himself, greatly amused. For a fifteen-year-old, that was one fine remark and the memory of it would keep him happy for a whole morning -more than likely. The sarcastic remark was mightier than the sword. Well, it was certainly less messy anyway.

If David remembered correctly, his father had fallen asleep after a couple of glasses of Scotch and none of the other adults had noticed for five minutes. - For a moment he had to think again, uncertain as to whether he had remembered or dreamt that particular detail.

David sniffed, scratched then abruptly realised that there was something strange about or that something strange had happened - he was not sure which. He sat up in the bed and looked around him at the familiar details of his cousin Michael's room. Everything was where it should be, everything as it had been before he had gone to sleep and yet something that he could not identify seemed to have changed. For a time he stared, squinted and eventually came to a satisfactory explanation. I am going crazy, he decided and slipped back under the covers.

Sunday morning was one of the ritualistic times in the holiday that he welcomed and enjoyed. Going to church was an entirely different experience at Lake Nipigen to that in Winnipeg. In the city it was seen as something that the school / the establishment wanted him to do and therefore there was pressure from the real establishment, his peers, not to go. In the rural community, it had a far greater social importance. It was a peerless experience and a great place to meet women. Geriatric women mostly but there were granddaughters too. David had a limited definition of "meeting women" which basically encompassed staring at the back of their necks for an hour or so. Not lustfully nor condescendingly. There was a great deal of enjoyment to be had from the contemplation of the beautifully formed aspects of the female anatomy. David stood in the foremost ranks of those who admired and adored and had deserted the army of the lustful forever when he was - oh - at least thirteen. David's soul and intentions were wholly noble - it was far and away the more comfortable path. Comfortable, it was either that or the fact that it was the only course where he knew where in hell he was going.

"Hell's bells." he muttered realising what the source of the strangeness had been. During the night he had dreamed of flying again. Now that was strange. He had had recurring dreams before but not the flight dream, not on two successive nights. There was no reason why he should not have, it was just that it had not happened before.

Somebody was moving on the other side of the door. Time to get up.

Being seen with his family was moderately embarrassing to David but it was not so going into church that day. The six of them almost took up a row and, for a moment he experienced that rare, uplifting, feeling of group solidarity which he had occasionally known with his friends but virtually never with his family.

Mass began and David's attention fell into decline. Then suddenly, perhaps quarter of an hour into the service, he stiffened and his heart began to beat faster as he grew inexplicably cold. Something - - something was not as it should be though he had no idea what. He turned and looked around the church. Devout -

disinterested some familiar -most unknown to him. Their faces were anything but abnormal. None of them seemed to be particularly interested in him and he could see nothing lurking beyond them.

"What is it?" his mother hissed, leaning towards him. Reluctantly, David faced forward again.

"Damned if I know - - oh, sorry God." he muttered the last two words being muffled by the apologetic hand that had risen to his mouth. He removed his glasses and began to clean them, a habitual means of gaining time and distraction.

It was probably just paranoia, he decided but the suspicion of something perversely wrong continued to bother him. It reminded him of the story that Mickey had told him once about the man who had left his house and while he was gone some thieves had stolen everything of his which they then replaced with perfect copies of the originals. Anyway the man returned to the house and his dog bit him. A strange story which, mindful of its source, was not surprising.

David briefly considered mentioning his suspicions to Uncle Manny but quickly rejected the idea. After all, what could he say? "Excuse me Uncle but have you noticed that everything is exactly where it should be, looks exactly as it should do, behaves exactly as it should and really is what it should be but that its being bloody weird about it?"

Sunday lunch and Sunday afternoon followed much as normal regardless of all premonitions of evil and of the paranoiac delusions that led to such premonitions. Uncle Manny and his father had talked of going fishing before being struck down by the weight of aunt Elaine's cooking and, instead, they spent the afternoon lying about digesting and giving fair to good impressions of turtles. Even David joined them in falling asleep in front of the T.V. It had never occurred before and it was perhaps unusual for a healthy, moderately mobile fifteen-year old but then there was to be just no escaping Aunt Elaine's chocolate cake. He had fallen asleep cradling Paul which made for a touching picture and an extremely abrupt wakening.

Rain threatened, bringing an end to the proposed fishing and dinner loomed sickeningly near. It was hard, damned hard, but David did his familial duty.

After dinner there was a very nearly interesting film on TV which the remainder of the family watched while David slouched from kitchen to den for a time before deciding to go for a walk.

He began the walk uncertainly, looking around the garden while an indefinable reluctance led him to hesitate. After a few minutes of admiring the few vegetables that he could name and the flowers that he could not, he decided to stop procrastinating and to make for the lake and, more immediately, the intervening trees.

The lake lay two miles beyond the first trees and, with the sun fast sinking behind the treetops, there was no question of his seeing it that evening. He decided that he would just walk amongst the trees for a while. It would be pleasant to remind himself of the smell of bark, to feel the forest underfoot. At the edge of the forest he paused, peering into the gloom where light ended. Inexplicably, he feared what might lie within the forest and his fear was irrational because it was of creatures that ought not to exist. It was conceivable that there might be a wild dog or suchlike hiding in there - just about - but his fear was not of any such animal though it may have been of tooth and claw. In the instant that he acknowledged the fear he realised, and accepted, that he had to enter the forest. His determination owed as much to the bloody-mindedness nurtured by the self-criticism and conscience of Catholicism as to his intuitive rejection of the childish fear and the vital need of the would-be adult to best such a rejection. Hurriedly, purposely disregarding the darkness to either side where childhood predators might lie, he entered the forest. He was reminded of the scene in every horror film that he had ever seen where the hero/heroine place themself in a position of vulnerability by entering the cellar/castle etc. For the life of him, he could never understand why they were flying in the face of all common sense and adrenaline-fuelled instinct. It got to the point where if they were going to be so stupid, well sod them, they deserved to be bitten, shredded or whatever. On the other hand, those were horror films, this was life and he should stop being so girlie. He walked on.

After a minute or two he slowed and eventually stopped, leaning against the low bough of an old pine tree which had all but fallen in a storm of several years ago. Ahead he could see the lightness of a clearing and, as he paused, the forest seemed to newly form about him as his memories falteringly aligned themselves with the dark trees around him. He knew the clearing having played there many times with his cousin Michael in the years before he went to college.

Even as he watched it and remembered, the light within the clearing lessened. To his left, though he dared not look, stood a woman her hair the russet-red of the forest in the fading light. She was young, pretty and stared not at him but through him, the focus of her eyes as unmoving and as taut as her every muscle. David was aware of her though she remained a peripheral image. He would not look at her, his innate politeness leading him to avoid the eye contact which would make them both overly conscious of how intent her gaze was. He watched the clearing waiting for the image to speak or move.

What she was doing there he could not imagine but as he wondered an inexplicable fragment of knowledge seemed to arrive, ready formed in his mind. The young woman was not human. She may have once been and physically was so in every respect but there was something, some attribute which had changed her.

The young woman - no girl - was tall, almost David's height and with a pleasingly curved face - beautiful? Yes, perhaps, though you would need a moment to decide that she was. For all that she might seem beautiful and to have such, normal, attributes - she was not, she was extraordinary - there was something about her that was mysterious, alien. - David had turned his head.

Turned his head and saw only shade where her body had been, bark for her hair and the last of the sun upon the tree where her face had been. "Idiot!" He slapped his thigh, which hurt, turned and stubbed his toe which hurt a great deal more. Fuming moderately, he cursed himself for his fantastic imaginings. The forest was too quiet for the approach of strangers and he had been reading too much H.P. Lovecraft. Such stupidity was all that he needed, it was hard enough being fifteen without reverting to childish imaginings. Paul would have been less afraid of the forest and yet, despite his anger, he did not go on into the clearing but returned by the shortest possible route to the house.

Back in the house the still-filled torpor of the others had not lessened but it had grown colder outside and the very nearly interesting film coupled with the warmth of the house was enough to persuade David to stay indoors. He watched the TV but could not concentrate and its images flickered meaninglessly before his eyes.

The phantom woman bothered him - not the illusion itself which was merely a consequence of his own disjointed imaginings but the power and potent attraction of the woman which he had glimpsed. They were the attributes not of any mythical creature but, to an innocent, of all women and of one in particular. He readily lapsed into his favourite leisure occupation - fantasies on the theme of their first for-real meeting and of nobly, pointlessly despatching terrorists. Yet, despite their appeal, he did not dwell for too long upon the fantasy, the mystery and attractions of Terri Egan being too closely related to those of the imagined woman to allow for their safe contemplation. The imagined woman had had a power that he had not understood and that had evoked an interest, a desire, whose rising he could not control and that was a thing which he feared far more than any unknown creatures of the wood.

By the film's end the imagined woman had faded until she appeared to threaten no more than any of the other sensations of slight disorientation which he had had and she was rightly confined to being nothing but a childish exaggeration, one that he ought to have grown out of.

When the pre-sleep dream of rescuing / impressing the inhibitions out of Terri came it was without any associated fear and though he felt the warmth of her gratitude too keenly, he drank a glass of water and his thoughts were not too sinful to necessitate prayer or self-loathing.

That night he slept deeply and dreamt little for the last time.

CHAPTER 4

For several minutes David lay with his eyes open, the contours of his pillow slowly coming into focus. Stupid, not a thought entered his mind until he idly considered the possibility of going back to sleep. He pushed himself up into a sitting position, glanced at the clock and felt his heart jump. Eleven o'clock! The day was almost over.

Hurriedly, he washed, dressed and made his way downstairs. His mother and aunt were sitting at the kitchen table with Paul upon the latter's knee. "Good morning sleepy." his mother said. He smiled inanely and sat at the place that had been prepared for him.

"Dad and Uncle Manny ...?" The question did not need completing. The Monday fishing trip was one of the holiday's rituals. David, either alone or with his uncle, would, thereafter, frequently go fishing but his father would rarely go after that first, obligatory, trip. "Yes" his mother replied needlessly, nodding, "they went hours ago."

He ate his breakfast as quickly as his self-consciousness would allow then hurried out of the house and through the forest towards the lake.

David arrived at the lakeside as his father and uncle were rowing back towards the quay. In his anxiety he scarcely noticed the lake - the first sight of which was ordinarily one of the comforting, familiar pleasures of the holiday. He waited nervously, unsure as to what he should do. Uncle Manny nodded at David when he first saw him but thereafter joined his brother-in-law in disregarding him until they had approached to within acceptable conversational range. Then his father smiled at him – a frightening, toothy grimace bespectably robbed as it was, of any warmth. "Where have you been?" A pointlessly asked question if ever there was one, thought David bitterly. "The fishing's over now. You'll have to be up before dawn if you want to keep up with the men."

It was typical of a father-to-David exchange. Well meant in intention but patronising in effect and rooted in a fatuous notion of youthful bonhomie. Yet, for all that their's was a relationship of uneasy role-playing, David had wanted very much to have been on the boat with him that morning and to have him around far more.

David's father clambered out of the boat with the ready ease and confidence of one for whom such an action was a biannual occurrence. Uncle Manny with a mildly taken aback but considerate slowness. "Look at these." said his father indicating their silvery catch and Uncle Manny motioned to slap David in the face with them. A thing which he had not succeeded in doing for - - almost eighteen months.

Once the boat was safely moored the three of them began back towards the house travelling slowly with their awkward tackle. "Have you just woken up?" asked his father.

"No," David lied. Prayers tonight. Killing terrorists was all right, white lies to extract oneself from conversational demands now they really counted. "Well not really but I thought that I'd come out to meet you. Are you going fishing again after lunch?"

"No we thought we'd try out Charley Bell's place - maybe the snooker table's flatter this year."

"The beer is." Muttered Uncle Manny drawing huge, forceful guffaws from David's father. It was not a funny remark but they were on holiday and David's father was going to enjoy himself whatever the opportunities.

As the house came into sight David abruptly recalled how his mother had looked that morning: calmer, less weary? She was already looking the better for the change.

"The warriors return," said his father in a voice that was supposed to sound like Johnny Weismuller's Tarzan, "bring food for woman." What he actually sounded like, thought David, was a jerk but he was still his father for all of that.

Lunch passed quickly with tales of lake serpents and other nearly-landed monsters which only served to put their actual catch into perspective. Inevitably, the father and uncle soon departed leaving David to choose between mother, aunt, brother and a solitary fish. He chose the latter.

Despite the curiosity which had grown into a firmly defined wish to glimpse phantom women in the forest, he saw nothing there that was more than a purposely misinterpreted shadow and he passed quietly through. Once at the lakeside he set himself up at the quay even though the fishing was usually poor there and waited for the vague possibility of a catch and the certainty of a mind cleansing examination of life, death and everything in between. A spectral topic which quickly resolved itself into a consideration of how best he might woo and win Terri Egan. Step 1: major plastic surgery; step 2: walk like John Wayne; step 3: practise swooping.

The afternoon hours passed quickly though not easily. Gradually, unwillingly, he was approaching a new perspective on his non-existent relationship with Terri. The daydreams persisted and idly pleasured him but would not do so for much longer. They were no longer adequate in themselves. He had known the smell of her as she walked past, had touched her arm once. He knew her face and figure in the minutest detail but she was no longer an image, a beauty whose emotions and form he could manipulate in his daydreams.

That was how it had been with the other girls that he had fallen for. All that he had required of them was a pretty exterior, one that he could project into his dreams and lavish his love upon. The dreams were no longer sufficient. The love had become more than an excuse for the dreams. He had to do something and he did not know what. Perhaps he could try one of the numerous "witty and frightfully amusing" remarks which he had thought out but then that was something which Roy Scotton and his like would do. "You say this ... ." "You say it like this ..." "You rub their ribs like this ..." Press the buttons and Paradise was yours. Something within David cried out against competing with their kind, with the new girl every fortnight braggarts. Admittedly their trading rate matched their boasts but that was not the point. The sad thing was that they were the greatly-envied ones of their year. They had status. It was heart that they lacked. The game itself was wrong and it was one that David would not play.

What then should he do or say? He had to say something. Nothing too clever, perhaps just, "Hi, notice me." A footstep upon the quay disturbed his thoughts and, turning, he saw his mother and aunt. "It's time that you came back," said his aunt, "it's getting late." Automatically, he followed her glance towards the lowing sun. "We thought that we'd take a look at the lake while we were fetching you." She added unnecessarily. David began to clear up his borrowed tackle.

The two women wandered about the quay slightly disinterestedly and talked though their conversation was not as free and as natural as it normally was having been robbed of these qualities by David's presence and the lack of its familiar setting.

For a moment, as they left, David found that his mother had hesitated - waiting courteously for him to precede her. It was an action with no source other than good manners and the inherent consideration that they implied. He thought then, as he had quite often since the birth of Paul, of how he would quite like his mother - as a person - even if she were not his mother or perhaps if only she were not his mother.

That evening the adults played cards for cents and continued into the early hours while a sleepy David opted for an early night. Overall it was not a remarkable day, nothing noticeably exciting happened and no great lover was born.

CHAPTER 5

In his dream he moved upwards until he sat. David's eyes opened and in the mirror's reflection he first became aware of the darkness behind him then of that which it framed, his own head and upper torso. What little light there was reflected dully from the sheen of sweat which covered his skin. His eyes met those of the dream reflection and he settled, almost slipping from the dream at the familiar, sure contact.

Slowly and with an utter terror, he became aware of what was behind him. It was alive. It was not a man nor woman and neither was it a creature. It was touching him.

He screamed yet before the scream could rise to his throat he had awoken and sat bolt upright in the bed. A light sheen of fear-sweat covered him - cooling. He could almost hear himself screaming in a dream that would not end.

David stared directly ahead of him at the wall where, in his dream, the mirror had been. For several moments he did not dare look around for fear of what he might see. When, finally, he did look there were no monsters to be seen. He lay back on the bed glad to find that there was only the pressure which the mattress exerted beneath him. Then, with a cowardliness which he was to regret deeply, he switched the light on and looked breathlessly for a mirror.

There was nothing behind him, nothing touching him. He had been used, through his fear, by the reality of a dream. When he returned to the bed he lay for a short time with the light on but soon switched it off telling himself that he was not quite so prone to childish habits and knowing besides, that the light could only extend so far. That the most that it could achieve would be to illuminate that which he dared not look upon.

Uneasily, unwillingly David waited for sleep. Initially, he had no desire to return to it not after the warm, corrective haven which his dreams were had been so obscenely violated but the needs of his body eventually reasserted themselves. Later he dreamed of Terri or perhaps it was of flying. Either way, it eased away the associated fear of dreaming and David slept soundly, safely thereafter.

Bleary-eyed, he took the mug of coffee and sipped. It tasted sweet but not too hot. He drained the mug greedily then, resting it upon his chest, he let his head fall back onto the pillow. The faint memory of the nightmare came back to him though its details were uncertain. Hunger forced him out of the bed and in search of breakfast.

Uncle Manny had finished eating but his mother, like David had only just arisen. "Do you want to go out on the boat?" Uncle Manny asked and slowly looked away once David had met his gaze and nodded. There was no sign of David's father. Three servings later they left the house. Or, at least, the adult's claimed that he had had three servings. David could only recall one bowl full and could not quite understand why they should claim otherwise. It was not that funny even if it had been true.

Uncle Manny said nothing to David during the walk down to the lake and only a few of the "Got your glasses? - Got the bait?" semi-instructional type of questions on the quay.

After ten minutes or so on the water he pulled a can of lager from his heavy, leather bag and offered David the first sip. The drink came from a local brewery. It was a particular favourite of his uncle's, quite rare and, to David's taste, indescribably foul but he accepted the sip in the spirit of friendship with which it had been offered. "Fine day." stated the uncle. David mumbled his agreement. "Your Pa' had to go somewhere. . . . Marie's looking well. How are you son?" David could almost hear the ting of a metal ball bearing as it moved in his uncle's mind from David's father to David's mother and inevitably down to David.

"Fine." David replied. The uncle considered the response, decided against its validity and stated,

"Something is bothering you."

"Well ..." It would be pointless trying to lie to him.

"I know the signs, son. I've experienced it myself - there's some little girl that's bothering you." David hummed, ahhed and eventually smiled pathetically. "I know - its hell." He looked out over the glassy surface of the lake completely missing the minor signs of tension flowing from his uncle. It did not have to be a girl. His uncle did not have a problem with that - if it was not a girl but, all things considered, it was less of a problem if it was a girl. "It's awful at your age. What is she - a girlfriend?"

"No - not yet."

"Well spoken." He commented, smiling.

"That - that's the problem really..." David's words trailed aimlessly away. He was unable to admit to his own embarrassing reticence.

"Have you asked her for a date yet?" David shook his head unable to meet his uncle's gaze. "Well?"

"Even if I had - I mean - would she - - do you think?" He looked at his uncle, his need to know overcoming his embarrassment. The uncle shrugged, looked away. "Damned if I know. - I can't lie to you, son, I've never understood what women see in men. Michael's my son and I love him but he was a real son-of-a-bitch - no disrespect to his mother -he was a real son-of-a-bitch when it came to women. He treated his girlfriends like dirt but they always saw something in him. Damned if I know what it was but he always had girlfriends - lovely girls -not stupid either. Now I would have thought that girls would have avoided him but they didn't and now you - I'd think that a girl could be really attracted to you but, you know, they're funny like that. You never can tell which way they're going to jump. I've spent my life trying to guess and I'm still no wiser." He shook his head as if to re-emphasise the inexplicable nature of women. "It's like as if they say "I know that he's a convicted felon with a history of arson and cannibalism but he's not like that with me -he's really sweet with me. Nobody else sees the real him -"

"It's not just that." David mumbled successfully intercepting locomotive Manny before David fell completely off the vehicle. "I mean, how do you - " he could feel himself reddening. "I mean how did you and Aunt Elaine first meet?"

Uncle Manny rubbed his jaw, ran his fingers over his light stubble and, eventually, said, "Well it wasn't anything special. She used to live near by and she used to date a friend of mine. We used to make a foursome. Anyway after a while they stopped seeing each other but we kept in contact through living so close and pretty much going to the same places. Anyway to cut the story short, we started dating and fell in love. It isn't particularly romantic but I expect that's how most marriages start – lasting ones anyway."

"Yes but how do you --" David suddenly developed an intense interest in the back of his hands and could speak no more.

"How do you start?" His uncle half-stated half-asked. David looked up into his uncle's face in time to see him, considerately, look away. "Well - - you say 'Hello' then she says 'Hello' back and you let your mouth take it from there."

"It's not as easy as that."

"Did I say that it was easy? No it's hard, hellishly hard especially first time but it’s got to be done. Maybe it would be best if you just blundered in before you gave yourself time to think about it. Don't worry about what you have to say the whole history of men and women together is founded upon the stupid things that men say to women. Maybe that's why they think were such idiots. Don't worry - hell she could be even more nervous than you are."

"Maybe," admitted David without enthusiasm though he was greatly heartened by the suggestion.

"Nice girl?" asked his uncle inviting a profusion of adjectives and the thorough detailing of all of the delightful details associated with Terri Egan, Goddess and dropper of textbooks. The invitation was hungrily accepted and almost forty minutes had passed before David's description ground to a reluctant halt.

"I've gone on haven't I?" apologised David. His uncle smiled though in the slightly distant way of a listener who had been entertained without ever having been entirely committed.

"We've all felt like that about somebody - all of us - even your father." The suggestion momentarily silenced David but he quickly recovered,

"I guess I'm besotted."

"Ummh. Extremely sotted."

Strange but it had never occurred to him that his father could have been like that or, indeed, that he could have had any life outside of the existing family context. Uncle Manny easily slipped into the conversational void that David had left and most of the remaining daylight hours were spent listening to his general observations on life and anecdotes. His stories were very familiar to David, strangely warming in the telling, unremarkable in the recording but, as David had long since realised, the stories were unimportant. It was the story-teller, a man with empathy, a man who cared, a man who was prepared to let David eat four-fifths of the lunch that aunt Elaine had prepared for the two of them.

David's father had returned to the house before David and his uncle. He was clearly restive by then and, sensing this, David decided to follow his substantial supper with an early night. His voice was slightly rough from the unusual amount of talking which he had done but, despite it, he soon fell asleep.

CHAPTER 6

Michael's room slowly came into focus. David picked up his glasses from beside the bed and pushed them on to his nose. The limited clarity that the room had gained was instantly lost. He looked over his glasses - through - over. Rising, he dropped them back into their case, scratched his head and trudged towards the toilet.

David nodded at the dishevelled head in the mirror then washed his face in the basin beneath it. It was only when drying his face that he realised that there had been something fundamentally wrong with the face that had stared back at him. A fleeting panic gripped him but the image that faced him in the mirror was his own. His own perfectly reflected and reproduced, not a single fault marring the perception of it. He saw his face as he had never seen it before. For several, stunned, moments the image stared disbelievingly back at him. It's jaw had fallen and, embarrassed, the image snapped it shut as David finally tore his gaze away. He could see perfectly. He was no longer myopic. The streaked-green wall tiles glared indecently clearly at him. He sat upon the edge of the bath and closed his eyes. Everything was impossibly clear. He could see. All of those damned swirly things were patterns and stuff. Textured, grainy patterns. It was stupid. It was impossible. It could not have happened.

It could have happened. He was growing, physically changing and, though rare, such things could happen. In fact it had been one the recurrent elements of his drug-crazed-grenade-throwing-terrorist-despatching daydreams. He could be cured of his myopia - it was possible - it was - was not.

He did not accept the possibility nor would he take pleasure in it. He was too good a Catholic to believe that any good fortune could come to him without at least complications and, more probably, a great and damning price.

Absently, he dried his face again and walked out onto the hall not knowing whether he should have run joyously from it or barricad himself within it. He almost walked into his mother. "David." she stated automatically, underlining her surprise then, "David?" she added upon seeing the horror in his expression. He smiled or, rather, tried to as the poorly executed leer which he produced fulfilled neither of its covering-embarrassment and reassuring functions. "What's the matter?" Surprised, frightened, he could not lie to his mother and he blurted out,

"I can see." He was instantly aware of the idiocy of his statement and added, "What I mean is that things don't look like they did - I don't think that I need my glasses anymore." Unthinkingly, his mother threw out the cry of mothers throughout the world who have been denied thinking space by their offspring.

"That's nice dear." She muttered then, mindful of the countless times that he had previously declared the latter part of his statement, "Well maybe we can have your eyes re-tested when we get back to Winnipeg." David grunted his agreement. "They're not hurting you are they?"

"No."

"Headaches?"

"No." He shook his head and, satisfied, she smiled.

"We'll leave it until then - it might just be the effect of the clean air here." He smiled with her as she passed and at her as she went down the staircase. What? Was there some sort of weird, visually distorting fog that obscured the whirly things in cities throughout the world? Somehow she had reduced an occurrence which was so improbable as to suggest the miraculous to no more than a case of teenage over-enthusiasm. Despite being a woman who was intelligent and veritably laden with common sense she had managed in a few sentences to utterly warp and bewilder his whole mental process. Still, at least it was nice to know that she had not handed in her mother's union card.

He hurried back into Michael's room then stared at the window - bed - wall. He could see perfectly, his mother was wrong. His legs began to feel weak and he sat upon the bed then lay upon it his eyes taking in every obscenely distinct characteristic of the room.

It could not have just *happened* overnight and, realising this, he accepted that it had not. The phantom woman in the forest and the strange sensations within the church had both been attempts by his unconscious mind to rationalise the changing perceptions of his eyes. It had happened and there was no denying the truth of it. Not for an instant was he cheered by the thought of it.

David stood unconsciously moving towards the horizons beyond the room's window and froze in terror at the sight beyond the glass. Sluggishly, stupidly he moved towards it. His fingers paused on the windowpane. Beyond them, and the glass, lay mile upon mile of low, grey cloud advancing upon him.

David, tried desperately to think of why the prospect of rain should so frighten him but failed in the effort. The emotion's origin was beyond understanding, was without reason. Whatever the source of the knowledge, he knew that there was something to be feared in the sight of the rain and all of his inclinations to tell his family about his perfect sight were ended through that knowledge. The rain was moving inexorably towards them and, with it, something to be feared. He opened the window and could all but taste the pre-storm atmosphere.

Whatever it was, he did not want to face it alone but for him to stay with the family would mean endangering them. Paul, Uncle Manny, his mother - they would all be drawn in to the approaching threat if he was to remain with them. Honour and intellect said that he should not let the rain keep him within the house every other instinct and emotion screamed at him to stay. To stay where his family could guard over him.

What should he do? The question reiterated endlessly within his mind until, with an undeniable abruptness, he came to a decision. Somehow he had to get away from them. Once he had accepted the decision his resolve did not falter even though he had chosen the option that he most feared. There was a certainty to the decision that he could not even contemplate questioning.

At the breakfast table he ate sulkily with many glances towards the others, looks which concealed feelings of near-contempt for their blind normality. They were threatened, their lives were in danger and yet none of them suspected, only he, only he knew.

The first drops of rain had begun to streak down the windows by the time that they had finished eating. "There'll be no fishing today." The uncle said to David, misinterpreting his resentful glances towards the window. David smiled in agreement though the expression quickly fled, driven out by a sudden and powerful anger at the man who could only see regret for a few lost hours when, in reality, David was prepared to die so that he could live.

The two men soon departed for town leaving David alone at the window staring deep into the forest and imagining the source of his strange thoughts.

The minutes - hours passed and David's brooding grew far worse. He was sarcastic to his aunt and rude to his mother. His frustration at their inability to see what was plainly before them and so, horrifically imminent developed at a rate which was only on a par with his impatience and desire to be away from them.

David's obsession was souring the atmosphere within the house and he ultimately found that the only - partial -source of relief was to stand outside it on the porch where he could see the rain but not be touched by it and watch the forest. Intensely, incessantly, he watched the forest.

At lunchtime his mother came out and stood on the porch beside him. He did not look to her, did not have to. She folded her arms. "David, what is it?" He made neither the slightest attempt to answer or to move. "David there's something bothering you. Is it to do with your eyes? Is there really something wrong with them?"

At first he did not reply but when he did his voice was distant and impersonal as though he were talking to a complete stranger.

"No, I was just being silly then."

"Then what is it, then? What is wrong then?" He blinked and his brow furrowed as he considered the question knowing that he understood the answer far less than she thought he did.

"I don't want to be here," he stated at length, "I want to be on my own somewhere - maybe I could go back to Winnipeg, on my own."

"But David you're on vacation." For the first time he looked at her, his gaze holding her with a disconcerting stillness and surety.

"I would like to be on my own for a while." He stated flatly. She shook her head but did not stifle his hope entirely.

"I'll speak to your father but, even if it was possible, I don't know that we would let you - you're only fifteen David." His head turned rigidly away. Reluctantly his mother turned back into the house.

Seemingly only moments later he heard the sound of his father returning through the glass behind him. "What's David doing out there?" He heard his father ask, then his mother's reply though he could not make out the words. "What? - Why?" Again he heard the sound of his mother's voice. "Does he?" It sounded as though his father's position had changed, David guessed that he had sat at the table but he would not turn his head to check. He would not look away from the rain-veiled forest. His mother's voice continued with occasional interjections from his father. He could not be certain of a single word that his mother said but he heard every consonant, every grunt of his father's.

More than once his father called him but he did not obey or even flinch in his watching of the forest.

After a time a third voice joined those of his parents. Again the words were indistinguishable but from the pitch it had to be his uncle Manny. How long it went on for David could not say but there was suddenly nothing but silence behind him. He heard the clunk of a car door and caught a glimpse of a large, dark green limousine moving almost silently away through the trees to his right. The door to his left opened. "Come in here." his father said levelly holding the door open for him. David chanced a single glance at his father's expressionless face then obeyed him his eyes fixed on the ground several feet before him.

Inside, his mother and uncle stood against the walls upon either side of the table unconsciously mimicking each other in their stern, arms-folded posture. Aunt Elaine was in the other room apparently watching T.V. with Paul asleep in his carrycot beside her. David sat at the table, his father before him with his back to the windows. "Now young man," said David's father, his favourite phrase when playing the part of the disciplinary parent, "let me make it very clear to you that there should be no childish sulking or outright rudeness in this family. You are a guest in this house and you should behave like one. Your uncle Manfred here has the kindness to offer you a place in his home and you repay that kindness by moping about..." The voice continued on and on. His father was fully into role and enjoying it. Gradually David's gaze rose from the tabletop to the window away to his father's right and beyond it to the forest. "Now your mother tells me that you want to be on your own. Well this is not the way to go about it and I don't want you to think that it is. Now your uncle Manfred, here, says that there is a cabin near to here which he has the use of and which - if we wanted to - we could let you use for a few days." Hope coupled with fear rose in David's heart. "Now your uncle thinks that you might be old enough to be trusted with a responsibility like that and to have a little independence, so does your mother but I have yet to be persuaded." Again he paused leaving David to realise what it was that was needed. He would have to beg for it.

"If you would let me, I'd be very, very grateful." He stated his gaze contritely upon the floor. "I'm sorry for the way that I've behaved - I know that it was wrong and I'm sorry. If you would just let me - if you'd show trust in me by letting me go then I wouldn't let you down. I promise that I'll never behave so childishly again." Hopefully, he looked up finding that the pleasure in his father's expression mirrored his own satisfaction with an apology well made.

"Well, we shall let you just for a few days. Your uncle says that by the time he was your age he had been hunting and camping on his own many times. Well you won't actually be going camping but I think that it would do you a lot of good-it'll make you grow up more." Still smiling, he looked to his brother-in-law. Act over, abdication imminent. "Manny?" he prompted.

"Right." said the uncle his symbolically folded arms falling away from each other. "Well it's a cabin that belongs to a college lecturer down in Toronto. Usually he only uses it for a couple of months a year and I'll keep a watch on it for the rest of the time. This year he's done a transfer to Europe and he said that I could use it for anything that I liked while he was gone. I'm sure that he won't mind your using it if you take reasonable care of it." David nodded enthusiastically. "Right. It's about 12 miles from here -got its own phone and generator still so it ain't exactly primitive. If you're willing I'm sure that we could make it habitable. What do you say? - Maybe we could do it tomorrow."

"No!" David exclaimed then ducked his gaze and head as he saw his father's indignation rise. "- I mean could we do it tonight? I'd really like to."

"What's your hurry?" asked his father.

"No hurry. It's just that we don't have to waste today. If we packed everything that I needed now then I could be in there before its dark." His father looked to the uncle who gave a non-committal shrug.

"All right." agreed his father, dully.

Even though the release that he needed was imminent, David's anxiety did not lessen but grew with every minute that he remained within the house. This time, however, David bore the taut, draining tension of his impatience in silence and with a covert desire to oblige which ensured that it was apparent to everybody else within the house. As every seemingly endless moment passed so David's ability to cope with the level of his own frustration declined. It was two maybe three hours after the decision had been made before David, his parents and uncle finally left the house by which time he was incapable of anything more than a grunted reply. His every inclination was, instead, to attack the dulled adults for their insistence on making the most unnecessary check and inane, not to mention patronising, statements when he, unknown to them, was about to die for them.

The packing and planning continued despite all of his will to the contrary but eventually all of the pretexts for delaying him there finally reached the limits of credibility and he made his monosyllabic farewells to his aunt and brother before joining the others in the station wagon.

As the vehicle pulled away he waved to the two of them then watched, fascinated, as the house which he loved and whose existence he could no longer bear dwindled into nothingness in the rear view mirror. The almost physical pressure which he had felt within it seemed to have been lifted and the urgency and purpose which he had been equally sure of, similarly dissipated.

David stared out of the vehicle's window but saw only the land and the rain upon it. Logically, he knew that the evil, which he had feared, was not there. After all, what could harm him? There were people who might, animals that might but he had feared neither of these. he had feared an unknown, inexplicable thing - the non-existent product of a harmless nightmare and his own inclination to brood. There was no evil monster out there. He knew as surely as anyone could and with a greater certainty than any other for he knew that it was in his imagination that the creature had had its origins and sole existence.

Throughout the drive his mother was silent having realised that the best way to stop him telephoning them would be to insist that he did thereby underlining that he would not be truly independent in the cabin. David's father showed no such reluctance though he was eventually quiet after quarter of an hour's fruitless attempts to draw a meaningful response from David.

Uncle Manny began to talk as they finally reached the track that led on to the cabin. "There will be enough tinned food for you to live off while you're there but, if you want to, all of his fishing and hunting gear will be there too. He's got a rifle - the same as mine, I think, but you'll know how to use it. Keep it by you if it'll make you feel safer but don't load it. There's a generator in the lean-to - its easy enough to start. I'll show you how when we get there." All that he said was either informational or, more importantly, encouragement but David could not concentrate upon what he said.

David felt empty without the monster. In a way it had been quite pleasant earlier when he had had certainty and had wanted to do something because... Accepting that his impatience and determination were no more than his tendencies toward heroic fantasies made manifest, he had obsessively worried and picked at why he should have such tendencies and had found his life wanting. If he had asked Terri Egan for a date then he would not need to fantasise about asking Terri Egan for a date. If he was not such an insignificant speck of nothingness then he would not have to fantasise about saving the world. He had long been a dreamer and, at best, it had been a harmless indulgence but, now, it would have to stop. It had been at its worse that morning. He had almost believed in the monster. He had been so sure and that - where fantasy threatened reality - was where fantasy would have to stop. As he stared through the station wagon's window he knew that even the "miracle" of his sight was no more than self-delusion. How could he be sure that his sight had improved? Could he be sure that he had not always seen the world as he saw it now? He could not and although the wish persisted, he knew that his vision need not be anything unusual let alone miraculous. His sight had never been that bad - not as bad as his father's for example – and he had not even worn glasses regularly until he was eight.

Having considered it all, he knew that the monsters had gone and was made lonely by the fact that his mind should have had need of them.

"The Smith place is about two miles North-East of here and we're probably only three of four miles if you went straight across the water." The branches of the trees above abruptly cleared as the cabin appeared before them. Unfortunately the weather was such that there was only the slightest increase in the amount of light and a considerable increase in the amount of rain falling upon the station wagon. "Here it is." David took a single look at the place and felt whatever hopes he might have had for it plummet into the most abject despair. At first, he did not know why. It was just a cabin, two or three room, indoor toilet -nothing too primitive, there must be thousands of others like it all over Canada and that, he realised, was why he was disappointed. His initial reasons for wanting to be there were very suspect if not downright stupid but some part of him had been quite pleased by the idea of being independent and to then discover that he would be living in a place which was just as comfortable as his uncle's was, inevitably, a disappointment.

The instructional tour of the cabin's facilities confirmed his fears. The only luxury which its owner had considered too luxurious was a TV, the absence of which left David undecided as to whether he faced the prospect of several days of brain-dulling boredom or had been spared the prospect of several days of brain-dulling boredom. The idea of being on his own there had quickly become an uninteresting one but he had committed himself to wanting it and in such a way that he could not back out of it.

If it had seemed an age before the three adults were prepared to leave his uncle's house then it seemed to be no more than a few minutes before they returned to it.

David stood uncomfortably in the cabin's door supposedly to say goodbye though his positioning and manner - despite his braver intentions - spoke more of a desire to prevent their leaving. His father gave him a hefty, companionable blow to the shoulder then passed out of the cabin. Just as her husband had not, his mother did not reply to his "Bye then." But she embraced him, pulling him into her warmth and the mixed smell of her perfume and of her own familiar –loved - smell. His uncle nodded to him, avoiding contact after seeing and carefully appreciating the significance of the touches which had preceded him. He mouthed the word, "Call," and followed his sister into the station wagon.

As they left David smiled and waved goodbye to them despite the sudden fear which urged him to run after them and beg them not to leave him there where the evil things could catch him. He closed the door and banished the thought knowing which part of his mind it had risen from. Almost unconsciously he fetched the lecturer's rifle from his cabinet. For a time David studied it, he knew the model, his uncle having formerly owned one. He loaded it, unloaded it, and loaded it. He sat in the armchair with its back to the wall, the light to his right then stared at the cabin's door and let the nightmares flood in. It was easy to visualise what would happen, how the door would be kicked in by a gross, clawed monstrosity its every step leaving the slime of decaying flesh in its path. Perhaps, more frighteningly, the door would be kicked in and he would see no monstrosity but only the trees beyond it.

Shape-changers, werewolves he could all but see them forcing their way in and him firing quickly, accurately. Each of the werewolves falling deceased before the floor. Werewolves in Winnipeg, he could see them roaming the streets. Yes that was much more like it. Werewolves in the school, Roy Scotton pushing the younger kids in front of himself when - TA RA! Enter Super-

Armitage and with Terri Egan to hand, yes this was definitely a fantasy that he could care for.

David took a deep, fresh breath. He blinked several times then sat up in the chair and looked around. The cabin was silent, a little darker than it had been, perhaps the lights were a little brighter. What had happened? He wondered for a dull instant before his memory answered the unspoken question. He had been daydreaming about Terri Egan, the last thing that he could remember was (having single-handedly despatched all of the drug-crazed grenade-throwing werewolves in Winnipeg) that he was organising the local populace (what they?) into cavalry units which under his direction would have cleansed Manitoba of the werewolf problem. Then he had gradually forgotten where the story was going and had fallen asleep. "Damn!" he muttered, realising that he had fallen asleep with a loaded rifle on the arms of the chair and his hands quickly began to correct the error. He glanced up at the clock on the wall. "Eleven O'clock." he read disbelievingly. How long had he been asleep for - seven hours - nine? His mind was still too confused to work it out. It did not feel as if he had slept for that long. Nine hours asleep in a chair ought to have left him feeling completely wrecked. As it was, he felt as if he had only napped for ten minutes or so.

David closed the rifle's breech and thumbed the safety catch into the "off" position. Something had changed. He stood, feeling the stiffness in his legs and walked towards the door. For a moment he paused with his fingers inches from the door's handle, the memory of his earlier fears haunting him. He swallowed, took a deep breath and opened the cabin's door. There were no cloven-hoofed monstrosities outside nor invisible creatures. He could see the trees and the grass, nothing more. One thing had changed, it had stopped raining.

He closed the door again and bolted it. Feeling embarrassed and somewhat pleased that his fears should have been shown to be so clearly foolish he walked back across the room and leaned the rifle against the armchair. Unbidden, his feet began towards the kitchen - he was completely famished.

Pain of a greater intensity than any sensation that he had ever known exploded deep within his torso. He fell not knowing that he fell and gasped in short, pained draughts of air. For an instant there was a silence in his mind - a relative calm giving him time enough to realise that he was upon the ground, that the pain was unendurable, that he would die swiftly and then the pain returned. It tore at him, toyed with him, its savage claws ripping at his body like a cat disembowelling a mouse. There was a second, briefer pause. He saw the telephone upon the desk several yards from him. He crawled towards it. One foot - two as the pain grew and peaked within him and he collapsed, unconscious.

CHAPTER 7

The pain had become like another creature living within him. It filled him, it saturated him. Its intensity was so total as to obliterate any thought and to make every sensation one of pain. At times though, the pain lessened sufficiently for something of David's awareness to creep in but such times were brief, rarely lasting for more than a few seconds. These respites, if such they were, served only to make the pain ever more unbearable. They were like the mention of heaven to the man in hell which David assuredly was.

After many hours of torment, perhaps a day, the pain declined, soon fixing itself at a lower, not quite, all-consuming level leaving sufficient space for David to think and to be aware of what was happening to him. At one time during that second phase David was even able to open his eyes. He thought of screaming but could not knowing that the effort would only increase the pain. He soon lost consciousness though his eye was held open by the floorboard which his head was pressed against.

Later, after several moments of consciousness, the pain had declined enough for him to be able to make a weak, pathetic moan. His moans grew louder, became screams and he was even able to move a hand - an arm, even a leg once though each time the pain of the effort thrust him back into unconsciousness.

Then there was the time when for a minute, perhaps even two, he was consciousness and there was no pain just the silence and the sensation of there being a great void within him. He was too tired to move though, every muscle in his body was spent. He could not even open his eyes. All of his life, his wishes, his desires became focussed upon one purpose, the need to curl up and die. The next time that he awoke it was to a screaming consciousness. In time, though the pain did not lessen, its nature changed. It reached, and remained at, a level which was not too great to make him senseless but which was sufficient to keep him low upon the ground not daring to move for fear of the pain it would cause. The hours passed and the first, lasting consciousness began to develop within his own mind. At that, it was a small part of his mind and in no other part of his body did David exist.

He cursed the pain, wondered what was happening to him and finally considered how he might stop it. The rifle was beside the chair if he could crawl over to it then he would use it upon himself. It was then that David realised that he could not move his body, that he was in a body which was no longer his. Perhaps the worst of his suffering followed that realisation and although thereafter the physical pain varied - at times even declining - the suffering did not.

Dreams occasionally harried him. Voids - great absences of all self-awareness - had their possession of him far more. When he dreamed, it was never without losing awareness of the pain and the dreams were a suffering in themselves in that they gave him a type of awareness so that he might feel the pain more keenly.

In one dream he was in the dark and the dark flowed about like a cold, substanceless liquid and he was of it, was part of it. He was in Terri Egan's bedroom watching her as she slept, the curves of her body hidden beneath her blankets, her flawless skin dully reflecting the moonlight that had filtered through into the room. He studied her longingly, wanting her but knowing that he could only watch and as he watched he accepted the reason why. Later, when he sadly reflected upon the dream he knew that the reason was to do with the fact that he was not the David that he knew but that he was another, altered individual. Altered or violated, he was not sure.

None of the other dreams were as related to anything that he knew though most had the same clarity to them. Most of his "dreams" had the substance of pure terror or pain. In some he would be lieing on his back in the middle of a desert staring at the sun knowing that in so doing, he was gradually blinding himself and that while he was doing this tiny armies of pincered, chitenous creatures tore at his flesh.

Understandably, torture and destruction were the common themes of his dreams. Once they took the form of an unbelievably rapid decomposition, his body falling apart while he lived - felt everything. Normally though his body was either being mutilated or consumed by other creatures. The creatures seemed always to be individually unthinking but to have a great collective purpose. Often they were beetle-like, at other times they had fang and fur and yet at other times they moved with something like a spider though neither their form nor texture was consistent.

In total, he had four major visions which were distinct from the persistent dreams of suffering. The visions were distinct in that they were not related directly to the pain and in that, more so than the suffering dreams, they were beyond any experiences of dreams that he had ever had. He would have said that they were more beyond his comprehension than the other dreams had he been able and had his understanding of their meaning, at a deep, intuitive level not been so absolute.

The first vision was of where he had seen Terri and it had been almost lost amongst several hours of the suffering dreams that were, in time, followed by the first of the great absences.

The second vision came after the absence and immediately prior to the bloody resumption of the suffering dreams.

The vision lasted for, at the most, ten or fifteen seconds. It was clear, unnaturally so. Every detail of it had its correct colour, perspective and depth even down to the completeness of his peripheral vision. It was as if he had opened his eyes and was there.

"There" seemed to be a gas-station in one of the western American states. they were in the diner next to the station having stopped there for a late breakfast. "They" were David and his two companions who faced him across their half eaten meals and the damp, red Formica of the table-top. Directly facing him was a young woman. She was tall perhaps five foot ten, slim and pretty. Her hair though dark, was auburn and expensively cut. She was saying something light, inconsequential, he did not know what but in the vision he heard himself make the appropriate response. The two of them had spoken with the ease and familiarity of long association. He loved her and she loved him though their love had grown through the things that they had experienced together, through the dangers that they had overcome together. They loved one another but were not lovers and might never be. They were partners, they relied implicitly upon one another and were set apart from all others not only through what they had achieved together but through what they were. They were not blind to each other's faults, there were aspects of each other's personalities which each disliked in the other, and they would die for one another.

Beside David's partner sat a young girl - no more than twelve or thirteen years old. She had the fine bone structure and evenness of features that were indicative of her beauty to come. At that moment she was intently reading a paperback. He knew that she had only recently joined them and that she was finding it difficult, crying a great deal and not readily accepting the truth about herself. Both she and David's partner were alike in that what set them apart from each other was a mental rather than a physical thing.

David turned his head at the sound of the door in time to see two men entering the diner. The first of them smiled momentarily at the sight of strangers in the diner. David looked away avoiding the challenge in the man's stare. He did not look away through fear but rather to avoid complicating things. Their work was not here but was another three hundred miles on. He looked again at his partner and she at him, unflinching, neither with anything to hide. Her expression was blank and David knew that few men would have met her gaze. "Nothing to worry about," she said, chewing, "Yet."

Perhaps a day passed between the second and third visions, a day with only the occasional absence to provide respite from the pain and the nightmares.

Of the four visions it was the third which was the most inexplicable and the one which, more than any other, struck to the very heart of his terror. It was the one that would allow no redeeming hope to survive beside it. Along with the pain, it was the most real experience that he would ever have.

The vision began in their Winnipeg home. David was in the kitchen while his mother was sitting just through the doorway reading. The room was brighter than it would ordinarily be, the air cleaner, sharper. Every detail of the room seemed to be sharper. At first, he did not understand how it was that everything seemed to be exactly as he remembered it but more so. Then he realised that it was he that had changed. His every sense was several times more acute than normal. He could almost taste the air and his sight was such that when he looked at the far, white wall it filled his vision, its brightness almost paining him and, if he focused upon it, the tiniest section grew larger before him and ever larger as he stared at it.

Benny scratched at the door to be let in. Benny was the dog that they had had three or four years before until his persistent excavations of their neighbours gardens had led to his being given to friends who lived further out in the country. David stood and walked the yard or two to the door. He opened the door and Benny scuttled hopefully past him towards his bowl. It was then, as he began to close the door, that it grabbed David about his throat. It had waited silently for the right moment than had come forward unbelievably quickly. Whatever it was did not matter, what did was the fact that it could crush his windpipe if it so wished and that its more immediate wish was to drag him out of the house to it.

Upon feeling the touch of the creature, David had, instinctively, jumped back as far as he had been allowed and, fortuitously, had grasped the doorframe. Realising that his grip upon it was all that had thus far, saved him, David hauled himself backwards until he could look back into the room where his mother sat. "Its got me," he gasped and she instantly stared at the ground in deep concentration her lips muttering the words which might help him. David knew that if he could apply himself in the same way that, together, they would have their only realistic chance of saving him.

His feet were already raised in the air before him as the creature had grabbed him with its other limb and finally, having tired of waiting, the creature began to draw him towards it. David looked out into the dark but could see nothing and knew that it had been a foolish expectation as the creature had no visible form.

The vital moment was upon him, if his and his mother's efforts could not prevent his being pulled out of the house then he was lost.

He awoke and stared dully at the sun-bleached wood of the floorboards. Strange, being in the house he could understand as well as the dog and the creature but his mother would not have reacted as she had. She would not have known how to even though it was the right, the only, thing to do.

The floorboards were dusty he noted in the few seconds or so that he had. He had forgotten about the pain as if the vision were the reality and the pain the dream. Then he remembered that the pain was still with him, that it had never left him and he quickly retreated back into unconsciousness.

The fourth and final vision followed soon after the third - perhaps no more than two hours and by then the more explicable dreams of suffering had effectively ended.

In the fourth vision, David - the changed David - the set-apart from-all-others David - was in a cramped, damp cavern, somewhere near to its entrance he presumed as he could see the dark, eroded rock of the cavern clearly enough. He looked further into the cavern to where the dark deepened and grew more oppressive. Annoyed, he sighed at first not knowing why then remembering what lay ahead of him. Deep within the cavern waiting for David to come to him was his nemesis the one who was unlike him in all that he despised and like him in all that he despised. He would not come to David, he would wait for David to come to him - on his conditions. They were too alike, too well matched. Only one of them would live.

Sadly, uncaringly, David began to walk forward. It was shortly after that, last, vision that he truly awoke.

CHAPTER 8

At first with a mounting sense of panic, then with a dull sense of disbelief, David awoke. He lay upon the bed wearing nothing but his jeans. The bedsheets were pulled and knotted about him, soaked and reeking of his sweat. With a pained slowness and weariness he began to disentangle himself. His head flopped over the edge of he bed and his body inexorably followed. Too weak to raise his hands, his face thudded onto the floor then was pushed painfully across its surface by the toppling mass of his body. He lay there for a time trying to assess whatever damage had been done. The great intensity of pain had gone leaving his every muscle aching and weary.

For a long, long time he lay unmoving upon the ground then, at first limb by limb, he began to move forward. He was soon crawling and with every yard he became more aware of the strength that remained within him and, in that knowledge, grew more determined. The bathroom was soon reached and, painfully, he pulled himself up onto the edge of the bath from where he could drink from the basin. The cold tap turned with a little reluctance and he drank thirstily straight from it.

He was unaware of what he had carried with him from the bed and so it was not until his thirst was satisfied that he looked up from the basin to the mirror on the splashboard and saw what was behind him. It was not of man nor woman nor animal. It was touching him.

In sheer revulsion he spewed the water which he had just drunk back into the basin then ducked so that he would not have to look in the mirror, inadvertently cracking his jaw against the basin's edge. Then he remembered what it was that he had dreamed of before and which his mind, at the time, had not allowed him to remember and he fainted in absolute terror. The blood began to pour from his back.

At the most, he was unconscious for ten minutes or so before he awoke again cursing that last vision but, all too soon, all too cruelly, he became aware of the pressure between his back and the wall. He brought his hands together then and prayed to Christ that it had not happened, that it would go away but while he was doing this, the blood flowed from his back and the pressure of it forced him further away from the wall and onto his front. He cried then too but that changed nothing.

The dark, light-boned membranes which he had seen grew stronger, grew fuller with the blood which was flowing into them but, like his every muscle, they were far too weak and could not maintain their structure or form. The blood flow to them was, at that stage, uncontrolled and first one then the other grew larger, weaker and again was once more filled.

David cried and prayed but neither brought the immediate and absolute cleansing that he needed. In time both stopped leaving him to the obscene sensations of his blood ebbing and flowing within him. Had he wanted to, he felt that he could control its flow but he did not dare attempt it for fear of his being damned in so doing.

Yet it could not continue, something had to change, something had to give and, eventually, it was David. It was his own weariness which finally betrayed him. He was too tired and he despaired of both prayer and tears. For a few minutes he just lay there until he realised what he had done, that, if only for a few minutes, he had not fought against the monstrosity that was upon his back. However brief an acceptance it had been, it had nevertheless been acceptance. He beat his head viciously against the ground until he was too sick to continue and at the end of it, despite his pain he had not awoken and it was not a dream.

David pulled himself back on to the edge of the bath and turned the faucet on to rid the basin of its contents. He did not look up from the basin, did not dare to. Again, after several moments, he came to accept that there would have to be a time when he did look and that it might as well be then. He could feel the weight behind him, he knew that they were filled with his blood and could grow no more.

David looked. Behind him the wings that he had dreamed of were full and broad not the dark and half-shrunken mass which he had seen before but larger, more powerful. The feathers no longer shrivelled fibres but expanded, they were a dark ashen grey in colour and he began to cry at the detail. In themself, they were not monstrous, in themself they were beautiful but their existence made a monster of him. He cried harder and for all of his tears it changed nothing.

He rose and stumbled out of the bathroom instinctively wishing to flee the mirror. He wandered aimlessly about the bedroom his gait unbalanced by the mutated flesh upon his back. He lay upon the bed and drew the sheets about himself until he lay protected within a dark, warm cocoon of cloth. As his tears began to flow again he began to bite upon his thumb nail but even that, partially excusable, vice soon gave way to its infantile precursor and he sucked upon his thumb then lay there a pathetic, stinking freak with the emotional hurt and dirtied soul of a child.

David cried, and prayed, for the obscenity to go away for it to have never happened. In time, the tears brought comfort, of a sort, and he slept.

After perhaps half an hour, David awoke again and lay there vacant-eyed, conscious of his wings and hating them. He was uncomfortably aware of his own stink and it was that, more than anything, which caused him to push away his sheets. The wings had diminished during his sleep. Having been drained of blood they had contracted to their smallest possible volume - yet they were still there. Some straps and a thick jacket might flatten them against his back enough for them to be imperceptible he realised and, in the same instant, knew that it would be pointless to attempt it, that they would still be there and that he would still be a freak, a monster.

David returned to the bathroom and urinated despising the thought that the obscenity which his body had become could be capable of so human an action. He began to leave the room only to pause in the doorway and to then abruptly jump backwards against it again and again as though, animal-like, he could knock the wings off. His actions achieved nothing perhaps the bruising of his own flesh but nothing more. He thought of crying then but doubted that he still had the capacity within him to do such a thing. Aimlessly, he began to wander about the cabin sometimes clearing up a little of the mess that his tortured threshing had made of it. But never looking to a mirror nor allowing his mind to consider the horror that had been thrust upon him. All too soon his apathetic course led him into the kitchen where the sight which met him cast a chill which struck deep into his soul once again.

A tap was running and the water had been splashed all about as if an animal had drunk from it, an animal that knew nothing of vessels and could not even cup its own hands to drink. Upon the floor were tins and packets of food that had been ripped and hacked open by the same animal. A broken knife testified to the creature's having had some intelligence but the state of the food's containers and of the food itself which had been eaten off the floor still told most powerfully of an animal, of David.

He staggered backwards out of the kitchen then turned abruptly so that he could no longer see inside it, his heart was beating frantically. During one, if not more of his "absences" he must have done it and if that was so, then what else might he have done? Unable to resist, he began to walk towards the cabin's door drawn compellingly on by his own fear. The porch was clear and the land before it still bore the tracks of his uncle's station wagon despite the rain which had accompanied his arrival at the hut. There were no new tracks, no sign of his having left the cabin. Yet it was not enough and he ran frantically around the cabin searching, oblivious to his own partial nakedness. There was no evidence of his ever having left the cabin he realised after the third circuit not unless he had... and he kicked the cabin's wall for his having put such a callous suggestion into his mind.

Wearily, he walked out into the centre of the small clearing that was directly in front of the cabin his wings, unconsciously, filling out. Then David looked upwards a surly resentment in his eyes and mouthed the single word, "Why?" There was no apparent reply. Again he asked, then ever more insistently, he went down upon his knees, asked -prayed - begged - demanded and still heard no reply. For perhaps forty minutes he knelt in the clearing saying Our Fathers and Hail Marys until the words ran into one another and became a breathless chant. David prayed to the God which then, more than ever, he believed intensely in. Then, as his increasing despair had almost grown strong enough to drive him away from that place and his vain invocation, he heard the unmistakeable sound of a telephone ringing. Slowly, feeling very cold and alone, he walked back into the cabin. The telephone was upon the lecturer's desktop untouched by the chaos which David had brought to the cabin. It was red and terribly, terribly loud.

He picked it up. "David?"

"Yes."

"Oh, good." It was his mother's voice. "I phoned this morning but there was no reply - you must n't have been in."

"No__." He mumbled, instinctively lying, not having the courage to tell the truth. "I must have been fishing."

"I thought so." He could sense the dissatisfaction in his mother's voice, hushed but nevertheless there. "I thought that you would have phoned before now."

"No - no - " a lie came readily to his lips but he could not speak.

"Well -never mind - you should have phoned."

"I'm sorry," he stated his voice falling away, "I'm so sorry mother."

"Never - mind. You sound so much better than when you called before, your cold must be better. - Listen it's been four days now so we'll come to pick you up about noon tomorrow. We still think that we should spend most of the holiday together, we are still a family after all."

"OK Mom -bye then."

"Bye -David - I love you."

"Bye - I love you." He heard the receiver being put down on the other end. Dully he replaced his own receiver and turned back to the centre of the room as if God were there more than anywhere. "Is that it?" he asked. "Is that your answer? -What does it mean? Does it mean, they're coming tomorrow and I'd better not be here then or that I'd better be here? Which? What the hell kind of sign is that?" Unconsciously, he took a step forward causing his left wing to painfully strike the edge of the desk. He touched the pained area instinctively then, realising this, he thrust it away. A sudden spasm of anguish caught in his throat then he walked forward, kneeled and prayed again.

As the sun set and the room darkened around him, he prayed. Endless Acts of Sorrows, endless Confiteors. Father I have sinned - spare me from thy vengeance.

As he prayed and the wings remained upon his back, filling and contracting at his whim, a fear which grew into a determined belief nagged at him until he could almost picture Father Heaton, his first parish priest, standing behind him, muttering, "Only demons would need to warp your body. God would just will it - like snapping his fingers - and there they would be. They'd be complete - probably invisible too."

Eventually he made the sign of the cross and stood rubbing the soreness from his knees. His path was clear.

David sat in the armchair, picked up the rifle, loaded it then placed its butt upon the floor and the end of its barrel in his mouth. No demons would use him. For a few moments he paused, thinking implausibly of Terri Egan amused by the realisation that -even though he was about to make a sacrifice of an order that he had often daydreamed about - he could not have cared less about whether she would know or understand. He removed the barrel from his mouth, released the safety catch, returned the wet, cold barrel into his mouth, reached down and pushed the rifle's trigger.

The rifle butt slipped pulling the barrel from his mouth and, clumsily, he caught it feeling an instinctive fear of its going off. His fingers had begun to return the barrel to his mouth when he paused, halted. Was this the sign? The miracle? Of course it could not be. Rifles of this calibre could not have hair-triggers, they would be far too dangerous to their owners and being the length that it was it had to be at such an angle that it would slip. He could do it a thousand times and the result would always be the same.

If he was going to do it then he would have to support the rifle butt. It could be done by standing but for some reason that did not appeal to him. David pulled the armchair over to the wall so that he could support the rifle butt at the junction of wall and floor. He sat in the chair then looked over its back. He would make one hell of a mess. The rifle's bullet would not just lodge in his skill, there would be blood and brains everywhere. He could do it in the bathroom of course, he thought and then stood. He knew that he would not sit there again with the barrel in his mouth.

David knew that he could not let his mother find him like that. It was not the suicide, he just could not let her find a dead monster where her son had been. The tears which had deserted him for the past few hours began to flow again. He cried for his mother, for himself and for the knowledge that he would rather live secretly hiding his monstrosity than die and let others know of it.

The tears did not abate but after a time he began to wonder. Had it been God's test? Had he passed? At some deep, unconscious level David knew that he had passed. After all he had pushed the trigger without realising that it could not have killed. It was not God's test. There was no explanation but there was certainty. He had done the right thing.

David knew that it was over, that the worst of his ordeal had been endured and completed. For a few moments he dared to believe that it had been nothing but a test and he rushed back into the bathroom hoping that his wings were no more than a temporary insanity which, now that he had redeemed himself, would have vanished.

The wings were still there, still full, still proud and his tears had stopped.

David clasped his hands together and bowed his head. "Lord Jesus Christ I love and honour you." he stated, "If it is your will that I be like this then I accept your will. If you have some purpose for me then I accept that purpose. I only ask that you answer my question. Lord, I would like to know why it is that you have chosen me - why have you done this to me." Speak Lord your servant has asked a question. He looked up, saw himself in the mirror. He looked to the left, right, listened intently.

"You no account son of a bitch!" he shouted. "You did this to me or you let this happen to me. Either way you knew all about it. Look at it - look at it! This is my body and you did it, I think that the least I deserve is one word -one word - one bastard revelation. It's not much to ask for." he said and wondered why it was that he was almost laughing. He looked at the face in the mirror, saw its grin broaden then he rubbed his nose and turned to leave the bathroom. "I guess I'm done. I guess I'll have to figure it out for myself."

CHAPTER 9

Mickey had finally persuaded David to go with him to the inappropriately named Young Catholics Social Club Night. An event that usually resulted in the most anti-social and unchristian of behaviour though, to be fair, it did take place at night, the participants were invariably young and clubs were often involved.

It was almost a month since David had taken the train to Lake Nipigen and his secret had remained just that. He was acutely conscious of it himself. In truth such was his own awkwardness, self-consciousness and paranoiac desire for privacy that nobody else had noticed any change in him. Hiding it while he slept was still a problem but the straps, a voluminous pyjama jacket and his mother's respect for his privacy had left him in comparative safety. He had taken to being the first to wake which did not come easily but which was justified in the defence of his secret and for the opportunity which it gave him to expand and flex his cramped wings.

Outside of the home his secret had become a far greater ordeal. The first day back at school had been a horrific succession of shaming possibilities. He had been constantly on the brink of vomiting, sickened by his misshapen body blaspheming against the mundanity of the school day. David quickly realised, however, that the thing which was most likely to expose him was his own sense of exposure and he was soon able to disguise it. Of necessity he had learned to live in shame and to hide that shame.

Throughout the bus ride to the club Mickey told David of how he was going to "do" some girl a favour tonight and of how "the only way to make girls come on to you was to disrespect them, let them know that you could get better if you wanted to. Keep them grateful and," above all, "don't let on that you're really after them." A fine theory with aeons of practical research behind it. Unfortunately, upon entering the club, his jaw dropped to somewhere about crutch level and he began to salivate excessively at the sight of vaguely female flesh. Like most would-be studs of his age Mickey had ambitions and belief which far outstripped his realism. To his credit, though, he usually gave up after the fifth rebuttal and sought after less optimistic company. He was not excessively particular -anything in a skirt that had shaved that morning would do. Mickey the Hammer was God's gift to the unlovely girls unfortunately for him, most of them had too much self-respect to share that perception.

David dragged Mickey over to the non-alcoholic bar where they bought themselves a coke each and stood for a time with the *boys*. Mickey slipped effortlessly into the social mode. In common with the others he would glance across the near-vacant floor at the "girls" with expressions that ranged between disinterest and contempt. He would also burst into semi-frantic jigging – it would not be accurate to call it dancing - for about ten seconds then stop seemingly without any self-awareness of his actions.

Automatically David began to move away from the crush of bodies with Mickey reluctantly following. David finally stopped with his back against the wall. Mickey stood for a few moments surveying the girls his weight shifting anxiously from one foot to the other. "Come on girls," he hissed, "which one of you is going to get lucky tonight?"

"Mickey - you're a jerk!" exclaimed David, one tenth appalled, one tenth amused and eight tenths bemused. What were girls for again? Relationships? He could no longer see the relevance.

"Yeah? Well what does that make you?" David shrugged - a gesture which he had only recently perfected.

"I guess it makes me a jerk's best friend."

"You're a jerk yourself."

"Maybe - nobody's perfect." Mickey nodded and commented on the obvious,

"Nobody's dancing."

Roy Scotton and his gang breezed into the club and straight on towards the bar pulling with them their counterpart group of girls and the interest of several other unclaimed girls. The hall's lights darkened and strobed as another CD was entered into the school's archaic P.A. system. The Scotton gang moved out onto the dance floor several of their members not deigning to dance. David watched with a certain degree of confusion. Part of him still wanted to respond emotionally and to be angry as hell but the major part of him could not care less. Mickey began to dance by himself. It was one of his most favoured ploys. He would proceed to dance alone until he was close to the most gorgeous girl that he could find and then ... Well there was no "And then" it was enough to be close and it generally worked until said girl noticed him. David began to edge away from him. "Hey, what about them?" asked Mickey abruptly coming to a halt and gesturing across to where two girls sat against the wall.

David removed his glasses apparently to rub the bridge of his nose but actually so that he could see who the two girls were: Josie Caffyn and Terri Egan. David smiled lightly, ironically, he had scarcely thought of Terri since the change and had not even noticed her in school. His own emotional reaction or, rather, the lack of amused him. I ought to be feeling pain here, he thought, and knew that he was not. A line from St. Paul came to him, "When I was a child, I thought like a child" now that I am a man I skulk in the shadows and keep my back to the wall. Skulk - lovely word that, he felt as if he had been born to it. "I reckon I could get somewhere there." said Mickey.

"With which one?"

"Josie girl, of course."

"But you called her a dwarf the other week." David remarked, gently mocking.

"Look some of us don't have a thyroid problem. Some of us were built for quality rather than quantity unlike some of us." David grinned and placed his glasses into their case. Nobody had noticed them either. Contact lenses he assumed not that anybody had commented. "Come with me then."

"What?"

"Come with me."

"No. You want to ask her, you ask her."

"Yeah but - " he jerked his thumb towards the dance floor, "I'm not going out there on my own."

"Hi girls." said Mickey, one of his better-rehearsed, better-executed lines. The two girls looked away from each other to Mickey and to his reluctantly following companion. Mickey gave Josie what he thought was a long, lingering stare. She giggled. "Do you want to dance?" She giggled again and looked to her friend.

"Why not?" Mickey almost gambolled with delight. He grabbed her by both wrists and dragged her out onto the dance floor before she could change her mind. David stood numbly for a moment. Terri avoided looking at him but it might have been a significant non-look, he mused whimsically.

"Hi," he said and she gave one of those not-looks and might have made a noise which, it could be argued, was the sort of non-response that was enough like "Hi" to avoid the charge of rudeness and enough unlike "Hi" to avoid the possibility of any further communication. David sat down leaving an empty chair between the two of them. He leaned back, resting his elbows on the two adjacent chairs and watched, without seeing, the couples on the dance floor.

So where do we go from here? He thought and the answer came swift and sure. We walk home alone, we go into our home alone, we go to our bed alone and we try to do something to fill in the empty time between now and then.

Should he talk to her? It would fill the time in and he knew, instinctively, that he did not care anymore. Not for her – other than in the, general, others matter sense - nor for what she thought about him. So what about? Girlie talk? Do you have problems getting the right shampoo type? Greasy? Dry? Feathered? Tell me about it. No, just talk. One person to another. He grinned as a bitter but curiously pleasing realisation struck him -wouldn't it be delightfully ironical if she had yearned for him too, now that nothing could come of it. He turned towards her, "Hi!" Don't fix it if it works. Her head inclined the merest fraction towards him, "You're name is Terri isn't it? My name is David - David Armitage." She looked at him.

In his sheltered existence up to that point David had lived under the misconception that men were supposedly the aggressive half of mankind. With that one look, he came to realise that men were not the truly competitive ones. Men placed their competitiveness into fantasy situations such as sports or careers. Even male violence was as often as not serious but bloody mindlessness. True aggression, true competitiveness, true viciousness belongs exclusively in social control. All of which was present in the look that his once-longed-for Terri turned upon him. Extreme violence having been done, she dismissed him from her awareness and looked forward again. There is nothing for it now, he thought, except to go as far away as possible, to dig a hole, lie in it and hold my breath until the world is no longer besmirched by my existence. But there again...

Since the change, strange thoughts had constantly nagged at his consciousness, mostly absurd comments on his absurd existence. "I have to go now - must fly." "Now then David, son, no point brooding on it..." Part of him embraced the irony of it all with something like joy, something like insanity. Whatever it was, it would not let this sixteen year old girl dismiss him from the ranks of humankind ... not without having first underlined (with a quill) one or two relevant facts. "David Armitage," he continued, "privileged to meet you." There is something intrinsically noble about somebody who does not know when they are beaten. Either that or intrinsically stupid. She continued to stare steadfastly ahead. He waited. After several minutes of her ignoring and him waiting she turned abruptly towards him,

"I know doesn't your mother work at Martin's Store?" Clearly he was human enough to talk to but mutually unrequited obsession was no longer a strong likelihood. She had been his God. He had been the son of that woman who worked at Martin's. A few months before his life would have ended, as it was, it did not hurt especially and he had found something to fill some time in.

"That's right," he answered cheerfully, "well she used to. She stopped when she had my baby brother Paul." Her face had begun to rotate slowly back towards the dancers. He suspected that each word from his lips equalled degrees of disinclination. Regardless of it all, his brain continued to churn words out which neither of them paid any particular attention to. "I suppose that he's quite cute now. Mind he wasn't always like that. When he was born, he was so ugly. My sister said that we should have kept the afterbirth and thrown him away." In a moment of rare concordance they both stiffened in shock. What? He thought, I don't say things like that! Her head could not have turned further away from him without her having had a gene transplant from an owl and, for the first time, he did not blame her. Time to go. He rose to leave then hesitated in front of her, "Sorry, bad joke," he muttered. For a moment her mouth seemed to twitch as if, automatically, she was going to respond but then she realised that, overall, she would much rather stay offended. Although he was directly in front of her, she managed to avoid noticing him completely. "I'll just get a Coke then."

"If you were thinking of getting me one, don't." she said, her eyes impaling him against the far wall. Fair enough, he mused, less insulted than she had hoped, and made his way across to the bar.

At the bar, he was served unusually quickly (an eagle-eyed barkeep!) and he retired to an empty stretch of wall.

What now? Walk home alone, into home alone, to bed alone. For reasons that she could not even guess at, she was quite right to detest him. The only sensible, realistic option for him was to be quiet and to hide. All of which he knew perfectly well. Be quiet and hide, he thought as he moved away from the wall. Be quiet and hide, he thought as danced for a yard or two. Be quiet and hide, he thought as he stood before her. He knew and he agreed intellectually that it was the right thing to do but at another, almost unconscious level, he had decided upon another approach. Damned if I do, damned if I don't, he thought as he hunkered down forcing her to look at him. "I used to love you," he said. A few months before he would have self-imploded at this point, tonight it just seemed like a reasonable jumping off point. She straightened her back in obvious fright. "Don't worry though. I don't anymore and I'm not the stalker from Hell either. You've nothing to worry about there. I didn't really love *you* - you just provided a rather lovely looking shell. I didn't love *you*, I didn't know *you*. I've only really just met you. But I loved and there was something fine and noble there- I was not in lust, I was in love. So what point am I making?" Exactly! He thought - an iron will and unhesitating courage had brought him this far but the capacity to reason seemed to have been swept overboard way back when. "I guess it's just that I am as human as anyone." As if. "I apologise for projecting my romantic fantasies into your body, I've no right to do that." She just looked stunned now - no, stunned *and* appalled. "But I am human too. You can try to deny it with a look, you can try to deny it with your words but you can not deny it." Where, he wondered in the desperate silence that followed, does this poor little girl figure in all of this? Why did I say all of this to her, it was not provoked by her, it was not intended for her. She sat there a bemused, perhaps frightened, sixteen-year old girl. He stood, slowly, an old, old sixteen-year old something. He smiled and bowed slightly, unconsciously, "I'm so sorry. From the bottom of my heart -I apologise for any and every hurt that I may have caused you." He had heard that on TV once, it seemed appropriate. "I'll go now and I swear that you will never so much as be aware of me again." He repeated the slight, unconscious bow and exited down stage with considerable haste.

Back at the wall he picked up his barely touched Coke and gulped a mouthful down. He turned his back to her, avoiding any form of contact. The hall was hers, the world was hers and he wouldn't be anywhere on it at least as far as she would ever know. He took another mouthful coming to the immediate and obvious conclusion that if he were to let his instincts make his decisions for him, that he was going to get himself into a great deal more trouble than this little incident. Poor child, there had been no need to go pecking at her.

"David." he jumped in fright, sickeningly feeling his wings contract. She stood behind him.

"Christ!" he turned to face her. Here it comes, he thought, she's either going to knife me or open her mouth and do me some serious damage. Whichever it was, the decent thing to do would be to stand there and take it. He allowed his gaze, and several hundred pounds of armour to drop to the floor.

"It was not... David." Something about her tone compelled him to look up. Their eyes met and crackled with mutual confusion and embarrassment. "I accept your apology." Here it comes, the noise between his ears anticipated but something was not right ... she looked ... like what she was - a shy teenage girl trying to establish some sort of contact with an utter stranger. She looked away awkwardly then back towards him, "I may have been rude, I'm sorry too." The impact of his jaw hitting the floor sent him into complete silence. She dropped the eye contact and began to retreat. That, he realised, had been a very hard thing to do.

"No problem," he muttered. She smiled fleetingly. It was not a warm smile, it was a "I'm done and I'm getting out of here," smile. She began to turn and walk away. "Bugger it!" She froze and he knew that if he was going to get all weird again that she would defend herself, that she would finish it. She looked at him, waiting. "Bugger," he said much more quietly. He did not know what to say, "let's just pretend that we're both two human type people. There's no need for both of us to sit alone. We could talk - nothing meant by it just talk -maybe while away some of the time before we both go home alone." but there again ... She looked at him, pouted, considered the possibility. "Why not?" they both knew that nothing would come of it. He saw that she had brought a drink with her. She took a sip on it and turned her back to the wall parallel to him. They both looked at the dancers neither spoke. They were not bothered about talking or about not talking it was not as if they did matter to each other.

"There is Thomas Scanlon," she commented after a time, "have you seen his brother lately?" His elder brother, Kiefer, was a notorious drug abuser.

"Yeah," replied David, one human type person to another, "Christ he's in a bad way. The drugs have done for him -he's lost so many brain cells now that he can hardly get to the end of a sandwich."

Brilliant.

CHAPTER 10

It should not have been as it was. Physically it was impossible, morally it was profane. Yet he could do it, it hurt nobody and it felt so undeniably good. It was wrong though. He knew it and could do nothing to stop himself. The concept was wrong, was blasphemous and the practice changed the world.

Mankind was meant to view the face of the world from its face not from above. David knew the facts, the morality, the practical implausibility of it and yet still he had wings and yet still he flew. He had tried, determinedly, not to. Believing that to use the wings would involve some perverse failure just as he had believed at the beginning that accepting their existence would.. Unlikely - even laughable -though it might seem, the wings were the temptation that Satan had cast before him and, to David, the thought of using them would be the equivalent of yielding to Satan, which was precisely what he did.

His decline began with a sneeze in the bathroom when, involuntarily, he had thrust his, full, wings backward and down. He had cracked his forehead open on the window frame above the window and had fallen, stupefied into the bath which he had easily cleared.

For several minutes he had lain there discomforted by the bulk of his wings and oblivious to the blood which, congealing, had streaked its way down his face. Birds, with their large wing area to low weight ratio could fly. For a man to be able to fly his wings would need to be many times greater than David's were. When filled, David's wingtips could extend to little more than half a metre below his feet. Even given the fact that his wings were too small to make flying feasible, the muscles that such flight needed would have to be powerful enough to rip his torso apart. David's flying was physically impossible and yet he had thrown himself across half of the bathroom. He lay in the bath and thought of crying because he knew that he had the power, however little he wanted it, and because there would come a time when, perhaps of necessity, he would use it.

That time came, less than a month after when he stood in an empty warehouse where he knew that he could not be seen and, head bowed, he let the blood flow into his wings.

When he was ready, he prayed for guidance and flexed the muscles which six months before had not existed and which now felt as natural and as responsive to him as any that he had been born with.

David thought then of which God to believe in. If his god was science then he would either not fly or would rip himself apart in the effort. If he believed in the One God.... he was still no nearer to understanding.

Scientifically, what then occurred was the redefinition of the impossible as the currently inexplicable. Raising himself into the air was impossible and not particularly difficult to him. Avoiding contact with girders, cables, walls, roofs and floors at excessive velocities was beyond him. He was heartened, however, by the difficulty of it, feeling that Satan would have made it considerably easier for him.

After many visits to the warehouse he eventually learned to master his power. During the course of his learning, David's attitude to the wings and to God changed. He would pray to God daily, hourly and not a feather did he lose or word hear. Eventually he came to accept his abnormality. His attitude to life and to his place in it had changed. The world had lost its context of inexplicable fears and of the disproportionate significance of so many petty things. Even if he were to lose his wings he would never again be the boy that he had been. Equally, he knew that he would never be a man amongst men.

To a large degree, David knew his fate: he would be discovered either through carelessness or bad luck. Most probably through illness as his changed physique extended to improved eyesight, the growing of wings and damned all else. He hoped and he prayed that it would not happen while his parents lived. Far too clearly he could picture what would happen once his shame became known and how he would become a monster, a freak, how in his being seen as such, he would be robbed of his own humanity. Initially, it was amongst his greatest fears but as he came to accept the inevitability of it so other motivations and desires came to the fore. One in particular was contrary to the fear: the wish - no, need - to fly in the open.

David wanted to fly in the cool night air as he had dreamt and, increasingly, dreamed. He had to fly on the wind, gliding between thermals, caressing and using the sea of currents that he could sense in the daylight.

He flew from the roof of his house usually two or three hours before the dawn and it was wonderful. It was his completion, the greatest experience and the greatest pleasure that he would ever know. It was a wholly primeval delight, untinged by the concepts of science and religion. It was his completion and on the third night there was a figure waiting upon the roof of his house.

At first David feared that it was his mother but the figure was clearly that of a man and there was something about his squatting, controlled posture which excluded the possibility of it being his father. In the second or so between David's seeing the man and his realisation that he had to do something, his flight had carried him to within twenty yards of the rooftop. David caught himself and hovered, thinking furiously. He could fly away never to return - the man clearly knew which house he had come from and whilst David's secret would be lost there was still the possibility of his sparing his parents. David took in the details of the man's face - eyes and knew then that he should not fly away. There was something missing, the single quality whose absence could prevent his fleeing: surprise.

David let the wind pull him on towards him then dropped, landing several yards away from him. The man stared at David as David stared at him an unnatural frankness and piercing quality to both of their gazes.

The man was about thirty years old. He was unshaven, tanned and there was a vague, indistinct quality to his hands, his clothes the wrinkling of his skin which made David aware of hardiness, a weathered quality to him. Homeless. The thought appeared shaming him through all of the pre-conceptions that it dragged along with it. Here was a man who slept in doorways, or worse yet, forests. Even more indefinably, there was something about the man which struck David as being both feral and menacing.

The two stared at one another for a long minute neither speaking nor moving. David had unconsciously clenched his wings behind himself, prepared to thrust forward or back, whichever was necessary.

The man glanced away and smiled showing broad, slightly uneven teeth. "I've been waiting a long time for you, boy," he stated.

David's hopes rose, fell, plummeted.

"And who am I then?" he asked and it was near to the question that had beset him for so many months.

"How the hell should I know?" The man shrugged. "I don't know who you are but I know what you are." He added anticipating the question. David stared at him and found his gaze met equally, hardness for hardness, hate for hate. "You're a smell in the wind," he acknowledged David's confusion with the hint of a humourless smile. "You're a freak," Despair, anger, the possibility of killing the man all flashed through David's mind before the sentence was completed. "I know because I'm one too." Disbelievingly, David searched in the man's face for contempt or amusement but found neither, only a sad, even cynical, calmness. There was to be no smile, no pleasure in their mutual distinctiveness. Their only bond was to be in their common shame and intuitively David knew that the man was like him, that he understood. Nevertheless, he asked,

"Where are your bloody wings then?"

"I've no wings," he replied curtly. "There are freaks and there are freaks and I'm not one of the feathered ones." He watched David, waiting for a response then looked away and patted the acutely sloping rooftop to his left. "Sit down and I'll tell you the story of my life - I guess yours will be similar." Uneasily, David sat managing only with considerable difficulty not to slide off. The stranger, seemingly, had no problems in remaining upon the rooftop. "Look at this," he stated and held his left hand up.

As David watched the angle between the man's wrist and the back of his hand grew more acute until it was something less than seventy degrees. In involuntary disgust David swore. "Believe it," said the man and he turned the hand so that David saw where his thumb had thickened and elongated until it lay alongside his fingers all of which, in common with it, seemed to have a greatly reduced movement of the knuckles.

"That's obscene!"

"You're no beauty yourself."

"Sorry," muttered David in apology, blushing.

"Yeah," grunted the man his hand slowly returning to its original form.

"How did that happen to you - to me? What are we?"

"We're freaks!" the man snapped, "Don't give me your questions. I don't know the answers. Do you?" David shook his head. "Then shut up and listen." Glumly, David nodded his assent. "All right." The man rubbed his jaw with a near-normal left hand. "What's your name?"

"D-david."

"Sullivan then if it's first names. Right - well it happened to me when I was twenty-two - seven years ago. I was married then. Two young girls - still just babies. I got - this feeling - no need - I had to get out, out of the house, the street - everything. It built up quite slowly over, maybe, eight months, by the end of it I just had to get out. I'd lost Helen and the girls by then," he paused, "it was for the best.

"I was out on my own for another four months before I could face anybody and by then it had happened. I was like I am now. I change, you see, not just my hands but my feet and my spine." He shrugged, "You fly. I run for hours, days if I had to."

"Are there others like us?" David asked tentatively. Sullivan shrugged,

"I've been looking for eight years - all over the continent then six months ago I smelled him ....or her. Everybody's got their own smells and everybody has got some common ones except for you and me. We're short on one."

"What do you mean him or her?"

"Couldn't follow them. I tried for four months then thought I'd try my luck somewhere else. I smelled you down town a week ago. It's taken me until now to trace you."

"Where did you smell the other one?"

"New York." Sullivan half-smiled and added David's thoughts, "Lots of sweaty bodies in New York."

"But there are three of us."

"That I know of." Their thoughts ran together.

"Why?" asked David, simply. Sullivan shrugged. "There has to be a reason. Look at what has happened - wings, strength. We can do things and look at the way we've changed: wings. I have changed to have the appearance of an angel - religious images it must be the hand of God." Sullivan took a long, hard look at David.

"Save us from the fucking child," he muttered and David's most optimistic scenario fell from the sky. He snarled and held his hand up before David's face the wrist cocked at its obscene angle. "I run, I hunt, I kill. I kill - same as you we've just got different ways of doing it." He smiled a cold, superior smile but, above all, a knowing smile.

Slowly, saddened, he let the blood flow from his wings. "Two in six months - maybe there are more of us changing now. What do we do?" Sullivan looked away.

"You do nothing. Stay here while you've still got some sort of life. If there are more, I'll find them. And do you think you could stop flying over Winnipeg. A city of this size there is always going to be somebody awake even in Canada. You may be stuck with being a freak but you don't have to be a jerk."

David stared at the rough features of the stranger's impassive face anger rising within him. All the months of self-abomination and contempt came together in an overpowering rage catalysed by the intense disappointment of finding that the dreamed of ally - confessor - friend was no more than another grimy freak who held him in contempt. "What gives you the right to call me a freak?" David asked though when he spoke it was deceptively quietly. Sullivan looked at him and again when he glimpsed the cold, cold anger within him.

"That's what you are," he stated baldly more curious than afraid. David stared at him for a minute or more not conceding a millimetre.

"I know," he said finally, "but it's the way that you said it." Sullivan looked then barked a harsh, unexpected laugh. He grinned at David. David did not smile at him. And it was there. There were a number of times when without knowing why or what the consequences would be, David instinctively knew what he had to do, what to say. And it was there. His hand rose between himself and Sullivan. Sullivan waved it away. Sullivan who had spent seven years alone, waiting not knowing for what. Sullivan who had lost his family and the best years of his life did not need the handshake. David held his hand just where it was. Eventually, he shook David's hand though not until his eyes, face and body language had spelled out that this did not change anything, that this did not mean anything. But he did shake David's hand.

Business finished with, they both looked out over the darkened city. "Do you want to hear a story?" David asked, Sullivan shrugged. "It's about two friends in the First World War - John and Mark. I heard about it a couple of months ago - church - " Sullivan smirked. "I don't know where." It was just there. "Anyway one of them was wounded out in no-man's land and the other told his captain that he was going out after him. The captain told him not to be so stupid, his friend was probably dead and there was no point getting both of them killed. Anyway he managed to get away from the captain and half an hour later he crawled back into the trench with his dead friend and he was wounded himself - mortally wounded. "What the hell were you doing!" said the captain, "I told you what would happen. Now was it worth it?"

"Yes, said the soldier because when I got there he was alive and he said to me, "John, I knew that you would come and get me." After a time, it became apparent to the stranger that there was no more to come. His head turned slowly until he faced David.

"What the hell is that supposed to mean?" David shrugged, his heartbeat had dropped enough for him to begin to feel the cold.

"It means that things matter. It means that there is something beyond the crappy bits of life we see. There has to be reasons." Sullivan gave a good-natured, dismissive shrug.

"There is something beyond, yeah," he agreed, "I don't know what but it scares the hell out of me."

CHAPTER 11

"Why not?" David rubbed his eyes avoiding the gaze of his persistent interrogator. "There is a reason and I want to know what it is." Absently, David ran his fingers over the outline of his Voyager model. Terri sat on the spare chair beside his desk compelling him to look at her. "David?" He smiled that same secretly-pleased infuriating-as-hell smile of his. "David we've been seeing each other for a year now and it's been a good year - I've enjoyed the time that we've had together but in that time we've never done anything more than kiss." He looked out of the window at the darkened street seemingly oblivious to her words. "At first I liked having a boyfriend who didn't paw me whenever he thought that nobody was watching but - well things happen. One thing follows on from another but it hasn't happened with you and me and I'd like to know why. The way that I see it there has to be something wrong and if it's something wrong with me then I'd like to know what it is. Do you find me unattractive?"

He gave a slight but unmistakable shake of his head, still smiling that damnable smile. He knew that it was a question that he had to respond to but he could not. "Then I can only think that there must be something wrong with you, that you must have a problem." He gave no indication as to whether he agreed or disagreed. "David - if it's because you're worried then don't. I think, no, I'm sure that our relationship would be strengthened by it. We've been together a long time now and - " She reached out to touch his face. "I do love you, David. If it's your first time then that's all right. Everybody has to begin somewhere." She smiled sensing, despite whatever else his blank expression might mask, that, for him, it would be the first time. "There's nothing wrong with that even at your age." She gave a nervous smile. "I know because you wouldn't be alone. I guess it's silly but -" She shook her head. A deep compassion and longing for her welled within him, a love and need which owed nothing to lust.

"I think that it's lovely," he stated and touched her face. She kissed him then, habitually, leaned back in her chair before he inevitably drew back.

"Is it that David?" She let her hand fall. "I still want to know why. I've had my say now it's your turn."

David studied her expression, wondering. She had a face which was often sombre, she did not show her happiness often enough or easily enough. To him she was the loveliest of all women - intelligent, mature beyond her years and if you stripped away the sex and the looks there was somebody underneath that he really, really liked. That he loved. "I do love you," he said. Wife of my dreams, thought. "And I will always love you but we can not become lovers and so," he shrugged, "unless you are prepared to have things exactly as they have been for the past year then we may have to end it." Her eyes became moist, instantly silencing him though her tears did not fall.

"All right," she stated with an acceptance that did not go beyond the words. "If you can not say why then so be it. Maybe there will be a time when you can tell me and maybe there will be a time when we might become lovers. David, when might that be?" He replied with his eyes cruelly dull.

"Not now, maybe never." She seemed to grow softer, less distinct as he tried to hold his own tears back. She cupped his hand with her own. Her eyes seemed darker, more insistent.

"It's not just the physical thing," she said, "I want that too but there's more. You have secrets and I want you to share them."

"I know." He said, nodding. "Maybe - - I don't want to have secrets but you are the last person in the world that I would want to have know my secrets. - Maybe - if the world was different maybe I could tell you then but I wouldn't want you to know."

"Will I ever know?"

"I don't want you to." She stared deeply into his face compelling him to look at her which he did and, though nothing was said, he knew that if any woman could love him despite his abnormality then it would be her. David bowed his head and for a time they remained like that with her cupping his hand watching him and he with tears upon his face.

Suddenly he sat bolt upright, unconsciously pulling his hand away from hers. A broad, enthusiastic smile brightened his wet face. "David, what is it?" He stood and retrieved his coat from the cupboard into which he had thrown it. She had rarely seen him looking so uninhibitedly, happy. There was something very different about him where before there were inner secrets and shame, now... now she did not know how but he shone from the knowledge that was within. Hastily, he pulled his coat on and stood by the desk looking out onto the dark street. "What is it, David?" He noticed her then and smiled at her and his smile was for her.

"Oh Terri -." He could barely speak then he was calm again and knew what he was going to do. "Maybe the world's about to change. I've got to go. It might be that I'll never see you again but don't worry I'm going to do what's right." He kneeled before her taking both of her hands in his. "I promise you that if I live, I'll come back and there will be no secrets then." His large, dark eyes watched her, delighting in her, filling her with his joy then he kissed her. For a few seconds she was too surprised to respond or speak.

He was standing again, buttoning his coat up and looking out of the window the warm, beatific smile still upon his face.

"David?" She reached out catching one of his busy hands, restraining him. He looked down at her the distant look temporarily leaving his eyes.

"Don't you hear it?" he asked, "Listen." Obligingly she complied but could hear nothing and said so. "Never mind," he stated then added with some satisfaction, "It's there - just there. It's a cry - the cry of a child."

Part Two

Part 2: Anything for Martin

CHAPTER 12

What do you say when you have used up all of the words?

You love somebody. You love each other. You come together, you marry. You are excited, entertained, devoted. You are at ease with one another. Too much at ease.

Their marriage had needed to develop, it had needed to be for something. Something other than each other, something other than each individual. They had needed a child. Suzanne was not going to go down that path. There was no momentum, no growth.

What do you say when you have used up all of the words? Their marriage had finally ended because he did not have the answer.

James Arthur sat alone in a diner seven miles East of Las Vegas. Tinted, floor to ceiling windows looked out onto the parking lot and the turn off the highway. He had finished his breakfast and was nursing a second coffee. His work lay out there and he had little desire to begin. He thought of Suzanne and of the break-up. The divorce was seven months past and it no longer hurt. In a strange way, he liked to think about it, to try to make sense of it all. There had been little pain by the time of the divorce.

For the last two years they had been gliding down towards it. Married seven years and at the end there was not enough to hold them together. There was enough love, he loved her now as then and she truly loved him though even now she did not believe it. She would have to go through a few relationships, he thought, she would have to put a few years on before she realised that she too, could not love more.

Suzanne was beautiful. Perfect skin, perfect face, perfect hair and a body that was to die for. She had worked very hard at keeping it that way. There had been no need. She could have grown fat and saggy and it would not have mattered to him which was the sort of thing that you said but, deep down, he knew the truth of it. He had never loved her for her appearance. It had led to the initial attraction and had been something of a bonus but he did not love it, he loved her. He had loved who she was and if only she had realised it too then they would be together still. Intellectually, she knew but, inside, she could not believe that anybody could really, really love her for herself. And there lay the reason for their separation, there and in two to twenty other things.

What do you say when you have used up all of the words? A thousand - ten thousand times he had said, "I love you." And at the end, and now, he still needed to say it but how can you say it after seven years when you have tried all of the other words? You want - need - to say it again but to say it in a new way, in a fresh way. To say it with all of the excitement and enthusiasm that you feel

bubbling within you but also with truth and simplicity. I love you. There is no simpler way. There is no more adequate way.
He sipped the last, bitter dregs from his cup. An improbably long Silver Bullet '07 pulled off the highway and disappeared from his line of vision to the right. Unusually, it had three or four satellite dishes bolted onto its roof.

College had been good. He had never had any dates worth mentioning in high school and then suddenly in college he was surrounded by gorgeous, wonderful women a steady supply of whom would give him the blessing of their company. In bed too not that he had ever worked particularly hard at it. Mostly he had just let them talk themselves into it. To that day he was not sure why. He sensed that they saw him as a safe bet - or even pair of hands. A little freedom, a little walk on the sexual side and there he was. Last of all there had been Suzanne. College had been very good.

His safeness was one of the two to twenty reasons for their separation. No real ambition. He was not lazy, he worked as hard as any man but, in retrospect, there was nothing out there to really go that extra mile for. Life was very pleasant, work was something that you did to pay where you had to. A goodish degree from a reasonable University whilst he met some wonderful women and had a very pleasant time thank you. A degree in design realisation whatever the hell that was. He knew, of course, but secretly suspected that he did not. Not really. In reality, he was lacking in that simple quality of real direction. He might have spent years

before he discovered that basic truth, as it was ten minutes with Grizelda the witch-queen had set him right on that.
Grizelda, also known as Gretchen the mother-in-law. Thankfully now an outlaw. He had never been good enough for Grizelda's little princess and perhaps she was right. That was another of the two to twenty. She had had nothing personally against him or his type. Some of her best friends might be gardeners or dog-walkers but one would hardly invite them to court the princess.

James Going-nowhere-and-enjoying-the-ride Arthur was not a suitable match for her daughter. Still it had happened and he was not angry not after the first three or four years anyway. Suzanne might have truly believed in her own beauty and value if she had ever stopped listening to her mother or, ironically, if she had listened enough to hear and believe in her mother's good opinion of her worth.

Still, he thought, we've all passed a lot of water since then. He waved his cup at the waitress who pointedly ignored him. She had the attitude of a woman who was not going to get up as early and as unwillingly as she had without making everybody in her path pay for it. It was the sort of pettiness which could have easily annoyed him had he not been too mature for that level of petulance. Besides, she had a big zit coming.

A man and a woman appeared to his right presumably from the silver bullet. The man reached the diner door first and held it open for the woman. He gave her a perfunctory smile as she passed, she ignored him. Married and under the cosh, thought James. He and Suzanne had never managed to hate with quite that intensity, shame really. You can not beat a bit of real emotional passion.

That was one of the two and twenty. Vertical toilet seats were in there too somewhere. The couple began to order a breakfast to go or rather the man began to order while the woman waited for him to get it wrong. James smiled wryly to himself, visualising a serious blow from a very large, foam hammer to his own head. Such cynicism in one so young and with such little sincerity.

The waitress began ostentatiously to write out his ticket. He was going to give her a big tip, he decided, just so that she could feel bad about ignoring him. That was his kind of vindictiveness: mess with her head but leave his own hands clean. The mental hammer began to reform in all its multi-foamed glory.

The couple sat down on the table between him and the door. They were not married he realised, suddenly. They had chosen a table and sat without a word in every imitation of the minimal or non-communication that only marriage or enforced confinement can achieve but their eyes were all wrong. There was something odd about the way that they failed to look at one another. Not that they were *not* looking at each other. Such avoidance was one of the finest flowerings of marital discord. No, it was something else. He was sure of it. In all of his sitting back and smelling the roses he had developed a keen sense of human observation. They could be brother and sister. Except that they did not look anything like it. She was auburn-haired, very pretty. He was tall, broad, blonde haired and grey eyed and with a huge set of shoulders on him. He looked the type to have played college football. A running back for certain not the slippery, nimble type more the "You in my way. You not in my way." type. Good teeth, all in all the sort that's a real catch. Probably as thick as a two by -- er -- two. And why in hell am I looking at him? James mused. Peripherally, he knew that he was mere yards from one of the most gorgeous women in a life full of glorious women and yet he could not look at her. Christ, I must be on the turn, he thought without any real conviction.

For the briefest moment he had a mental image of how he must have looked to the couple as they sat at their table. James Arthur - ordinary face not unpleasant but neither did it bring words such as granite and sculpted to mind. Only his large, brown eyes and thick eyelashes managed to be striking about it. Brown was too non-descript a word for his liking. He preferred to think of them as a kind of chocolate - perhaps that was the source of his appeal to all those lonely college girls. Thickish, ordinary coloured hair. Ordinary body not fat, not thin more sort of .. ordinary. Decent clothes given a little straightening and tightening which he would undertake a minute before meeting the client and undo a minute afterwards, if he remembered.

The waitress sulked past him letting his ticket free-fall a foot or so above his table. Mesmerised, he watched it drop wondering how it was that a piece of paper could manage to float with such undiluted contempt. He began to search his pockets for money. Oh well, the life of a machine parts salesman beckons. James Arthur reaches thirty and turns gay, he smiled, Grizelda would have loved that. No mucky men lusting after her princess' purity. Not that he should mock - there are many wondrous things in life and a mother's love for her daughter has to be right up there. Right up there with the smell of wood shavings and that first mouthful of ice-cold water.

James Arthur, the repressed gay. That had to be it, why else would he sleep with so many women? Well six or seven was not too many. Maybe nine or ten not that it was a competition. Not that it mattered. Oh Suzanne, he thought with regret as he stood. I was put on this earth to love you, if only you had believed. So what now? Simply find the other one that I was put on this earth to love. I wonder what shape she might come in? Female would be decidedly good. Female would be good.

I love you. He stood transfixed, his eyes drawn irresistibly and inexplicably to those of the woman. She stared back at him completely uninhibited. It was one of those rare and powerful moments when amongst all of the social protocols two people really look at each other. No fear, no shame, connection. "Christ...," he heard himself mutter. She was gorgeous, drop dead, kick in the head gorgeous. Her hair was fine, beautifully cut - some haircuts are just stuck on to the head hers definitely framed her face. Rounded cheekbones, the lines of her jaw were finely drawn, a slightly elf-like chin. Her eyes were a warm, if unflinching, hazel. Despite the bulk of her coat and the fact that he was too busy feasting on her face to notice it anything more than peripherally he noted that her body was all where it ought to be and in the requisite quantities. None of the above mattered a jot, he thought, other than to take the breath away. It was her eyes and what lay beyond them. She smiled. He sat again - too heavily – forcing his chair back several inches. Her companion slipped out of his vision to the left. It was how she looked at him. Somehow, he knew that she saw everything in him and liked it. Here was somebody with whom there would be no communication difficulties here was someone who was completely open to him as he was to her. "Christ...." What on earth could he say when so much was being communicated? He began to lever his legs from beneath the table. He had to get over there.

"Drop it." The man had returned carrying two paper bags which, presumably, contained their breakfast. James managed to tear his gaze away from the woman but the man had not spoken to him. His words and whole attention were directed at the woman. James looked back at the woman who had already risen. To his utter amazement she was already leaving. He struggled to follow, his body feeling as if he was wearing it for a friend. By the time that he had cleared the table and felt confident enough in his direction to look up, the man was half out of the door and she followed drawn on invisible threads. She smiled,

"Just enjoy the moment," she said in a distinct but not unpleasant New York accent. And she was gone. He froze in complete incomprehension, how could she let it go like that? In all of life there could only ever be one or two moments when two humans could truly connect as they had and, even given that they were complete strangers, he could not understand how she could just walk away from it. From what might be. He began to walk forward pushing the door open. Outside, he came to an abrupt halt as the Silver Bullet revved past him. The first window that he saw was empty, she watched him from the second. She watched him as he watched her. A few seconds before the link was broken. He saw her regret, her sadness and knew with a certainty that he would come to doubt but which in that instant was absolute, that she was in that vehicle against her wishes.

The back set of wheels pulled on to the highway and the silver bullet disappeared eastward behind the diner.

"Hey you!" Bemused, he turned. The diner chef had followed him out. Panting, sweating and carrying a ten-inch cleaving knife. James' expression must have asked the question. "The bill, you fuck!"

"Sorry," he muttered and searched his pockets. The waitress stood in the doorway chewing non-existent gum, sneering. He handed a twenty over. "Sorry I forgot myself. Keep it all."

"Yeah," he snatched the money ungraciously, "and you'd better not forget it." He turned and walked the rolling walk of the truly hugely thighed back into the diner. The waitress turned with him as he entered and, James thought, if the world is to make any sort of sense, she said something to him that began with the words : "The noyve ..."

Screw it, thought James. For a moment he had glimpsed heaven and what was he left with? The back view of a fat, sweaty chef. Reality, that was what he was left with. Disconsolately, he walked back to his car. He climbed in started the engine and searched in the glove compartment for a mint. Back to reality. Kaleph Machine Parts. West to Vegas. Not a bad job - considering. He had just fallen into it after Suzanne and it had taken him away from the West Coast to where he needed to be, away from Suzanne. The pay was crap but steady not that he had anything to spend it on. He popped the mint into his mouth and switched the air - conditioning on. It was such a specialist field that the manufacturers did not really have anybody else to go to for the machine parts. If their needs changed Kaleph changed the specifications. There was no real hard sell. He was more of a courtesy caller than a salesman. He pulled the car out to the edge of the highway. It was just the job for James Going-nowhere Arthur. West to Vegas. He pulled out onto the Eastbound lane and floored the accelerator. How else would he ever know?

CHAPTER 13

James had been driving for an hour before he came to the triple Junction. He pulled off the highway mounted the grass verge and cut the engine. It was impossible for him not to have caught the Silver Bullet. The road had been clear and, old though it was, his Corsican should have brought him to within sight of the vehicle within five or ten miles. It must have turned off. There had been a number of smaller, unpromising junctions. He had even stopped to check the last two. His choices were clear: he could retrace his path or he could give her up for lost. If the Silver Bullet had reached this point ahead of him, he had a one in three chance of following them - if that. "You fool," he muttered. It was an almighty nonsense - chasing a woman who had spoken two sentences to him and whom he imagined to be in some sort of difficulty. So choose.

He had already cancelled today's appointment with Danelli Brothers using the mobile and Vegas was Westward. The engine fired. There was nothing at all to be lost in making a slow return.

An hour and a half later he found a little-used gas stop that he had no recollection of. He was now perhaps four miles from the diner and every turn off the highway had been possible if unlikely departure points but, more importantly, he had clearly noted each one in his adrenaline-fuelled outbound journey. So close to the diner, he could not believe that he would have missed it. He drove on past. The landscape was equally unfamiliar not that one stretch of Nevada scrubland looked greatly different from any other stretch. Nevertheless, he could not shake the feeling of wrongness about it. He decided to drive on to the diner turn about and look at it from the same direction as he had approached it by in the early morning.

Half an hour. Four clear miles of unremembered highway including the gas stop. He had asked inside if the attendant had seen a Silver Bullet earlier in the day. The attendant's denial was almost as persuasive as his confirmation would have been. James drove slowly along the near dirt track leaning out of the window. His experience of tracking amounted to watching old Westerns as a child. There were tracks. They could belong to a Silver bullet ... or a thresher, dumpster - practically anything for all that he could tell. His car breasted a slight incline, he looked up and floored the clutch and brake. Ahead he could see the track widen out and join another major East-West road.

They could well have gone this way three hours before. The vehicle was gone, she was lost. There was nothing to do but to give it up and he would have done. Except for the fuel station. Except for the four miles. Except for the fact that when he really thought about it, he could not remember her saying "I love you." he just knew that she had and there were enough things that meant nothing individually but which collectively worried at him and which just would not let go. He brought the car around and headed towards Vegas on his original route.

Two things occurred to him almost simultaneously. The first was that they had to have parked and in all probability stayed overnight somewhere within half an hour's driving of the diner. The second was that he was enjoying - in an admittedly very strange manner - the mystery of the whole thing.

A meal, four hours and several trailer sites later he came to Glenrolling trailer and campsite. James parked near to the showers and consulted the tourist map that he had bought on his second visit to the diner. He was willing to go on but his backside had had enough. Glenrolling was crossed off before he left the car. He had converted his impossible mission to a manageable checklist. There were three more likely sites after this before he started on the "unlikelys" and crossing off was a damned sight easier than asking himself what he was doing and why.

Glenrolling had the ever-present cheap plastic furniture some distinctive, cheap plastic outdoor "plants" and a would-be ornamental lake. He ducked into the dark of the site office. "How're you?" His eyes adjusted slowly, eventually taking in the sight of a high wood-veneer bench dividing him from a smiling, dark-haired young man of about twenty. "What can I do for youse?" He was wearing a faded Shamrock Rovers T-shirt and had a distinct Dublin accent. James slipped into his, by-now, well-rehearsed story.

" I'm looking for a Silver Bullet '07 which might have stayed with you recently." He knew from previous sites that they kept records because of possible defaulters. "It trashed my car and drove off earlier this morning." Even his thumb outwards was automatic at this stage. "That's a hired car out there. I've seen the cops but unless I can get some more information I've no hope of getting them on insurance. I was hoping that you could give me their plates - if they'd stayed here-"

"Sure-." The Irishman had already flicked open the register.

"Sorry?" James had become so schooled into expecting disappointment that he completely missed the rest of the sentence. "What did you say?"

"I said 'Sure there was one here.' It stayed four days. Kept himself very quiet." He jabbed his finger down at the register. "We keep a paper copy." James was already scribbling frantically as though the clerk would pull the information away. "I shouldn't be doing this.."

"You shouldn't be doing this." James echoed.

"What the hell though, he screwed you. You get what you're entitled to."

"California plates?"

"Yeah."

"What time did they leave this morning?" The Irishman shrugged.

"Seven -start of my shift." Touchdown!

"It could still be the wrong one - did you see the people in it? A young woman very good looking - red hair almost brown looking. Kind of full-wavy." His head shook,

"Nope, I'd have remembered her."

"How about the guy? Blonde, big shoulders?"

"Nah." He moved his finger along to a signature on the register that James had missed in his excitement. The writing was unrecognisable. James shook his head. "Sullivan - not a trace of Irish in him though. He looked more sort of Greek. Irish-Greek-American I guess."

"No woman or the other man?"

"Could be," he shrugged again, "it was big enough. We don't have a lot to do with them. We sign them in and clear up after them, that's it. He paid cash so we've no address. Kept himself quiet. I've been on most of the week. I haven't seen anybody else."

"Is there anything else that you could tell me? Anything at all? Do you know where they were going?" Shrug, shrug, smile. "You could ask the Night guy but he's too pissed to notice anything."

For a moment, James stood silently staring at the Irishman. He had had a lucky, lucky break and was reluctant to accept that there was no more to come. He pulled a twenty, the largest note that he had, from his pocket and handed it across. "Thanks you've been really helpful."

"S'right. I hope you get your dues."

James left at a half trot. A few minutes before he did not even have a plan beyond trying to find out where the Silver Bullet had been. Now he was heading out to the forgotten gas station on to the second highway and at the first motel he would phone every trailer site with his new information and another creative lie.

If there was an afterlife, front desk duty on the 10 till 6 shift at Neustrass police station had to be it. The problem was, thought Deputy Halberg, that he could not remember ever having done anything wrong enough to justify his being there.

If anybody with any intelligence organised the rotas then you would have enough daytime shifts to build up a backlog of paperwork and then enough night shifts to clear them. As it was he was filling in crime sheets for crimes that were due to happen sometime next July. He was no book reader - yet. Desperation might force him to it. He could not play any games on the reception desk computer not after three states systems had gone down because of real-time memory being used up by desk and dispatch officers playing Mechagodzilla Takes a Dump last Fall. He could transfer into Vegas where night shift was generally considered to be the busiest shift of the day. The only flaw in that possibility was that he would have to transfer into Vegas. He could patch into the control lines - if he wanted to listen to two fat, hick officers discussing "Women we laid 1997-1999" there having been no action worth mentioning since then.

Deputy Halberg had requisitioned the backs of some crime support sheets and was drawing on them. Deputy Halberg could not draw. Deputy Halberg knew that he could not draw and that he would never be able to draw.

To an odd feeling of relief he saw a shape bulk in the doorway and the door began to open. What has Satan sent to lighten my darkness now? He wondered.

A seemingly ordinary-looking man walked uncertainly in. Five foot ten, Caucasian, brown eyes - no distinguishing features. Surreptitiously, he slipped the leather catch off his holster. It had to be a crank. If it walked through that door at 2.15 in the morning, it had to be a crank. If it walked through that door, it had to be a crank. "What can I do for you Sir?" Halberg asked politely. The man smiled seemingly embarrassed.

"Well, this might seem kind of silly," said James Arthur. Here we go, thought Deputy Halberg not bothering to keep his scepticism out of his expression. "I think that I want to report a kidnapping."

"Just a minute." Halberg keyed the crime report page on to his screen and pointedly checked that he had entered the correct sub-directory before looking at the crank. "Right then, Sir. Name?"

"James Arthur"

"Place of residence?"

"Er.." That was significant, thought Halberg. "Worthington, Washington State."

"Right." Halberg looked away from the screen. "Just fill me in on the story and then we'll go back to the details."

"OK -well. It happened this morning - yesterday now" Halberg's expression almost stopped him. "I was sitting in a diner about ten miles west of Vegas when this couple game in ordered breakfast and left." James paused for breath and to watch Halberg's expression. "The woman tried to talk to me but the guy chased her out - so I followed and, well, as they drove off I could see her being held there - she was trying to get out but.." He was in serious credibility trouble now but persisted. "She was being held there. I tried to chase them but lost them.." James had finally run aground.

"What time did you say this happened?"

"Seven-thirty- eight."

"And you waited until now to report this?"

"Yes - no. Look I've been trying to find the Silver Bullet all day. I've been ringing around trailer homes for hours." Halberg's expression would have lost out to a concrete wall in a softness competition. Having decided to finally come forward with the truth, James' resolve was collapsing fast before him. "Look I wasn't entirely sure of what I saw. I didn't want to waste police time when I could be wrong. I'm sorry - you must think that I am wasting your time." Amen to that, thought Halberg.

"Not at all. This woman, when she was driving off what did you see? How was she being held?"

"Well - - I'm not sure." James took another breath. "Mostly it's more kind of a feeling that I got from her - it was just wrong, you know how you can get a feeling that somebody is in trouble?"

"Yes, I do but then I am a trained police officer. What are you Mr Arthur?" James looked acutely discomforted.

"I'm a machine parts salesman." For the first time, Halberg began to take an interest in what James had to say. A chord had been struck in his trained police psyche. If James admitted to being a machine parts salesman then there might be something to his report. Had he admitted to being the High Priestess of Vlad the Inhaler then the case for crankdom would have been complete. Nevertheless.

"Did you really see anything Mr Arthur?"

"It was more in her eyes...."

"You could have been mistaken."

"Yes I could - but if I'm wrong - I just couldn't let it go by in case something was happening to her." Halberg nodded, respectfully.

"It could be -" Arthur placed a slip of paper on the desktop. "I got the licence number." Halberg's interest continued to grow. At 2 am in Nuestrass there was not a lot of competition for light.

"Hold on." He turned to the computer screen, cleared the crime report and headed into a different directory. Within the minute he had James Arthur's police details in front of him. One report from sixteen years before as a collaborative witness in a High School arson case. No convictions. Current address checked out. Recently divorced. No history of lunacy which might mean that this was his time or that he was being straight. Halberg decided to check the licence number. "What vehicle did you say this was?"

"A Silver Bullet '07." Halberg accessed the relevant query programme, entered the details and waited. He frowned and entered the details again. His frown did not lessen. "What is it?" asked James. Halberg glanced at him, muttered something unintelligible and stared disbelievingly at the screen. After a third attempt to enter the data he came to an obvious decision, hit several buttons and turned to James. A paper form began to chunter out of his computer. "What is it?" James repeated. Halberg shrugged, contemplated and decided to communicate - it did not amount to much but he did have something of a genuine "feel" about James.

"It's something I've never seen before. Look, all of the California plates that ever existed or that are ever going to be used are stored on a database in here. There are three conditions for each plate: Used - no longer in existence; Used - in existence; Unused - in existence. Those plates are not really anywhere. They're just waiting for dealers to call on them." The printer had stopped. Halberg passed the paperwork to James and hit several buttons on his keyboard. "Could you have been mistaken? Are you sure that these were California plates?"

"I'm pretty sure." Halberg made a dismissive gesture towards the latest information on the screen.

"You couldn't have mixed it up with an Oregon motorcycle?" he asked rhetorically.

"No. -Tell me what is going on." Halberg met his gaze with sheer perplexity.

"It's the plates. They don't exist, they have never existed and they are not on the database waiting to come into existence. I've checked other states and there's nothing resembling a Silver Bullet." James became acutely aware of the lateness and coldness of the hour. "It's worse than you think - Fed's and other - er - government agencies are on here too. They just have a "keep off" flag on them. Every mathematically possible plate is on here but yours isn't."

"What does that mean?" Halberg stared back at him. In the silence both of them understood exactly what it could mean.

"It could just be a computer error." Halberg lied transparently. "I want you to fill out this Crime Report. Put absolutely everything that you can think into it - any detail. Don't forget your contact number then you had better go home. Thanks for reporting this now you should leave it to us."

"I need to know." Halberg's eyebrows rose a fraction. "This is sort of personal now. I don't just want to wait a year and a half and get some letter in the post. This - there is something very wrong here. I've been a good citizen bringing this to you and now I want to know what happens. I'm not asking for a lot." Halberg thought hard before responding his eyes never leaving James'.

"I'll run a search through today's reports then I'll patch into control and we'll have the current units look out for it - I'll be putting out an APB. We'll take it from there." James swallowed, it was easier telling an all-out lie than merely giving out a misleading intention.

"I guess that you will do all of this after I've filled out this report - you wouldn't want me overhearing anything that's not my concern now, would you?"

"That's right," said Halberg not unkindly and, to James' relief he waited passively whilst James filled out the report.

James waited while he checked through the report. At a couple of points Halberg smiled wryly but said nothing until he had finished. "Thanks," he said then, "this might be something. It might be nothing but you just leave it in our hands. This is our job now." James nodded. Halberg glanced significantly at the door and waited until James began to edge away. "Take care now."

James left and when he was sure that he could not be seen through the door's glass he sprinted towards his car. Once inside, he turned the car radio on, lowered the volume and frantically re-tuned. He had to wait twenty anxious minutes.

"Unit 36 please investigate a report from Unit 21 made at 19.30 concerning an '07 Silver bullet. Approach with caution there may be a possible kidnapping situation. Repeat extreme caution. The location of the vehicle is at Master's ranch off junction...."

He scribbled the details down before consulting his map. He was a good hour's drive away. There was no possibility of his getting there before the police car - which was no bad thing.

Thirty minutes later he had to pull off the deserted highway as unit 36 reported back.

"All clear - " the radio crackled, "we can confirm that there is no kidnapping situation. The vehicle's owners were very cooperative. We have searched the vehicle and it's immediate locality. Nothing untoward to report."

So how was it that if they approached with due caution, wondered James incredulously, that the vehicle's owners encouraged them to search? What did they do? Knock and ask if there were any hostages inside?

Halberg's voice suddenly cut in on the radio. "Deputy Halberg here. Can you confirm the vehicle's licence plate?" The disembodied voice of the first officer duly confirmed the number that James had passed on. "Please confirm that you have investigated the earlier report?"

"We can confirm. The vehicle is completely in order." Not a trace of anger apparent in the officer's voice even given that Halberg had just questioned his professional competence.

"In that case," said Halberg, "I am over-riding your existing duty details. I want you to make this report directly to me. Is that agreeable Unit 36?"

"It is, we will make our way back now." Or whatever the hell else was necessary to make that unwelcome police interest go away.

James gunned his engine into life. What could they report directly to Halberg? Selective memory loss? That is if they did not miss it out entirely.

The miles passed monotonously by. After ten minutes had gone he passed a police car heading in the opposite direction. Shortly after that, his brain began to function. Why am I doing this? He wondered. There were all sorts of justifications to pick from.

Because something was very wrong and it would nag away at his conscience until he found out, until he could make sense of it all.

Because it was gone three in the morning and he was not thinking too straight. There was an odd logic to the motivations of men at that time of the night.

Because he was enjoying playing detective. It was strange but there was a definite thrill to be had in testing himself like this.

Because of her. The strangest reason of all was probably the truest. She was a fine looking woman but the world was filled with... This one was or rather could be different. She could be the one. Life with Suzanne had been very pleasant but unreal. She had liked fantasy - Mountie and the Bride all that sort of pretend nonsense. He had not minded it - if it worked for her that was good for him - but he had never seen the point of it. Why not the pipe fitter and the receptionist? Why not anything? Why the fantasy? He had met the woman who had seen him through to the core. Everything that he was and she had loved him. Or perhaps, it was the possibility that she could love *him* not what he did for her or what he might become but who he really was. And that, of course, was a damned sight more pretend nonsense than Suzanne had ever sought. They had spent perhaps ten minutes in the same room. She had not said, I love you. He had just wanted to hear it.

He pulled off the road and onto a dirt track signposted to the Master's Farm. There was no lighting other than his headlamps. It was rutted and slow going.

This was in no way sensible, he realised which just about sealed it for him. He did not want to be sensible. He had spent seven years married to a very nice girl living a very nice life. The prospect of finding a woman who could love him or hate him enough to rip his head off in her passion was enough. If only for once in his life, he wanted to be loved, or even hated, with passion.

CHAPTER 14

There was the dark, brooding outline of a hillock with a few straggly trees cresting it. The road swerved out to the left past what he presumed was the Masters' ranch. A long, plastic-looking vehicle nestled where the hillock rose and the road turned. He slowed but did not let the Corsican stop. Two professional police officers had been turned away without raising their suspicions. Something had worked on him too. If she was being held it was by some mysterious ultra-covert government agency with some kind of secret brain weapon. It was probably hypnotic - sub-sonic or super-sonic. Something like that. One of those mackerel technologies. At four in the morning, it seemed, to him, to be a very credible theory. The curve was getting very close and the potential embarrassment of waking them at this hour and blurting out his vague anxieties and paranoid assumptions seemed to be every bit as strong a reason for driving on as the brain weapon. The car began to slew to the left. He braked, stopped the engine, climbed out and all of the nonsense ended.

He had walked perhaps ten yards when lights came on in the vehicle and the door opened. She stood there framed for a moment before she stepped down and walked towards him. They both stopped perhaps ten yards apart. She looked as angry as hell. "You stupid, stupid man," she spat out. "I don't want you here. I don't want you! I am not being kidnapped. This is where I belong. The only thing that should not be here is you." His shame was absolute, he tried to recall a suitably similarly shaming moment from his childhood. He surfaced empty-handed. "You are going to go away and never see me again." She said more coldly, mechanically as if reading from a script - badly. " I have no interest in you and you have no interest in me. Now get the hell out of here and don't stop driving until you are in Texas." He had turned, his feet were moving, he was going but something stopped him, making him turn back. She looked mildly surprised. "What is it?" He felt as if a gag had been removed from his mouth.

"My bit," he said forlornly.

"What do you mean your bit?"

"I haven't said my bit." She smiled, a coldly amused smile. There was nothing in it for him.

"All right. I tried, now do you want me to make something clear to you?" He nodded. "Well, you have two choices: you can stand there and get killed or you can run." Two vague shapes exited from the rear of the Silver bullet. They were illuminated momentarily before he lost them in the dark. James looked at her. She watched him coolly, uncaring. He knew, as he seemed to know everything around her, with utter certainty that she would watch him being ripped apart without lifting a finger to prevent it. The shapes were coming for him. He ran for the car. He heard or perhaps just imagined the sound of something or things pursuing him. He half expected to be struck from behind just as he slowed at the car door. Nothing hit him. He half-climbed half-dived into the driver's seat pulling the door too behind him. He punched the lock down before starting the engine. Something large slammed into the door inches from his head. A glance to his right revealed the mid-part of a man's body and two hands tearing at his door handle. He had already engaged first gear and spun the car away sliding it to the left in the hope of running over the man's feet. The body disappeared from his field of vision. Something struck his right-rear wing he ignored it concentrating only on acquiring velocity. His nose was practically over the wheel.

It was perhaps a minute or so before he began if not to relax then at least to breathe. He glanced at the speedometer which was pushing forty. If he could maintain this speed over the dirt track, he would be clear. For the first time he glanced in the mirror expecting to see her in the distance standing, watching. "Shit!" It was still coming after him perhaps thirty yards back and maintaining its distance. The speedometer had to have been trashed. No man could maintain that speed and it was running in a crazy half-diving half-falling gait. A small ditch appeared before him, the car bucked it's bonnet rising and his front wheels losing traction. Somehow he managed to right it and to buckle himself in. He glanced behind again. The man was closing. It was not the blonde man from the diner it had to be the other one. Irish-Greek American the Irishman had said, he had forgotten to mention the non-human component. Suddenly the dirt road flattened and broadened -he had reached a concreted section of road and perhaps half a mile ahead he could see where it rejoined the highway. James floored the accelerator. Fifty – sixty - seventy. His pursuer was still following but rapidly diminishing in the mirror.

The Corsican joined the highway heading left at 300 degrees to his original course. James had driven perhaps one hundred yards when something smashed into his left rear passenger window. For an instant he thought that he might have been shot before he realised that something was on the roof of his car. He could hear the sound of it scrabbling for a grip, the metal buckled and he caught a glimpse of something like fingers or talons gripping the top of his windshield. He slewed the car to the right and the left hoping to dislodge it. Nothing appeared in his rear-view mirror but there were further buckles and noises above confirming that there was something up there. He considered slamming his brakes on and rejected the thought, he had no wish to see or to hit whatever was above. Before he could take any further action the windscreen shattered. For a terrifying instant he had the distinct belief that whatever was up there was about to peel the car roof off like the top of a tin of sardines. The car spun and there was an almighty crash to his left.

James sat there for an interminably long ten seconds. The car engine had stopped and all that he could hear was the pinking of an overheated engine abruptly stopped. The car had turned completely about before stopping. Subconsciously he ran a quick check on himself for injuries. He was sore in most places and covered in a sheen of sweat but there was nothing broken, nothing to stop him moving. Through the space where his windscreen had been he could see a very good reason for moving. The running man had reached the junction with the highway. He crossed onto the deserted road and began to jog, pacing himself carefully. James' attempt to re-start the car did not even draw a cough from the engine. He unbuckled himself and stepped out. The scene seemed to have a dreamlike quality to it, he would remember that moment with absolute clarity for the rest of his life. The car had skidded off the highway and slammed into a telegraph pole. There was no sign of anything on the car roof or lying injured on the road. There was a dense conifer forest twenty yards beyond the car. The highway was completely deserted apart from the running man who continued his confident, measured approach. James' only option seemed to be to head for the forest where the trees might reduce his opponent's advantage in speed. He took two steps towards it before something hit him.

Something very large where a second before he was convinced that nothing was within a hundred metres of him. He struggled to find which way up was before becoming aware of his surroundings. He realised that he had been carried five metres nearer to the trees by whatever it was that had hit him. There was something warm and wet on the right side of his skull. He scrambled on all fours until he was underneath the first tree. For perhaps a second, he continued resting before allowing his momentum to carry him on. It was a dark night, visibility was poor and it was as much as he could do to avoid the tree trunks and hope that his weight would force him through the branches. They were young trees but even keeping low as he did was painful. Pain and his own breathless become increasingly relevant as the adrenaline began to ebb from his system.

After several minutes, he reached a section of more established trees and despite much tripping, he was able to skirt the trees and make faster progress. There was no sight or sound of anything behind him. A hidden rise ahead and slightly to the right disappeared leaving him with the sudden, exhilarating vision of lights. They were small, clearly quite distant but they gave him something to head towards, to hope for.

Another minutes' dodging brought him to a clearing where he paused. He could clearly see a faint corona of light behind the trees directly ahead.

Something large and somehow bat-like flickered down through the light. Almost immediately it flew up and away again. James' eye was caught by a black shape where it had briefly landed. He stood, immobile, waiting as it walked calmly towards him. The running man. Recognition snapped him out of his paralysis and he tried to retreat all the while not daring to look away from him. From *it*. It came at him with an incredible rush of speed. It struck him heavily in the chest winding him and felt the pain of a tree slamming spikily into his back. It held him by the throat, smiling. Human face, human body. There was nothing visible to say that it was anything other than a man but it was not. James had scarcely thought of round-arming it when he was struck violently on the side of his head and then on the forehead against the tree trunk on the backhand. "Don't think of it." Its face was now inches from his. It could not speak without its breath flooding James' own open mouth and nostrils. A fleck of its spittle landed on James' cheek. "You're dead. You don't matter." It's breath should have reeked of rotting meat it was merely slightly acidic.

James felt himself lifted into the air and thrown through some lesser branches back into the direction of his car. "You'd better run." James ran. This time he staggered back avoiding the trees as he struggled to take enough oxygen into his lungs. His first few glances back revealed that the monster was following him. It was in no hurry to catch him. He caught enough breath to put on a trot and create some distance. The monster was going to kill him and there was nothing that he could do. He could not fight against something that knew his intentions at the same time that he did. He could not outrun it. Alone, for reasons he did not know and by a creature whose origins he could only guess at, he was going to die. Physically, he was all but spent, mentally he was completely bereft of any ideas. Fight or flight? Both would lead to his death. "No!" The cry from behind him spurred him into sudden flight. After a few seconds he began to wonder about the cry. The monster was coming for him but, with that cry, it was not the confident, calm monster as certain of James' death as James had been.

The pain in his chest was intense and he had to fight against the desire to stop. A dip in the ground forced him to look up. He saw light ahead, not the distant lights of a town but huge, white rectangular light. He charged ahead completely oblivious to the branches tearing at his face. The shape of it registered with the familiarity of the last few trees. A greyhound bus had pulled up alongside the wreck of his car. He burst through the last tree and on to the roadside, swayed and staggered to a halt. A surprised older, black driver looked away from the car and at James. "Jeez.." he muttered through his teeth. There were a number of pale, frightened passengers watching through the windows. James staggered towards the driver. He had a wispy, grey moustache and was the most beautiful sight that James had ever seen. He fell into the driver's arms, his legs completely giving out beneath him. The driver could not take James' weight and half dragged him to the side of the road. "Jeez, are you alright?" James could not muster the breath to answer him. For an instant his vision blacked then he began to gain self-control again. Everything seemed to be slowly, painfully returning to normal. "That was some crash you had." James could sense the anger in the forest. Remembering, he looked back but there was nothing to be seen. A large, concerned woman stepped off the bus and kneeled uncomfortably beside James. "We'd better take you into town," said the driver indicating the car, "do you want me to fetch anything from your car?"

"No – nothing. Let's just get out of here."

"Sure." They were both watching James, only he saw the flicker of light in the sky above his car before it burst into flame.

"Jeez!" The two of them dragged him onto the bus then the driver pulled it forwards a hundred yards away from his car. He stopped it again and made a tentative return to the burning wreck. James sat upon the front seat whilst the woman found some chemical wipes to clear the blood from his face. All of her attention was on him while the rest of the passengers were watching out of the rear window. Only James looked ahead. Cold, drained he could not react only watch. He saw the Silver Bullet pull out ahead of them and drive on for two hundred yards before stopping. James could only make out the brake lights but it was enough. He saw them come on as the vehicle stopped, he guessed, to pick up two passengers then dim as it began to drive off.

Go away. Do not follow us. Do not look for us. Then He felt the warmth of his bladder emptying in sheer terror and he began to cry.

CHAPTER 15

The driver proved to be a kind man. He put James into a hotel in the town, called a doctor into him and paid for James' first two days. It took James two days of crying, and sleeping before he had the courage to leave the room. The driver had left town by then. It was a cliche, but he had saved James' life and he did not even know his name. The doctor sealed several cuts, diagnosed shock and checked on him at twelve and then twenty-four hour intervals. James did not tell him about the Silver bullet, he knew that his only hope of living was to keep his mouth shut and not to make a nuisance of himself.

James awoke on the third morning feeling almost normal. His emotions no longer held sway. He was scared, ashamed and confused but for the first time since it had happened some part of him stood outside of what had happened. Intellectually and emotionally he knew what to do: he had to go away and never look again. And yet...

For more than an hour, he lay there trying to come to terms with what had happened. By the end of that time three things freed him from the compulsion that had been forced into his mind.

Gratitude. He was just so unbelievably, pathetically grateful to the driver and his kindness. He could not think of him without tears flowing however much he tried to stand outside his emotions. In his entire life he had never owed so much to anybody.

Shame. He had run in absolute terror and had no real problem with that - it seemed to be a reasonable response to the situation but he had soiled himself in front of two people who had shown the utmost respect and consideration towards him. He had been forced to walk off the bus and into the hotel with everybody knowing. He held no great macho notions of what a man should or should not be, nevertheless, he knew that he had not acted as a man should.

Anger. Somebody on the Silver Bullet had made him do it. He had already been through utter terror. If he was going to wet himself it would have been when the running man -Sullivan - came for him. There had been nothing in his life to compare with that instant of fear, nothing. Somebody on that vehicle had made him do it to show him how powerful they were and how weak he was. Somebody, or something, that did not have any compassion.
James Arthur's life turned on that moment. It was not the woman, he realised that. Although he did not know how or why, she was hip-deep in what was happening. It was not fear for his life. It was not the fact that he had discovered something enormous. It was the fact that he had pissed himself that allowed him to uncover a meaning and strength of resolution that his life had been singularly lacking in.

He dressed, signed out of the hotel, hired a car and drove out to Nuestrass.

CHAPTER 16

James paused at the police station door, reflecting that it had only been three nights before when he had last entered. He did not prolong the moment. Inside there was nobody ahead of him though there were several other police officers working at screens beyond the front desk. As before Deputy Halberg greeted his entrance with a sceptical glance. My lucky day, thought James, he had been prepared to wait until Halberg came on duty however long that might be. "Deputy Halberg.." James said affably and paused, momentarily distracted, by Halberg's shocked expression and apparent fixation with his empty right hand.

"Just stop there!" Halberg snapped. "Drop the weapon."

"What weapon?" asked James raising his empty hands outwards.

"I'm going to count to three and you will drop the gun."

"But I haven't got a gun." Halberg's eyes did not leave James' empty right hand.

"One ... " A number of the other police officers were beginning to take an interest in what was happening. "Two..." James was certain that he did not have a gun in his hands, he had no such confidence that Halberg was not holding a weapon behind the high desk. He dropped to all fours, turned and dived for the doorway. A shot thundered in the confined space. He pulled the door open and scuttled out. Another shot followed sprinkling him with splinters. He rose and sprinted for the hired car. Halberg clearly had difficulty negotiating the desk as James had reached a clear sixty miles per hour before the third shot followed.

Turning a corner, he accepted this situation far more readily than what had happened before. He had to leave the state immediately not in fear or because he had been told to but because the entire state force would be hunting him down. After all he had, apparently, entered a police station brandishing a bazooka or some such weapon. They had gotten to Halberg. Halberg had really believed that he had been carrying something and there had been nobody near enough to see or say otherwise. James' first and most credible ally had shot at him on sight. Now he had to withdraw and come back at them from a safe distance.

It was not until he had safely cleared the state border that he found the bullet-hole in his coat.

CHAPTER 17

Milk cartons. Two months after the "Encounter" as James liked to think of it, he was established in a God-awful apartment, doing a new God-awful night-watchman's job in God-awful New York. He sat in the local public library resting his eyes after another heavy session with the local and regional newspapers screen. During the past two months he had personally read every missing person's report within a two hundred mile radius of New York for the past two years. Nothing.

Next to the keyboard rested a computer generated picture of the woman. The visit to the imaging artist had been the most expensive of his many recent expenses. The apartment had cost way too much. The Corsican had cost. A month's unemployment had cost. It had all bitten deeply into the savings which seven childless years and a divorce from his financial superior had accrued.

The night-watchman's job had come not merely as a financial relief - it had been the first time that he had dared check his financial and criminal record. It made a callous kind of sense that Halberg would not have even recognised him. James' face had

probably been nothing more than the sub-conscious stimulus that would trigger his deceive and destroy programme.
The librarian - correction - information assistant appeared behind James with a portable pay-phone and several photocopied pages. She passed by him just that fraction too close again, before placing everything on the work surface next to the picture. James might have been misreading the signals but he was vaguely aware of her interest in him. She was Italian looking, which was nice, overweight, which was irrelevant, and married which was more than he could be bothered with at that time. "I found you that information that you asked for," she said.

"Thanks Mary, you're very kind." She lingered until he began to scrutinise the list that she had provided. When she left it was not, he flattered himself, without some slight disappointment. James continued to stare at the list taking none of it in. The thought of involvement was still there but it was no more than a thought. He told himself that he ought to, it was not as if his current job brought him into contact with any females. None that weren't Alsatian looking anyway. Neither did he have any sort of social existence. Work, eat, sleep, library - that was it. There had been a time when he would have leaped at the possibility. Any time prior to the past two months to be precise. "Registered Government Information Inquirers," he read and chose a name at random.

The first company only dealt with agricultural information, the second with current legislation, the third with milk cartons - as it were. There was a fifty dollars logging on charge. He hesitated, it was not an insignificant amount if it was going to get him nowhere and it was a significantly greater risk than ploughing through newspaper reports on his own - they might well be armed and waiting for him - but what alternatives were there? He was not going to do anything other than take the necessary steps. He pressed the accept button. "Good morning, how may we help you?" he just knew that the owner of that voice had a blonde, bubble cut.

"Er - yes, can you tell me if you do inquiries into the National Missing Persons database?"

"Yes we do, sir."

"Great I'm trying to locate a missing person's report but I don't have a lot to go on."

"What exactly have you got sir?" He could feel himself getting smaller by the minute.

"A physical description - brief - and a computer generated image."

"Do you have a name? Address? Age?"

"No - nothing more than I have said. Can I send you those details." There was a significant pause on the other end of the line.

"I think that you had better come into the office, sir."

"When?"

"Any time that you like, sir."

"I don't have to make an appointment or anything?"

"You can come in any time that you like to make an appointment."

The office was two and a half hours' travelling time away from the Library. Fifteen minutes if you could fly and twenty-five if they had not bothered to put all of the people and things in the way. James was significantly disappointed not to meet Miss blonde bubble cut. He had to wait fifteen minutes before he could be seen by a be-suited teenager who recorded every detail that James gave him on the appropriate form before deciding that James needed to see somebody who knew what they were doing. He was ushered into a small white room where he waited for another ten minutes.

A young man breezed into the room shaking James' hand before he had time to respond. He had dark curly hair, wore glasses unusually and, even more uncommonly in a building full of suits, had no jacket or tie. "Canute Lacey," he announced and flopped heavily down into the room's other chair. "What can we do for you?" he asked whilst studying the teenager's form. When James did not reply, he gave no acknowledgement. "Can I see this picture?" he asked, folding the read form. James handed it over. "It's not a lot to work with?"

"Can you find anything?" Lacey smiled.

"Yes." James had a good instinctive feeling about the man, he seemed to be honest, somebody who enjoyed the problem-solving nature of his work but then the fact that he had not yet fired at James was a major plus in itself. "If I can copy this it should speed things along. Business then - there is a basic charge of two hundred and fifty dollars for any enquiry that we make. It's free after that until we go over half an hour then you pay four hundred dollars per hour." He smiled sympathetically.

"How long do you think this enquiry will take?" Lacey pursed his lips,

"Five to ten minutes - I don't anticipate there being any problems with it. Is there likely to be?"

"No -what if the record had been removed?" Lacey shrugged.

"It shouldn't be a problem. Do you want me to chase up the details if it has been removed? - Within the legal framework of course." James nodded, Lacey stood. "I'll get you the contract then." He offered his hand again.

James did not have a telephone and therefore had to call Lacey at the end of his shift. On the third morning Lacey arranged to meet him at a bar near to his offices during his lunch break. James was there an hour early nursing his drink and watching everybody who entered for signs of potential psycho-assassin programming. What that would amount to he was not sure of, guns and glazed expressions would be strong possibilities.

Lacey, when he entered looked reassuringly out of place. The bar in keeping with the area was a distinct "suits" location. Lacey was wearing a bobbly, patterned jumper. He recognised James, waved and ordered a drink before joining him at his relatively secluded table. "How are you?" he asked unconsciously testing the simulation-leather chair for its slideability.

"Fine. - Why did you want to meet here?" Lacey pursed his lips.

"Too many ears." Lacey's drink arrived, something in pineapple juice. He took a long sip whilst the waitress disappeared. "I've done your research - up to a point." he sipped again, smacked his lips and sipped.

"And?"

"Sorry." He passed a manila folder over. "That's horse-shit," he commented before James could open it. "Very approximate look-a-likes. If your picture is as good as you say it is then she ain't there."

"It is." Lacey shrugged non-commitedly.

"Well she is not on the currently missing list.." James waited, it was obvious that Lacey would reveal all, eventually. "Somebody fitting her description may have been but .. she has not been found."

"But her record has been removed."

"Exactly." Sip.

"And..." James had a distinct feeling of deja vu. He hoped that it would not extend to Lacey pulling a gun on him, if it was under the jumper he would have time to call a taxi.

"The method of removal was unusual." Lacey watched him for his reaction, or non-reaction. "There is no difficulty with taking somebody off the data-base. People are found - but you have to fill in a record file ... OK sometimes that does not happen but there was no flag left and the trace was also cleared up. All that I've got now is a time of removal."

"Which was when?" Lacey raised a hand.

"This is where we are now Mr Arthur. Your half an hour is up. I need to

have your permission to go on."

"You have that already." Lacey nodded.

"It's not just the money. I need to know from you if this is all right."

"And if it is not?" James felt that he knew the answer to that question already. Why else would Lacey be meeting him here?

"I can proceed," Lacey continued evasively, "there are very few people who could remove that record. I can access duty rosters and authorisation schedules but people are going to start asking questions if I do. The company is very strict about us staying within the legal framework. So.."

"So?"

"So why do you want to find this woman, for example?" James drained his own five-dollar drink before answering.

"I don't know what it is that you would be dealing with. What I can tell you is that I have done nothing wrong .. and that there may be some powerful forces watching over this woman but I don't know who or what." Lacey sipped then smiled.

"That sounds interesting enough for me to proceed." James gave a rare smile. "I've never seen a record removed like hers was. .... I've seen two others now though. Both removed within twenty minutes of hers on the same day three and a half years ago."

"I'll bet you they're both men - one blonde, six foot the other five seven or eight, Greek looking?" Lacey opened his hands.

"That I don't know. I realised it was time to take a rest." He drained his drink and stood giving James a huge, conspiratorial grin. "Give me a few of days Mr Arthur. I'll meet you here next Tuesday."

"Fine, I'll be here." James shook his hand vigorously.

CHAPTER 18

Thursday to Friday in the library produced nothing but backache and a persistent migraine. On Saturday, James bought a gun. He spent most of the weekend practising at a gun club that he had been obliged to join in order to get the permit. The membership, the range and the ammunition cost plenty. The gun - a second hand desert eagle - was cheap. He practised with little enthusiasm, standing still to fire back had always seemed more dangerous than running like buggery but he had every expectation that Lacey would have turned into a homicidal assassin by Tuesday.

Monday was again, fruitlessly, spent in the library the only consolation being that he could easily have wasted several months searching back to his new point of investigation had he not contacted Lacey. An over-active imagination and over-tiredness had deprived him of sleep for several days and he was obliged to spend most of Monday night at work catching up.

Tuesday found him at the same table in the same bar with the handgun held inside a bag under the table. This time he was two hours early. His mid-term and long-term strategy were thoroughly mentally, rehearsed. There were two ways that Lacey could go. James was prepared for both but all of his hopes lay with the peaceful course. He had no wish to shoot Lacey just as he had no wish to be shot at. If they were on to him despite his discretion and his having crossed the continent then there would be little hope of his ever getting close to them. Even his finances were becoming exhausted. He was down to his last thousand.

When Lacey appeared James answered his wave with his left hand and kept the concealed gun trained on him with the right. Lacey stayed at the bar for several anti-climactic minutes whilst first a tray then two pineapple-whatever drinks and finally two chilli dogs were produced for him from behind the bar. James would have been significantly less surprised if they had pulled a baby elephant out for him. He wondered if anybody else was paying the prices that he was paying for drinks.

Lacey manoeuvred his tray over to James' table placed it down and dropped a slightly sweat stained green folder on to the table near to James. "It's all there," Lacey commented and gulped his first mouthful. "I've done good work for you and I'm afraid that that is going to be the end of our ever-so-brief relationship." James tensed, the gun felt sticky.

"Why is that then?"

"Because I don't like where the trail has led."

"Which is where?" Lacey shrugged.

"It's all in there."

"And you don't want to give me any verbal commentary?"

"Well," James flicked the folder open with his free hand. He could visualise what the desert eagle would do to Lacey at this range and felt sick. "I don't know where it's going. Don't get me wrong - there are plenty of leads in there for you to follow up but I don't know that I would." James pulled out a photograph of a woman in her late teens or very early twenties. He had forgotten that she was beautiful, it just had not seemed relevant.

"Is that a threat?"

"What? Don't follow it up? No, you do what the hell you like. It's just that my interest ends here." As if to emphasise his words he began to eat.

"Has somebody warned you off?" He shook his head dismissively.

"The only two people that I've spoken to about this are yourself and Benjamin Edward Smith -his number is in there. He would very much like to talk to you. He's a worried man. You see he removed the records and he has no recollection of doing it. OK it was four years ago - so what? Well I know the man he's got pretty well a photographic memory - he remembers - but he does not remember doing this. He's worried."

"Why don't you want to get involved?" Swallow, chew.

"It smells wrong."

"Who do you think it is? Or is it in there?"

"No, just facts no speculation. I don't know who it is but I know who it isn't.."

"Which is?"

"The government. They are usually way too sloppy. This is quiet and this is clean." James thought very hard and very quickly. On balance, he was relieved. He came to a decision.

"I guess you are being straight with me then." Lacey shrugged.

"I've no reason to lie to you."

"I guess I can take this gun off you then," said James, testing Lacey. Lacey jumped back as far as his seat would allow.

"Christ!" He half rose, "What the hell do you think you're doing?" There followed a long, communicative few seconds between them. Lacey had passed. James placed the gun and its bag to his side. "What the bloody hell do you think you are doing? What sort of an amateur stunt is that? You paid me for a service, I provided it there's no need to play bloody stupid gangsters."

"I'm sorry," said James, "but I think that you should know you may be in danger having done this."

"That figures - go on, I'm listening."

"Right - well I went to a cop with the number plate of the car she was in. The cop isn't interested until he runs it through the computer and then he finds out that it can't exist. He sends a patrol out which I follow to find her," he held up the picture, "she's there and she tells me where to go. Then this blonde guy and this Greek try to kill me. Luckily I run into a greyhound bus. When I go back to the first cop he pulls a gun on me and tries to shoot me. They've tried to kill me twice and all that I've done is to show an interest in them. So, what I am saying is keep clear but look after yourself."

"I'm very good at what I do Mr Arthur." James expression must have shown his incomprehension as Lacey leaned forward and explained, "I left no footprints - nobody will be able to trace me." He indicated the folder. "All of that I did outside of company time and I ran up you some company time to make it look as if you had some legitimate business with me." He shrugged, "I shouldn't ask but what is this about?"

"Would you believe mind-control weapons? Or drugs? Human experimentation?"

"No, I would not believe." Lacey replied very firmly.

"Nor would I but I know what I've seen ... and what Michael the Leprechaun tells me." Lacey was not amused. "Of course if you are asked about this you know now that I have lied some."

"I'm sure of that." Lacey decided to finish his lunch, drink his drinks and not talk to James.

"Just one more thing," James asked as he took the hint and stood to leave, "how much time did you run up to cover our tracks?"

"Five hundred dollars." James stuffed the folder in alongside the Desert Eagle he was not sure which was the more dangerous. "It's on account though - have a good life," Lacey added avoiding eye contact.

CHAPTER 19

Back in the dingy apartment, James opened the folder and extracted each item carefully, savouring each new item of information. There were three sheets one for each of the Missing persons and a fourth detailing the information trail that Lacey had followed to Benjamin Edward Smith.

The "woman" was in fact Elizabeth "Liz" Hastings, 22 -23 next month, her parents had posted a substantial reward when she had disappeared one evening on her way back from school. She was the only New Yorker.

The blonde man was David Armitage from Winnipeg in Canada. He had been missing for seven years having walked out of his house as a sixteen year old. His teenage photograph bore little resemblance to the man that he had seen in the diner, they had missed out the bat's wings for one.

The third man was not Sullivan but another man called Robert Danjule who looked like Lurch's shorter, bald brother. He had disappeared four years before. No known relatives, his entry had been posted by Chloe Bennet one of the nurses at the residential psychiatric hospice that he lived in near to Boston. Money was low thanks to Lacey's careful covering of his tracks. He could visit all three places if he was prepared to be forgetful with respect to returning the hire-car. Unfortunately all three trails were at least four years cold. The alternative, given that Lacey had not pulled a gun on him, was ....

Benjamin Edward Smith an assistant senior supervisor at the National Missing Persons Database Agency. James had not wanted to meet him in the agency, Smith had chosen a park bench in preference to a bar.

Everything about Smith said solid, dependable, sensible. He was about forty, black. Comfortably well filled and with a full moustache which bordered on the unkempt. "Mr Arthur?" James did not offer his left hand to shake or remove his right hand from the gun in the bag on his lap.

"Mr Smith." Smith sat down.

"You want to know about the Armitage, Hastings and Danjule records." James nodded. "I would too," he paused, "I've a very good memory Mr Arthur and I mean very good. It's played a big part in my getting my job. ... The job matters, it matters a lot, you know, we're not just bureaucrats. Every one that we take off the list is very important. Sometimes they're losses, you know, when they turn up dead, sometimes they're wins. Families put back together. They are our victories. I remember every one that I have taken off - every one. I could not have taken three off without my knowing. When Lacey contacted me I checked the records – my authorisation was used - nobody knows my codes. Nobody could know my codes - I was a manager even then." Lacey had been right, he was very worried.

"Do you remember anything at all about it?"

"Nothing."

"You want to help me, I want to help you but you're not offering me anything." Smith took a deep breath,

"I know but there is a way."

"Which is?"

"Hypnotism. They can't have drugged me or anything like that- I would have remembered afterwards. I wouldn't be struggling to find out three years afterwards. So I reckon they must have used hypnotism, you know, and another hypnotist could undo what they have done. I'd be willing to have hypnotherapy."

James released his grip on the Desert Eagle having released that this was not an elaborate assassination set up. It was something far worse. "This hypnotism," he asked, "who would pay for it?"

The hypnotism sessions could not be set up until the following Saturday which allowed James to earn a few more night's pay. In the day he finally located the newspaper reports on the disappearance of Liz Hastings. Without Lacey's information he would have spent, at his best estimate, six months searching. He also checked her home address and established that her parents were still living there but, timidly, he found several valid reasons to postpone visiting them until after the hypnosis sessions.

Smith had a *remarkably* good memory. The hypnotherapist spent almost forty minutes of James' money following false trails and getting caught up in the minutia of Smith's remarkable memory. Having established that his breakfast that morning was not relevant, Doctor Mears, the hypnotherapist, finally began to move on to the afternoon.

Had Mrs Justine Smith not been present James would have urged the Doctor on far more insistently.

The bureaucrat's wife was a surprise. She was ten, perhaps fifteen years younger than her husband, extremely attractive, extremely suspicious of James. Divorced, living in a hole, James could not help but to speculate as to how the seemingly staid official had managed to land such a beautiful specimen. His best guess was sweetness of nature, that or the fact that he would remember birthdays and the like. James was realistic enough to know that he would not be thinking of her in terms of conquests to be won if he was not quite so lacking in female company himself. He knew that he ought to talk to her, to communicate to her as one human being to another even as one gorgeous human being to a grubby near-destitute human being. Not that she had given any indication in their brief, distant introduction to one another. Before he had ever opened his mouth, it was apparent that she was extremely hostile towards him. James hoped that it was a black thing, he'd hate to think that it was personal.

Mrs Smith was video-taping the entire session. Not an unreasonable precaution, he could hardly object given that the Desert Eagle was in his bag.

Doctor Mears had tried, unsuccessfully, to skirt around the afternoon's events several times. Smith's memory was too exact and his mind too literal to make the connections that Mear was alluding to. He made the most progress when he asked the direct question. "Benjamin," he asked, "why did you remove those three records?"

"He told me to." James leaned forward impatiently. He was under strict instructions not to interfere and had only bludgeoned his way into the session by insisting on his rights as He Who Paid The Bill.

"Who told you to?"

"The man." From Smith, this was unbelievably vague.

"Which man? What was his name?" Smith paused.

"I don't know. He did not say and I did not ask."

"Did he work at the agency?"

"No. He visited me that afternoon." Smith was beginning to show some slight signs of discomfort.

"Why did he visit you?"

"He told me to remove the records."

"Then what?"

"He left."

"Did he tell you anything else?"

"Just to clear away the traces and to forget that I had done it and that I had met him." The Doctor paused, uncertain as to where he should go next.

"How did he make you forget?" asked James, the Doctor scowled at him but said nothing.

"He told me to. He told me and I forgot."

"Can you remember anything else about how he made you forget? Did he use anything on you?"

"No. He just told me to forget."

"Did he suggest it? Was it like hypnotism?"

"He just told me and I forgot." The Doctor was becoming quite caught up in the mystery now, asking two questions whereas before had he restricted himself, professionally to single questions.

"Did he stay with you long?"

"No, just long enough to see me remove the records."

"Did anybody else see him? Would they remember him?"

"Other people saw him but they would not remember ... it was just an ordinary matter." The Doctor referred to James' and Smith's own written list of questions.

"Did he introduce himself?"

"No."

"How did he get an appointment to see you?"

"I don't know. He was referred on to me by the reception desk. They did not give me any details."

"Did he show you or them any authorisation?"

"Yes."

"What sort of authorisation?"

"A card. He showed me a card and then told me that it gave him authority and that I would have to do what he said." James and the Doctor exchanged glances.

"What was on the card? What did it say?" Smith giggled.

"Nothing. There was just a pattern. It looked like something that he had ripped of a cereal packet and put in to a card folder. It did not say anything."
"But you thought that it gave him permission to tell you what to do?" The Doctor mused out loud, Smith's literal mind interpreted it as a question.

"Yes."

"What did he look like?" asked James, the Doctor turned angrily and waved a finger at James.

"Answer the question." he instructed calmly.

"I don't know."

"Why don't you?"

"Because he told me to forget it."

"What did his face look like?"

"Blank. Just hair and a blank face. No eyes, mouth, nose, eyebrows, chin -just blank."

"Did he really look like that?"

"No."

"Then why did you say that he did?"

"Because he told me to forget it."

"Ben - if somebody else saw him - the receptionist or whoever. If they saw him and he had not told them to forget would they have seen eyes and a mouth - things like that?"

"Yes."

"And what would these eyes look like?"

"I don't know."

"Why not?"

"Because he told me to forget."

"What did he look like -apart from the face?" asked James. The doctor was about to launch into James when Smith's reply cut him off.

"Six foot tall. Dark brown -nearly black hair, slightly wavy, fine. Expensive cut. Slim build. Caucasian hands - Caucasian. Expensive, very well cut suit. It was green -very dark green almost black. Jacket and trousers, white shirt. Emerald green tie. No pattern -silk. Highly polished black leather shoes." Smith appeared to have stopped.

"And the face, Benjamin?"

"No face, just blank."

"Is there anything else that you can tell me about him. How he spoke - anything else that might tell us more about him?"

"He had a dark green car. An expensive car."

"How do you know that?"

"After I had cleared the records up, he told me to take him out to reception. I saw the car waiting for him. It was parked right in front where nobody is allowed to but nobody had stopped him or moved it on."

"Could you draw the car for us if I asked you to?" James held his hand up indicating that he had further questions. The Doctor shrugged.

"Did he give you any instructions?" asked James. "In case anybody asked you about the records?"

"No."

"Did he let you know how you could contact him?"

"No."

"Did he make you remove any other records?"

"No."

"Did he talk about any other records?"

"No."

"Do you think that he was FBI?"

"No."

"Had you met him before or since?"

"No."

"Who knows about these records?"

"You, Doctor Mears, Justine and ...." he paused apparently, significantly "Canute Lacey and .. the man who told me to remove them."

"Who is he?"

"He did not say."

"Do you know anything significant about those records?"

"No." The Doctor held his hand up to stop James.

"Benjamin, I want to go back to the face."

Which the Doctor duly did. Despite the earlier limit which he had insisted on, the Doctor continued to try and chip away at the details of Smith's memory block for another hour. At the end of that time he was no closer. Smith drew a detailed picture of a large, green expensive car. He had not seen any significant information on it that would have helped to identify it. James thought that it could have been one of several makes which he could equally well have selected by simply naming a number of expensive makes of car.

Smith was brought around and after the broad details had been discussed he and his wife returned to their well ordered life whilst James remained with the Doctor to pay the amended bill.

James signed the cheque and passed it to the Doctor. Mears was clearly exhausted from the nervous energy that he had put in to the session. "I'm not really inclined to tell you this, having to hand this over, but you might have put yourself into a dangerous situation having done this." Mears took the cheque.

"What's this all about?" he indicated the chair that Smith had sat in. "Really?"

"Really."

"Really?"

"The truth is that I don't know."

"FBI?"

"It could be but I don't know. Smith does not think so. I've spoken to somebody else about it and they don't think that it's government." For a moment they stared at one another communicating their mutual confusion.

"I've never come up against a block like he had. Mighty walls and barriers, yes, but you can see how they got there and there's always some powerful emotions holding them up. This one is, well, just like this Green man told him to forget it and that's it."

"Do you think that you could break it down?" Mears thought carefully before answering.

"No and that's another first but I can assure you that I will not be writing to any journals about this case."

"That's very wise." Another understanding flickered between them. The Doctor nodded to James then shook his head.

"I hope that he does not come back in, I can't do anything for him."

"It's probably best if he just forgets."

"That's it though - a man like that, forgetting. It would be like telling anybody else to just stop breathing." James smiled a humourless smile,

"What's the betting that if this Green Man told you to stop breathing that you would?" The truth of it floated intangibly in the air between them. Had he wished it, James knew that he had an ally here, a fellow believer and, just as he realised it, so he knew that the decent thing was to leave the Doctor completely out of it. "Can I take this?" James asked, indicating Smith's sketch and breaking the uncomfortable silence between them.

"You paid for it," said the Doctor, distantly. They shook hands and David left him to his life.

In the lift on the way down, David clutched his bag to his side and pondered on the injustice of his quest. It had become the most important thing in his life not just since he had dropped out of a normal life on divorcing Suzanne but for his entire life. This was the big one. This mattered and yet everybody that he had brought into it: Halberg; Lacey; Smith: Mears - no matter how limited their involvement, he was, in effect, allowing a non-metaphorical gun to be pointed at their heads.

The next step would not be easy either to do or to avoid. There were others to whom this mattered too.

CHAPTER 20

There was a bite to the evening. It was barely October but the first taste of winter was in the air. James had invested in a respectable overcoat and a briefcase both of which felt as if they were still dangling their labels. Justine Smith's reaction had bothered him in so far as it reflected on his plummeting social status. There had been a time when he had been on everybody's party list not that he dominated social gatherings rather that a lot of people had found him exceedingly inoffensive if not to say rather pleasant company. He wanted to impress the next two people that he would meet. Elizabeth Hastings mattered to them.

James stood on the other side of the street from her parent's house in a suburb off New Rochelle. There were lights on inside. He took the first step and the others followed easily enough. The door had an old fashioned-knocker which he struck, satisfyingly, twice. The temptation to adjust his tie proved all too irresistible and, mirror-less, he succeeded in pulling it completely askew. The door opened revealing a fifty-something man. He was grey haired, overweight particularly around the jowls where several chins had long since achieved seamless unity. There was a decent stomach too though James had the feeling that it would take a fairly substantial punch. He wore glasses, slippers and a holed but comfortable sweater. "Mr Hastings?" The man's frown inclined slightly. "If you could spare me a few moments.." The door began to close unconsciously in the approved home improvements salesman manner. "About your daughter."

Had James not been looking for it, he would have missed the surprise, the pain and the anger that flickered in his expression before finally settling into clear hostility. "What about her?"

"Well -- " James had considered several plausible lies all of which fell away. "I don't want you to get your hopes up but I think that I have seen her." Elizabeth's father stared him down for several awkward moments before letting the door swing open.

"You'd better come in," he muttered then turned his back and moved back into the house. James closed the door carefully and followed him.

Mr Hastings led him into a warm, open plan den. He sat on a large, leather chair and indicated that James should sit on its partner facing him across a glass-topped table. "Let's have it then. My wife is due back in half an hour and I don't want you here then."

"That's fine," James delved into his briefcase uncomfortably aware of the zipped compartment that held the Desert Eagle. He withdrew the Computer image which he had had made and passed it over. "I don't want to lead you on because if you were to ask me where she is now or what she might be doing I just don't know." Hastings examined the picture carefully keeping any emotion from his expression. He passed it back. "That's not a photograph," Hastings' face registered mild surprise. "It's a computer image that I had made up after I met her and before I did some research."

"You'd better start telling me what this is all about before I throw you out." There it was again, from party man to parasite in four difficult months.

"OK. I'll start and you just chip in and let me know when I start sounding like something believable and not like some lunatic who just walked in off the street." Hastings did not give him the satisfaction of a response. "Well I was sitting in a diner about three - no four - months ago near to Las Vegas when she walked in with this guy. I got the impression that something was wrong then he started to drag her out - metaphorically not literally - so I followed." Evidence for credibility part two was produced and handed over. "They got into a Silver Bullet with that registration. You can have it checked out but I suggest that you lie about it, give a false name and say that it hit your car and drove on or something. I went to the police with the straight story and the first thing that they did was to tell me that it did not exist. It should do but it does not. The second thing is that they pulled a gun on me and tried to shoot me before bringing that plate number up." Hasting's expression became increasingly doubtful. "Look I know it sounds crazy but you can check this one out. When I've gone try it but please be cautious." Hastings placed the number on the table. "Ok. So I went to the police and before they turned on me I found out where the camper was parked. I went there, I met her and her companions attacked me." There was a world of disbelief facing James across the table, his confidence began to slip away. "Look - what I'm saying is that I think she's connected with some dangerous people. I don't believe that she's in danger or hurt or anything. But she's involved. She didn't try to hold these two guys back and I was bloody lucky to get out of it alive."

"Well that's where you're wrong," Hastings snarled, "my daughter is a good girl - she wouldn't have anything to do with violence -"

"But-"

"What the hell do you know about it?" Somehow, James did not respond to the challenge. He stared back at Hastings waiting for the anger to pass.

"Ok," he conceded finally, "I don't know anything. She's your daughter I just met her briefly but I believe that it was her and I believe that she's not in danger. That's all that it is - my opinion."

"She would not be involved in anything wrong and if she wasn't being held against her will she'd have gotten in touch with us."

James knew better than to push against the pillars.

"No. I'm sure your right." He handed over the third piece of evidence. Hastings shrugged dismissively.

"I entered this - what's new about this?"

"I know - I'll come to it... So I escaped, went to the police who fired at me so I ran away then I started to find things out. This for example." He tapped the record, "Four years ago you put that information on to the National Missing Persons Database, three and a half years ago somebody removed it." For the first time Hastings' expression began to register a degree of tenuous acceptance. "Now you might think that I'm from way out there but you can check this fact." Evidence number four. "That's the name and number of the man who removed the record and he is worried as hell about it. Somebody forced him to do it and completely wiped his memory." Hastings picked up the last piece of paper and waved it absently. "This is all fantasy," he said without conviction.

"As far as you know, yes, there are not many facts there but what there are you can check. If you wish, I can go away, you can check these facts and when you are sure of them we'll talk again."

"All right," said Hastings with such finality that James began to stand prior to leaving. "No wait." James sat again. "I need to know something."

"What's that?"

"I need to know why? I need to know what it is that you are after?" Of all the answers that James could give him, this was the big one. James opted for honesty.

"I'd like to find her again, I'd like to know what has been going on. Why? I guess it's got everything to do with the fact that I ran away. I was scared. I was very, very scared. I embarrassed myself Mr Hastings and until I've found some answers to all of this I don't feel very comfortable with myself. To be honest, I was interested for perhaps half an hour because I thought that she was a babe. Now - I don't know that I'm interested in her, I just want answers."

"Would a little money help you to find those answers?"

"Mr Hastings I don't want a reward not now not ever. Don't you insult me and I won't insult you." James had recognised the feint for what it was and responded appropriately. He and Hastings stared at one another for several seconds at the end of which there was some, grudging, understanding.

"A name might help." Hastings muttered.

"What? Oh Christ, yes, sorry my name is James Arthur." Hastings stared at the hand which unconsciously risen before him. With a certain amount of reluctance he shook it slowly and firmly.

"Well, Mr Arthur, I love my daughter very much. There isn't a day that goes by when I don't feel the pain of her going. You wouldn't be exploiting an father's despair would you?" James thought carefully before replying.

"Guilty - I suppose because I'm here and I'm talking about her. If I'm doing that there's got to be some pain especially if there's hope involved. I'm not promising anything but I'm trying to find her. I've got a few leads and talking to you is one of them."

"What you've got is a crock." Hastings commented with an ironic smile.

"There's more."

"How much more?"

"Not much more." James produced another two pieces of evidence. "These two records were removed at the same time and in the same peculiar way." He indicated the first, "This was the guy with her in the diner."

"It's not a lot."

"No but I might learn something by talking to the three people who posted the records - you're the first."

"So what have you learned?" James shrugged,

"That's she's a good girl." Hastings finger jabbed instinctively at him.

"And you'd better believe it." He became aware of the gesture and let his hand fall on to the table. He shook his head. "Only children, I reckon that you're always ready to fight for them. What do you want to know about Liz?"

"Anything. Have you had any contact at all with her?"

"None."

"Tell me about how she left was there anything suspicious - anything at all?" Hastings began to look away.

"Her friend left her on the subway with two stops to go. We spent months following her journey. Met the trains with pictures and idiot sandwich boards."

"Did you find any witnesses?"

"Yes, paid them too. Nothing happened on the train. She got off a station early on her own then where she went we do not know."

"She got off voluntarily then?"

"That seems to be the case."

"Had she met anybody prior to her disappearance?"

"No, quite the opposite. She'd split up with her boyfriend a couple of months ago. He was a .. reasonable boy - he had nothing to do with this. I know, I've checked." He looked anxiously towards the front door. "Don't breathe a word of this but she just seemed to drop all of her friends at the same time, she became very down. Her grades dropped and she was a straight "A" student. Looking back at it I have to think that she might have maybe had some sort of break-down." Having voiced his fear, he appeared reluctant to go on.

"Was there anything in particular?"

"No ..." he shrugged, "well you know how it is when your kids hit the dreaded teenage years and nothing that you do is good enough for them?" James smiled in a manner which he hoped would be taken as signalling understanding. Hastings continued on regardless. "Well we'd gotten through all of that with her years ago but then the last few months it was like she'd just woken up to the fact that we were real people and she was not happy." There was a moment's silence as James considered. A change in behaviour would seem to fit with a number of speculative possibilities none of which was he prepared to share.

"Did you see anybody new around at the time of her disappearance?"

"No - believe me we've been down that road. If there had been, we would have known." James produced the sketch of the car and the description of the green man. Hastings studied them carefully. "No. Who is this? How is he involved?"

"I don't know who he is but he removed the records."

"Do you have anything else?"

"No."

"So where do you go from here?"

"I'll chase up the other people who posted the two records. I'll see what I can learn just as I have here." Hastings gave him a studied, intense stare.

"You haven't learned anything new here, have you?"

"Yes, I have."

"What? That she is a good girl?"

"Not just that - I'm seeing a bigger picture. The more I see, the more I understand." The distinct sound of a key in a lock echoed through behind James. Hastings leaned forward and grabbed James' hand. He stared intensely into James' face from no more than a few inches.

"I need to know - if you find out any more I have to know."

"It could be dangerous," mumbled James embarrassed by the contact and the closeness. Hastings withdrew slightly, physically and emotionally.

"That does not matter - " he released his grip on James' hand. "We aren't living like this. We can't go on." James spread his hands.

"I don't know but the worst things that you could imagine - I don't think that that has happened to her."

"The worst that you can imagine is not knowing," said Hastings quietly. Footsteps sounded softly behind James. Hastings smiled at the figure beyond him. James turned to see Mrs Hastings small, slight, defeated. "This is Mr Arthur, Jean. He's a private investigator who is investigating some other disappearances he was collecting some background information." James smiled unwilling to condone the lie with anything other than his silence. "Jean - Mr Arthur. Mr Arthur - Jean."

"Call me James."

An hour later James left having accepted their hospitality and having maintained Hastings' fabrication. Two hours before his motivation was basically self-respect during the course of the meeting he had acquired several more powerful reasons for finding their daughter none of them particularly uncomplicated none of them particularly welcome. He would like to believe in their daughter as they did. He would like to believe that their little girl was the woman that he had met. He had found them in grief and his instinctive feeling was that if he succeeded that that would be precisely where he would leave them.

CHAPTER 21

The night watchman's job had long since gone. James had changed it for a seasonal job at an apartment store where he gloried in the paper title of assistant sales manager and a somewhat improved wage. For two frantic weeks he had combined it with the night watchman's job before their joint demands had led to an inevitable sacrificing of the lesser income. For the four weeks leading up to Christmas he had worked at a postal sorting centre. Working three nights out of six had been tolerable. As had the company. Without exception, his fellow workers were students in the seventeen to twenty age range. In a perverse, grandfatherly way he had enjoyed their enthusiasm and egocentric horizons. None of them saw the picture that he saw though they'd have willingly believed in it too not that he mentioned a word of it. Almost six months had passed since Las Vegas and he was weakened by persistent doubt. Things came to a head on Christmas day, his first alone, when in his whiskey-numbed state he seemed to have three clear choices. Firstly, he could give it all up and try to make himself a life. Secondly, he could follow it through to wherever it would lead. Thirdly, he could address the real problem that faced him at that hour by getting himself seriously laid.

Yet even there, the image of Liz Hastings haunted him. James had to find her. It was not that he loved her or even liked her, he simply had to bring things to an end.

January the 18th found him driving a newly bought pick-up towards Boston. His desires had not been satisfied nor itches scratched but he had enough money to finance the three trips that he needed to make and, if nothing else, his purpose remained pure.

A telephone conversation had allowed psychiatric nurse Bennet to clear her schedules and James to contemplate a thousand paranoid scenarios. The nurse's house, for example, had two beautiful gables either of which would have served a sniper ideally. Then there was the fortyish woman who shuffled out onto the porch when he pulled up. The housecoat and the dangling cigarette were an easy give away to one of James' increasingly paranoiac tendencies. The image of her inviting him into the house and then sinking her teeth into his neck flashed through his mind as he walked up her path. "Chloe Bennet?" he asked at the foot of her porch whilst keeping his hands in his coat pockets. He had sewn an extra-large pocket into the right pocket so that he could hold the Desert Eagle.

"You must be Mr Arthur then?" She held her hand out to him.

"Yes." He had not planned on this. Reluctantly he released the weapon and shook her hand.

"Come inside."

The house was tidy, empty. Very much what he would expect of a bitter, divorced nurse living alone. The only thing that grabbed him by the throat was the smell and taste of nicotine. They observed the niceties of polite conversation and she made him coffee and fetched notes that she had made shortly after Danjule's disappearance.

"So - you want to know about Robert Danjule?" she asked. "Everything that you can think of particularly to do with his disappearance." She shrugged and began to busy herself with a cigarette.

"Do you mind?" she asked.

"Not at all and it's your house." She took her first, longed-for inhalation, visibly relaxing.

"I shouldn't really - but you know how they say that each one takes five minutes off your life?" He nodded. "Well it takes ten minutes to smoke one so I reckon I'm coming out ahead." Nothing more having been said, James knew that he was going to like her.

"What was your connection with Mr Danjule?" She shrugged again.

"Nothing at all. I just worked on the ward - so you might ask why I posted his missing report? Well it was the injustice of it I guess." She took another puff on the cigarette. James considered diving into the silence but rejected the idea in favour of letting her. "It was just that - we have all sorts up there. Believe me, all sorts and he was just so harmless and when he went there was nobody to give a dam. Nobody cared - nobody was interested and trying to get the people who saw him off to talk about it was like getting blood out of the proverbial stone. It wasn't right how he went. He wasn't signed out, no location. Somebody just walked in off the street took him out and nobody gave it a moments' thought."

"Who took him?"

"That's just it. Nobody seemed to know and if you pushed them on it - these were the people who walked him out the door -if you asked them about it, they couldn't tell you it was like they weren't lying about it it was just like they couldn't..."

"Remember?"

"That's just it. He'd been gone a day and not one of them could remember anything."

"Do you know anything about how he was taken?"

"Yes, I do. I saw him being taken out although I didn't know it at the time. I just saw him and the man who took him for a second. I was walking past with some laundry. I didn't know that he was going then. Didn't find out until later." "What did the man look like?" Shrug, thoughtful puff.

"Just normal, good looking - expensive looking. You know the sort of guy who has a manicure. Dark hair. Suit and tie type of guy."

"What was the suit like?" She referred to her notebook. "Yes - it was flashy - green a very dark green." Touchdown.

"What about Danjule? What was he like?"

"Nothing really severely autistic - supposed to be.. Exceptionally withdrawn from being a baby really."

"Did he have any special talents?"

"What do you mean anything that would make somebody want to kidnap him for?" James nodded. "No. He was unusually lacking really. He was diagnosed as autistic but I don't think that he was really. I think that it was more likely that he had been brain damaged perhaps in childbirth. He could feed himself some of the time - toilet himself very occasionally. There was nothing there really. With the autistic there can be very little contact but you know that there is something going on behind the curtains. There was nobody home."

"What about family?"

"None. There had been but they died fifteen years ago. There was enough money to see his life out in the hospital but it was all in trust there was no way that anybody could get it."

"Why do you think that he was taken?" She sighed and stubbed the cigarette out.

"The only think that I can think of is just silly."

"What is it?"

"Organs. That's all that he had. He was just a walking set of organs." Stranger and stranger.

"Would I be able to see the records at the hospital?"

"You could ask, there are very few of the same staff left but you can ask."

Which was just what James did. He spent the best part of a week chasing up every scrap of information that he could but gained nothing more than he had gained in that first hour's conversation with Chloe Bennet. James had liked her more than he wished to admit. A kind woman acting decently because she was moved by the injustice that she saw. He hoped that his motivations were as worthy. Perhaps they were but the fact that he felt the need to be judged as being worthy inclined him to doubt. Nevertheless, Sir Galahad, rode on across the Canadian border.

CHAPTER 22

"So you are investigating missing persons but not my David particularly. You are just looking for similarities in the cases."

"That's right," said James feeling very small.

Rachel Armitage seemed to stare straight through him. The private investigator lie had worked very well with Chloe Bennet not that he had wished to lie to her but it had, he hoped, placed a distance between her and the danger that he was in. After no more than two minutes in Rachel Armitage's house he knew that it was only a matter of time before the biplane Honourable Deception went down in flames.

"So who is paying you to investigate?"

"Nobody," half-truths were often the best lies, "I'm filling out some time between jobs - trying to tidy up some old files."

"Have you got some form of identification?"

"Yes," he began to delve into his pockets, "nothing to say that I'm a private investigator though. I'm on a seventy-two hour visa and the border officials are holding on to it. I'm not licensed to work in Canada." She waved away his wallet and fixed him with The Look again.

He had come across The Look in his previous jobs especially when he had been a salesman and had encountered company owners. How would he describe it? It spoke pretty well for itself and what it said was, "You have two minutes to convince me that you have something of value to offer me and then you are out the door into the realm of front door secretaries and assistant managers." Not all of the company owners were like that of course, some were as pleasant and as well mannered as you could hope for but the truth was that the men or women who owned the company had the real power. Rachel Armitage had real power and he would have to justify himself very quickly.

"So, what do you want to know?" she asked.

"I'd like to know about the circumstances in which he disappeared."

"He put his coat on and walked out that door babbling something about a child, seven years ago." No green man, no unexplained memory loss. For a moment James could not believe what he was hearing until he came back to her fixed, resolute expression.

"If you don't mind," clearly she did, "I have quite a few more questions."

"So have I." He waited, fruitlessly for her to continue.

"There's a lot more that I would like to deal with."

"There's a great deal that I would like to deal with. Mostly it's anger with him for going. Part of me would like to hurt him but I'd give all of that up just to see him again." It was uncomfortable being so close to her intensity far worse than the Hastings and their despair. She had The Look and like Elizabeth Hastings she had the eyes. James knew that she could slice him open if she so chose.

"Can I press you on the circumstances in which he went?" She bowed her head and rubbed the heels of her hand into her forehead for several seconds.

"My son disappeared seven years ago, it killed his father. I have been through a great deal, Mr Arthur, I can not be dealing with this nonsense."

"What nonsense?"

"I mean you."

"What can I say?" The question had escaped him before he could think about it.

"You can tell me the truth." Various lies occurred to him none of which seemed to have any purpose and so he began to tell her the truth.

James told her about the past eight months and about the day that had begun it all though he omitted the bat-creature and the man that could out-run a car and the unexplained mental powers. He had no difficulty in keeping those things from her because although they were true, he knew that they would have undermined the essential truth of what he was saying. And all the time she watched him knowingly, wisely. She was an intelligent woman who had dealt with her own losses. She understood how people worked, she could read people - certainly he had been no challenge to her. When he was finished she questioned him on one aspect of his story.

"When you saw him, this was eight months ago?" He nodded. "That would be Las Vegas then." He sat there completely dumbfounded, there had been no real need to name places and he had not. She stood before he could question her. "I'm going to call a friend over and then I'll make you something to eat.

Despite his protestations, she made him a very good Spanish omelette and declined to answer his questions with anything other than a polite, "After you've eaten."

The "friend" appeared before he could finish the omelette. Her name was Terri George, she was aged about twenty-five, in the first smug bloom of matrimony and she was what in High School James and his friends would have described as a "Wahey fwor" girl. There really good-looking girls walked past and you went "Fwor!" Terri George was on a higher plane, she was undoubtedly "Wahey fwor!" He finished the very good omelette tasting none of it and then had to repeat his story for the new audience. Whilst he did this he noticed several significant looks between the two women. They clearly had a very close friendship far more than was likely between a fifty plus matron and a young wife who was half her age. Without being told, he knew that they had come through something together, he surmised that her son was the cause of their suffering.

When he had finished they exchanged another of those looks. "Well?" he asked, the question seemingly interrupted their communication. He knew that it was almost certainly paranoia on his part but he could not help but to be suspicious of them.

"Well what?" responded the elder woman.

"I've told you why I am here. Believe it or not, I'm trying to help. I'm trying to find your David and these others and I'd appreciate any help that you can give me. I'm assuming that you do want to find him."

"Oh, yes." She answered with a confident edge. Nothing ventured ...

"And that you don't know where he is." James mirrored her certainty, pushing her fixedly for a response.

"I don't know where he is," she said levelly before taking off on another tack, "Terri was David's girlfriend for the two years before he disappeared. She was there on the night that he disappeared."

"What can you tell me about his disappearance?" The younger woman glanced at her friend for permission which was granted with an abrupt nod.

"It was very strange. We had been having a real teenage heart to heart then he just sat up grinned his head off and said that he had to go."

"Why?"

"Because he heard the voice of a child."

"Sorry?"

"He heard a child calling for him." James thought for a moment. Where did a child come into it?

"Did you hear it?"

"No," she replied adding damningly, "it was in his head."

"Had he acted strangely in any way prior to his disappearance?" There was yet another meaningful exchange of glances between the two women the understanding of which was denied to James.

"Well David was just...an incredibly sweet boy to date but there was no ... physical aspect to our relationship." For the first time since meeting the mother, James began to feel as if he had knowledge that they did not have. He had no difficulty in believing that there had been no physical aspect to the relationship. "On the night I sort of confronted him with it and I have to think, looking back on it that it might have led him to go. I asked him if he was homosexual." James smiled became aware of the inappropriate nature of the expression at that point of intensity and felt as if he had to justify himself,

"I don't think that he is homosexual. I'd be pretty sure of it." It was difficult to tell which of the two women looked more relieved.

"Why is that Mr Arthur?" asked the mother. James shrugged,

"Just an impression I got - or didn't get really."

"There's got to be more to it than that. We are both dealing in trust here aren't we?"

"Of course," he replied musing on how the use of his first name might have helped the a fore mentioned trust. He shrugged, "Look I've no reason to say that really - I don't know - it's just that I didn't get the impression that he was homosexual." Non-human bat-type creature certainly but being a homosexual non-human bat-type creature as well was certainly stacking the statistical improbabilities rather high.

"It's strange," said the mother, "but I had some hopes. I know that now-a-days and certainly in this house, homosexuality is no reason to run away from home but it seemed to be somehow better than ..." her eyes held him, examined him and decided that he could be trusted this far. "It just seemed better than the fact that he might have turned loopy and started hearing voices."

"Maybe he did hear voices."

"Voices that nobody else could hear? What do you mean by that?"

"Simply that nothing should be ruled out until it absolutely has to be ruled out. Didn't Philip Marlowe say that when you have eliminated the possible ...?"

"No, he didn't that was Sherlock Holmes." An onomatopoeic four-letter word bounced around James' mind, he really was not cutting it with the private investigator story.

"What do you know about voices Mr Arthur?"

"Nothing." Nevertheless he thought that this was a good idea to produce some diversionary evidence. "Did you see anybody unusual around the time that David disappeared?" Both women shook their heads simultaneously. "What about these?" He produced the pictures of Liz Hastings and Robert Danjule but received negative responses to both, which was as he had expected their disappearances having occurred after David Armitage's. The sketch of the green man, his car and James' own, crude drawing of Sullivan proved to be equally unrewarding. "Nothing at all?" He asked, forlornly. "There was no detail at all - nothing?"

"No."

"Well - " Minor significant looks, "David didn't like to be touched - I always assumed that he might have had some sort of rash or something that he kept quiet."

"That's right," the mother agreed, "for the past two years he became really paranoid about being seen undressed - I don't think that I ever saw him undressed during that time." Not 'think' thought James, you can be certain that you did not see him naked.

"Unfortunately I didn't think that this was too different from normal teenage behaviour." Both women looked blankly at him. Their conversation appeared to have reached a natural end. "So where do we go from here?" James took a long, thoughtful sip of his cold coffee.

"I think that we deal in some more trust," he stated. "How did you know that I met your son in Las Vegas?" She nodded compliantly then walked over to one of her cupboard drawers. She retrieved and placed before him a bundle of cards and letters.

"Whatever he has done - and it's not in there -he's a good boy Mr Arthur. Whenever he can, he writes."

CHAPTER 23

Washington had been the final, independent option. If the Hastings, Miss Bennet and Mrs Armitage had produced nothing he would still have had hopes for Washington. As it was, his suspicious had been confirmed before the last visit, if little more than that, whilst Mrs Armitage had given him a seeming abundance of additional information.

James stopped in a motel on the border for the night. In the morning he would start the long journey down South to Washington but the night held the intriguing allure of matching the contents of his briefcase against ten dollars worth of photocopies. He spread the material out on the table then the bed and the floor. He read it carefully itemising each fact and slowly, thoughtfully he began to develop new conclusions. Most of David Armitage's writing added little to his knowledge except that he had been full of hope, full of joy. Except that he was a decent, well meaning man. Yet another of his assailants seemed to be a blameless, upright citizen.

Armitage had spent the first two years after his disappearance in or around Brownesville, Iowa. It was afterwards that the cards and letters were postmarked from all over the country and that the letters had changed. In so far as it was possible to tell, Armitage had matured dramatically at that point. The letters were no longer those of a boy on a great jaunt. Some of the enthusiasm had gone, some of the joy.

Over the seven years he had probably written every two months on average although there was little by way of content. Most of the issues concerning him were not available for consideration - where he was, what he was doing, why he was doing it. Add to that the fact that he was writing to a mother who could not respond to him and the letters developed a sad, repetitive familiarity. James was sure that Armitage did not even know about his father's death.

There was little for James to cling on to. In an offhand, early comment Armitage had mentioned that he was "watching over Martin" which James presumed to mean the child. Erudite comments on the landscape that he passed through did not offer much assistance to James' quest. The date marks, postmarks and points of origin would perform that service in Washington.

James had attempted, recklessly, to reach Washington in a day's drive. He checked into a motel in the early hours when common sense finally took precedence. The room smelled. He slept for ten hours. A few hours later brought him, refreshed, into the suburbs and to the Tele-communications Quadrangle.

During the course of his library research James had discovered the NC database. Apparently every news story that was ever reported in the States had been entered on to it and could be accessed through open-ended questions. The claim was immense the fees, at just under seven hundred dollars per hour, similarly phenomenal. James spent the best part of an hour preparing his own information and lines of enquiry in a small cubicle with an interface and printer. To his great disappointment when he reported that he was ready to begin the clerk simply returned him to the cubicle and accessed the database from there. He had hoped to be taken into an enormous smoke filled chamber preferably with lots of scuttling data recorders, valves and the blue glowing tube things. The reality was an insincere welcome message and a green screen with a time elapsed on-line reminder.

The dates and places that he had prepared were entered on to a map of the States with major road networks being superimposed. At this stage with David's letters, he could have already predicted a few likely spots. The fact that one card had placed David and the Silver Bullet in New Mexico within two days of the green man wiping the records was a strong indication that the green man operated away from the others. The car had been another indicator, together they had drawn James to the inevitable conclusion: contact points. The Silver Bullet might well be travelling throughout the country on evasive routes but there would have to be places which they would return to in order to pick up or send materials to or from the green man.

At the first prompt he typed: "Superimpose reports of flying men or unusually large birds on map with dates as colour coded. Disregard reports by witnesses previously linked with reports of other bizarre phenomenon." Twelve minutes passed before the map began to fill. He had logged fifteen minutes before the search ended. A second search adding in local postal despatch locations and paper copies of all of the maps and reports took him up to the three hundred dollar mark while a repeat search with the parameters of "Citizens of previously good character" and "Flying persons" proved too vague for even the NC database to produce anything meaningful. James removed himself from the line and pored over the information in a neighbouring cubicle having decided that just because he was paranoid it did not mean that everybody was not after him.

Two reports he could dismiss out of hand because they reported sightings at wildly divergent locations. Four were disregarded because they described un-corroborated daytime sightings in heavily populated areas which James just could not bring himself to accept. Twenty-one reports hit the reject file because the eye-witnesses looked to James like Bob and Mary Honeydewblossom from the planet Zarg which left him with eighteen reports spread over seven years two of them, significantly, from Brownsville, Idaho. All of the surviving reports seemed to come from decent people who were not seeking publicity with nothing to gain and everything to lose. They just happened to have seen something extraordinary and had to speak out as he had and as he had not.

Another, significantly cheaper, hour with the conventional computer produced a refined map linking the reports to the letters and postal points. There were five possibilities, three of them strong possibilities : Tonopah, Nevada; Everett, Seattle and Greengate near to Holdrege in Nebraska. The last location was the strongest in that there had been two sightings within a week of each other three years before, two letters posted within two hundred miles and a further one from only four months before. By extrapolating the overall movement patterns James concluded that the Silver Bullet visited there every six months and that he had two months in hand before the next dropping off or picking up. It was the best three hundred and seventy-five dollars that he had ever spent.

CHAPTER 24

Greengate near to Holdrege in Nebraska consisted principally of, depending on your point of view, either a prosperous, well designed modern conference and leisure facility or a ramshackle collection of ten cent stores, trailer parks and recycling facilities. The former point of view occurred if you stood on the only street worthy of the name and looked West the latter if you looked East. To James' eye the earlier and shabbier half had "To be cleared for imminent development" written all over it. He parked in the Hotel's extensive forecourt car park and considered his options.

The Hotel had an extensive external security system which looked out on to the road. There was every possibility that it was new and modern enough to have a video-disk system which was likely to have several years worth of footage. He could try to lie his way into viewing their tapes. That would eat up most of the two months remaining to him or he could just wander into the local shops and draw upon the bank of human curiosity.

The first store was staffed by an Iranian who spoke little English and had only worked in Greengate for the past twenty-two minutes. James experience in commerce had long since taught him that the world was peopled by pleasant people from various ethnic groups who lived there and had no idea where it was that you were going.

The second store would have been staffed by another Iranian but it was clearly his day off. The moon-faced, elderly general wholesaler who was filling in moved arthritically to the front counter to help James, "What can I do you for?" he asked confusingly.

"Yes. Could you help me? I'm looking for the owners of a large Silver Bullet '07. I believe that they may have stayed in town during the past few years. I think that they come here every six months or so. They may have been here four months ago."

"What do you want to know for?" He settled onto a leather high stool.

"It's to do with an insurance claim. I think that the owners may have witnessed an accident in which my car was involved but I don't think that they even know that they did."

"You got the licence?" James searched into his briefcase and handed it over.

"Don't recognise it but then who gives a damn about remembering."

"Yes."

"What colour did you say it was?"

"Silver. It is a Silver Bullet." The old man's hand suddenly rose gun-like. He fired off the first round in his index finger.

"You mean Sullivan's rig."

"Yes and the girl -"

"Liz whatsit and the other guy - whatever." James began to feel himself going very cold. "Yes regular customers here, mostly Sullivan - nice guy. They keep themselves to themselves mostly. Now that you do say it they probably do come around every six months or so. They park just left of here between here and the Dinomeats store."

"Do you know when they are coming back next?"

"Nope they come they go, never say where or when."

Thirty minutes and several purchases later James returned to his car. He had not learned anything new merely information which confirmed that he was at the right place and that the people (monsters?) who had tried to kill him were in fact very nice, if somewhat reserved people. He settled into the driver's seat and pulled a writing pad and pencil from the glove compartment. He tapped the pencil aimlessly on the pad. One reason why his story would not be believed was that elements of it were too fantastic. Another was that the neighbours always thought that serial killers were such nice, if somewhat reserved people. There was more to it than that though, he had spoken to their families, they loved them, they believed in them. Perhaps the same could be said of serial killer's families but James doubted it. His would-be killers seemed to come from stable, adequate backgrounds. He began to write:

"To do :- Find somewhere cheap to rent;

write up latest findings;

mail latest findings on to Mrs Armitage etc;

find a job to tide me over - preferably in the hotel, preferably with access to security footage;

buy car - recorder;

buy toothpaste;

buy glue to plug ears when I confront the Silver
Bullet and it's murderous crew ..."

He threw the pencil and pad expertly into the glove. The first priority had to be to come up with some sort of plan for when he actually confronted them. Reason would not do not if, as looked likely, they had kidnapped a child years before. Pulling his gun was not likely to work either - they had other weapons which would do for him before he could react.

Despite his annoyance, he could feel tiredness creeping up on him and eased his seat back. He was not paying to park where he was and hence might as well catch an hour's sleep before finding somewhere to stay. He part lowered his window and allowed himself to drift off into comforting speculations as to how things might go. He could rescue the child, free the woman who would turn out to be as good as her looks demanded and who might fall deeply, passionately in love with him. The thought of holding her seemed to be the best inducement to sleep that he could find at that moment and gently, contentedly he began to drift away.

The sun was low, shining almost directly into his eyes. James rubbed the sleep out of his eyes and massaged his temples feeling a headache coming on. He checked behind then fired the engine and began to back out of his parking space. There had been a motel half a mile out of town, he decided to try that first. The auto-park had filled up somewhat during his sleep and he had to edge carefully past several poorly parked saloons. With care he pulled away from the hotel and up to the junction with the main road.

His unconscious mind slammed the brakes on before his conscious mind could take in what he had seen. Across the road, beyond the fenced-in recycling plant on some wasteland next to the old man's store was the Silver bullet. James' first thought was to drive away as quickly as he could. They were two months early - admittedly on their random schedule but he had no real plan, he was not ready. But then they could be gone by morning. He was pretty sure that this town was little more than a mail pick-up point. Drive off, urged his common sense but all the while, he knew that this could be his only chance. They would change their route if they knew that he was on to them and they would know - they might know already. When he had come upon them in the dark they had known that he was coming well before he had reached them. Run away, that was what they had told him, that was what they had wanted. He accelerated and pulled the wheel to the left then almost immediately to the right. It occurred to him to get his speed up and to ram the vehicle. An illegally parked pick-up prevented that. James slammed the brakes on before the store. He left the engine running and stuffed the desert eagle into his coat pocket. He did not bother to close his door. Six steps to the low wall bordering the wasteland. A low hurdle then ten steps to the door. It opened at his pull, he climbed in before there was time to hesitate. The scene that met him was to remain with him to his grave.

It was hard to say what it was that he had expected to find never having, seriously, thought it through but the ideas had lain dormant at the back of his mind. Robert Danjule, had played the part of the secret monster, Sullivan he knew was a monster and James had to believe that the child that, much to his surprise, stood looking angrily before him, was the innocent victim of whatever was happening.

Danjule sat at a bench before a bank of four television screens and a monitor. Large, expensive headphones straddled his now, completely bald, head. He did not look away from the screens despite the noise of James' entry.

Sullivan lay upon a bunk behind Danjule stirring reluctantly and looking surprisingly young. The child stood before him.

James knew within the instant, instinctively and undeniably, that the child was the monster. It had the body of a child but the head was too old for the body and if not the head then the expression. James had annoyed it greatly. "Breant weckon," it said turning toward Sullivan. James pulled the Desert Eagle clumsily from his pocket realising that there was nobody there that he particularly wanted to rescue. Sullivan jumped on his bed as if he had been given an abrupt electrical shock. The "child" began to back away to James' right. "Fas dev onp." It said, "Fas dev onp." Sullivan stood reluctantly. James raised the gun holding it braced in his two hands, he levelled it at Sullivan. There was less than a yard between Sullivan and the gun.

"Look," said Sullivan apologetically, he looked and sounded disconcertingly normal. "I'd rather you didn't. It's no good threatening me. I haven't got any choice." He had begun to advance then stopped as did James. Sullivan watched knowingly,

James incredulously as the gun rolled harmlessly on his trigger finger and hands, his but not his, placed the gun on the bench where Danjule's fingers flickered across a keyboard oblivious to everything else. "I guess you don't have any choice either." James looked up into Sullivan's eyes and for an instant they shared an understanding. The child did what it would with them.

"Fas dev onp!" Unwillingly, Sullivan reached for the gun. James' hand whipped out catching him a light but unbalancing blow across his face. He struggled for a comic moment for his balance before tripping to the floor. James backed away before he could recover or the child could compel him to remain. He was down the steps and over the wall before he could think what to do. Standing besides his car he hesitated. A handsome man and a beautiful woman were running towards him from the direction of the hotel. Armitage and Hastings. An explosion thundered behind him. Almost instantaneously his windscreen iced into a thousand fragments. Turning he saw Sullivan, white-faced, at the top of the silver bullet's steps the Desert Eagle in his hand. He began to raise the weapon again. James sprinted towards the other two thinking that if Sullivan's accuracy with his second shot was anything like the first that he would have to risk shooting one of the other two. Seconds passed, he darted left then right. There was nothing immediate to dive behind. The woman was nearer. Armitage, having stopped twenty metres further back, was removing his coat. Hastings waited feet apart, confident. He knew within a few seconds why. His legs began to abruptly slow, to stumble, he went down on both knees, his hands flat on the ground, he was unable to look up.

It was much the same as when the child had exercised control on him but not quite. He could feel the control in his legs, arms, neck. The limbs were as surely not his but there had been the sensation of her control entering him. He sensed that her control was not as absolute as the child's for all the good that he could do about it. Peripherally, he saw her feet approaching then grow until they stood immediately in front of him. As legs go, they went. What was the saying? Life's a bitch and then you die? Suddenly he felt hands pulling him to his feet. The child would not have had to touch him, making him stand would not have risked the child's control. He began to salivate. Then they were face to beautiful face. He knew now that when they had connected before that she had wanted him to find her attractive but not this second time. This time there was only sadness, openness and a kind of manic, defiant humour in her expression. She was simply astoundingly beautiful. Stunning would be a correct but entirely inappropriate adjective given the circumstances. "You stupid man," she said without malice, "why did you keep coming back? You should have just walked away and lived your life. I didn't want you to be hurt." James could hear footsteps behind him, he saw a flash of pink flesh behind her where Armitage stood and then it was all gone as she pulled his face towards hers. Her lips paused centimetres from his as she hesitated, watching him, smelling, questioning. Then her lips pressed against his, he felt the shape of them, the touch of them as they moved to cover his then they were gone. For a bewildering instant he seemed to catch a glimpse of himself then he heard, in his mind, "You stupid - stupid ---beautiful man." James saw it all so clearly in his mind's eye, saw Sullivan behind him.. Saw her step back as Sullivan raised the gun to his head and finished him as she held him still, he saw the intention perfectly. She had not moved back thirty centimetres when he spat in her face.

The control was gone. He wheeled about on Sullivan kicking him heavily in the stomach, he went down but rolled still holding on to the Desert Eagle. James turned again and threw himself forwards knocking her heavily to the ground. Her control had gone but he was still connected with her and in that vague sense of knowing he could feel the child rising angry and contemptuous. He began to run.

Sullivan was winded. He would have a few seconds perhaps enough to reach the shelter of the cars in the hotel auto-park. Armitage stood between him and the cover of two nearer cars.

Armitage. Armitage! Physically he did not slow but emotionally he recoiled from the sight ahead of him. Armitage had stripped to the waist and his back was unfurling grey, feathered abominations. James leaped at him this time only catching him a glancing blow on the thigh. It sent him backwards but did not knock him over. Behind him, James could sense Sullivan raising the gun, he veered right putting Armitage and then two cars in the line of sight. There was no shot. He could feel the knowledge, the certainty growing weaker as he reached the car park, could feel it being switched off or rather him being excluded from it but not before he momentarily sensed her delight, her laughter. He dived between two rows of cars running all the harder for knowing that it was what she wanted.

The Desert Eagle fired behind him. Where the bullet went he did not know but he was unhurt and crouching low, almost on all fours, he had nearly reached the hotel's entrance. Most of the hotel's front was glass panelled so he could clearly see the untenanted reception desk. The main lobby was to the right, he had glanced at it earlier in the day. It was too empty, too big. To the left as he looked at it was an open corridor passing elevators and stairs. He saw one of the elevators opening, full of passengers. If he could just make it to the safety of other people he would be all right. He needed witnesses, more people than they could control. Rising he risked a glance behind only to be met by the eerie sight of the three of them reaching the car park. Armitage's wings were fully extended. James ducked again and skidded into the hotel's entrance. The desk broke his momentum and he headed towards the elevator almost running along the wall. Then he was amongst them, surrounded by people as more and more suited businessmen sleep-walked out of the elevator. He screamed at the first, grabbed the second by the collar but they and all of the others blithely ignored him and his frantic explanation died on his lips. Not one of them could hear or see him. He turned numbly out towards the car park where he could see her walking carefully towards him, her companions by now, well ahead of her. It was no wonder that he had been able to break free from her control she was, after all, keeping everybody in the vicinity from seeing what was happening.

His attention was broken by the sound and sight of Armitage reproducing the violence of his entry into the building although he had to give him the edge as his trajectory was entirely above the ground. James backed into the press of somnambulists. To his surprise he found a sudden gap and was inside the elevator. Knocking the sole business man occupying it to the side, he hit the close button. The doors began to shut painfully slowly. It was more inevitable than surprising when the last few business men outside were bowled out of the way arresting Armitage's momentum. He paused before reaching in, the doors were half closed. James' fist snaked out made satisfying contact and withdrew before the doors closed.

There was a numbing silence during which he realised that he was temporarily safe but that temporarily was for just as long as it took Armitage to hit the "Open" button. He scanned the levels then frantically hit the top button. It claimed to lead to the restaurant and if there was one place in the building where there would be too many people it had to be there. After a few despairing seconds the elevator began to rise. James turned to his silent companion. The businessman hardly seemed to have noticed his rough treatment. "Can you hear me?" No reaction. "Can you hear me!" Still no reaction. "Have you got a pen?" James began to search his pockets. A weapon would have been a wonderful bonus as it was he had to content himself with a permanent marker but what to write? And where? He lifted the man's shirt front, satisfied himself that the ink would not be easily erased and wrote, shakily on his stomach. He had barely finished tucking his shirt back in when the elevator's doors opened.

James stepped out half expecting the same confusion of bodies that he had left below to greet him but instead found a bland, light blue carpeted corridor. He stepped away from the elevator as its doors closed and it began its downwards journey. Facing the elevator, there was a swing doorway to the left marked "Stairs" and to the right the first elevator whose numbers indicated its steady rising. At his back he could hear the sounds of people talking and of cutlery on plates through two swing doors. He did not head straight through them because, unconsciously, he had picked up another sound and when Sullivan burst through the doorway to his left, James was ready for him. He charged at him dipping at the last minute to catch him heavily in the chest. They slammed against the far wall going down together then James pulled back to give himself enough space to strike Sullivan with a short armed back-handed blow across the face. He pulled his hand back and aimed carefully driving his fist into Sullivan's unprotected solar plexus. Simultaneously, James heard Sullivan's forced exhalation and the sound of the Desert Eagle hitting the carpet several feet away. James rose, his knee, partly, unintentionally catching Sullivan another hefty blow under the chin. He scurried over to the gun watching Sullivan who looked for all purposes done for. James picked up the gun feeling its reassuring weight and coldness. Sullivan had not been able to shoot for squat but he knew what he was doing. He moved towards Sullivan never for a moment thinking to use the gun on him, he was heading for the restaurant where there would be witnesses to whatever might happen. The thought had occurred, however, to Sullivan and he moved suddenly betraying the fact that he was not as hurt as James had thought. For a moment there eyes met then he jumped from an angle and in a way that no ordinarily limbed human could.

For a few seconds there was a frantic changing and exchanging of advantages before they wrestled themselves into a position halfway through the restaurant doors with Sullivan almost on top of James, almost on his back both arms locked around James' gun hand and James' other arm pinned to the ground beneath the weight of the two of them. The static position continued for a minute or so before Sullivan's two arms managed to force the pistol away from the two of them. He began to re-apply his grip trying to keep James on the ground, whilst he was doing this, however, James had managed to free his other hand.

The first elevator's doors opened. Liz Hastings exited closely followed by Armitage. Calmly, she picked up the gun and directed it towards the contorted heap on the floor that was James and Sullivan. "You won't do that." said James with more confidence than he felt.

"Why not?" she asked, as was appropriate.

"Because you don't want to." Of all the things that he could have said, this was to prove the decisive response. She raised the gun towards his head.

"When have my wants ever had anything to do with what I have to do?" When had James sent the message to his hand to put the gun down in the Silver Bullet? Never.

"Oh shit." he muttered. Then he jabbed Sullivan in the eye with his thumb and managed to twist him around between him and the gun. In the instant's time that this bought him, he dived into the restaurant. There were perhaps fifty diners eating at tables to his right a couple of barkeeps in front of a long, mirrored bar further to his right. "Help me!" screamed James at the top of his voice. Not a conversation faltered not a head turned. He began to run at full speed for the gap between bar and tables. There was a set of wooden stairs leading upwards to a second level. Beyond that he did not know but it was the only remote hope of an exit. As he ran he became aware of several things: the enormous windows beyond the diners and the stairs - the restaurant was clearly on this level for the view of the county; the reflection of his pursuers stepping through the restaurant door; Armitage launching himself into the air and Liz Hastings firing.

The first shot shattered the window beyond the stairs. It had to be very strong glass but, as he knew from experience, the Desert Eagle had a phenomenal kick on it. The second shot seemed to catch his left foot or it may simply have been the inadvertent foot or luggage of a diner. Either way, it served to turn his last few metres before the stairs into an uncontrolled plummet. He caught the banister extremely hard on the right hip which served to turn him and to launch him backwards through the window.

The rest followed with a lazy, almost dreamlike slowness. The glass lacerating his flesh was simply a recorded fact, a thing of no importance. The sudden flash of blue, fading to red as he left the building that was important. The sight of the glass splintering and falling above him as he looked up that mattered. The beauty of it was enhanced by the winged man bursting out into the glass shower. He turned, heading downward after James in his slow descent, seeming to be the only thing that moved at normal speed. The winged man's face growing closer, ever closer as he reached down to save him. In his face James saw determination, desperation and finally anger as he felt the back of his skull collapsing on the sidewalk behind him. The winged man banked, landing painfully and then kneeled at his side as James Arthur faded from the world.

Some things did not matter, some things did. He understood which and his passing was a happy thing. The winged man had tried to save him, the woman loved him. It was not her doing that she was not allowed.

He would never be able to tell Mrs Armitage or the Hastings that their children were alive - that they were well intentioned people. Perhaps nobody would ever know why he had died. That did not matter. He could have walked away, perhaps he should have walked away but he was proud that he had not. Today he had fought monsters. Today he had kissed the love of his life.

In a way, the past year had seen his increasing separation from the life and loves that had gone before but it had been a good time, lived with nobility, left with nobility.

Kneeling over him, David Armitage screamed his anger and, with his last thought, James wished him understanding and peace.

CHAPTER 25

David and Sullivan climbed despairingly into the trailer. Sullivan went straight to the basin to apply a wet cloth to his eye which was already swelling. David stood and began the shaming process of emptying and strapping his wings away. Danjule was at his screens as ever, the Lord stared out of the window. He was adding his strength to Liz's. The fact that he was doing this told David all that he needed to know of the importance of what had happened. Dahenro-sat served the Corast. No Corast ever helped dahenro-sat but then he was ultimately only protecting himself. If the people in this place did not remember what the Corast wanted them to remember then the ripples would spread and spread. As it was one human had died and there was every chance that they would be safely on their way within the hour. No great cost, no loss merely inconvenience. David knew that the Corast would judge it so. Not that he dared to touch his mind, dahenro-sat that he was.

Sullivan's posture, his carefully neutral expression told David of his feelings. There was no need to touch his mind and, in respect, David did not. The black eye served its purpose, it was something to do. Two or three times, Sullivan could have killed the man but David kept that thought down skirting over it in English and not in the speech, hoping that the Corast would not deign to notice. Not that it mattered - there would be an accounting later, the man was dead. The dahenro-sat had served their purpose.

David reached out to Liz and saw her for a few moments standing near to the body. There were vague shapes - uniformed men near to her. "Get away." She commanded him. "I don't want your flippancy. I've just seen a man that I could have .... liked very well ...die. I don't want you near to me." David withdrew. The thought occurred that he had held the man as he had died but there was no justification for bringing that up.

Sullivan sat behind Danjule pressing the cloth against his eye. David thought of how, at the end, he had tried to save the man then pushed the thought away and back again. Waving it before the Lord like the rag before a bull except that that was altogether too crude a simile. It was more like a fish several metres below the surface. Whatever. However he struggled to describe it if it kept his real thoughts from the Lord then it too would serve.

The Lord: Corast except that that was not quite it. There was no direct translation in English. You had to throw in other things. Such as concepts like apex - those who matter. Dahenro-sat. The nearest, closest fitting concept was disposable. Yet even within dahenro-sat there were divisions. Danjule was the highest - mest - the storage place. Then Hendy - hub - a pusher. Some distance below was Liz - juyti - a listener. As far below Hendy as Liz was would come David and Sullivan - lydrinn. In five years, the Corast had never bothered to hold a conversation with either of them. Instructions – orders there were no other aspects to a lydrinn's relationship with his Corast. If David's name had not been present in his own consciousness the Corast would never have known it.

"The first two years were the best, weren't they?" David asked Sullivan rhetorically. Sullivan gave a grudging non-committal shrug. "Watching over him. That was fun wasn't it?" It had been. They had spent the best part of two years struggling to live, never daring to leave his house unwatched. It had been difficult until Hendy established contact with Sullivan whereupon they had had money to spare but they had both had real belief, they had had a cause until the day came when they were handed that cause. Neither of them would ever forget the mother's expression. The emptiness, the despair and ultimately, the relief. It had not taken long to find their place. The Corast had told them. "Do you remember how we were then? How we would have done anything for Martin?" Until they got him home and found out that they had no choice in the matter. Sullivan gave him the briefest, suspicious glance. It was years since the Corast's given name had been mentioned. Sullivan occupied himself with re-folding the cloth. They could both sense that Liz was about to finish outside. Neither of them wanted to be present at the burning that she was due. David turned his attention to Danjule's screens which he had switched over to the news channels. At least it made a change from his normal viewing. Guns, guns and more guns. A thousand necessary facts in the production of advanced armaments.

David checked his finger nails for dirt. There was no point in attempting to plan things - there was no leeway for that – he had to act. He reached up into the cupboard and pulled out their pistol. The Corast turned to him and spoke directly to him for the first time in four years. "Don't!" He commanded. English, I must be worrying him! Noted David with that sense of contemptible flippancy. He lowered the pistol. "If you attempt that I won't hold back. You'll be in so much pain that you'll lose control of every muscle in your body." He had sent that one rather than risk slowing it with words. David hesitated, most surprised that he had had a warning. The fire began behind his eyes, he knew from painful, repeated experience that he would be unconscious within seconds. He aimed and fired.

There should have been blood and bone all over the walls, there should have been fireworks and a choir. The child's eyes dimmed, blood flowed from the bullet hole in his forehead. There was a sighing sound as he fell against the wall. There was a distinctive thud to his left where Danjule's head landed on the desktop. That saddened David. It did not surprise him having known for years that the Corast had erased all trace of who Robert Danjule was from the prime information storage space of his mind. It was a great pity that Danjule could not live independently but then the Corast had killed him years before, he had been the first victim not the man today. Like water escaping suddenly from the tank that they had been completely immersed in, the oneness left them leaving the three barely connected and weak from shock. Sullivan stood uncertainly, his hands shaking violently. "What in Christ's name have you done?" he gasped. David replaced the pistol neatly in its cupboard as Sullivan staggered towards him. "How the hell did you do that?" And before David could think about replying he struck him a high round-armed blow to the chin. David crumpled unresistingly to the floor. Sullivan kicked him once - twice then screamed at him, "What have you done? We've got nothing now! You've killed us!" David shook his head.

"No - we're alive." The Corast had gone. "Robert's dead - " Another poorly aimed kick trapped his fingers against his knee – the pain of which action told him that he had broken one or more of his fingers.

"Just don't answer!" Sullivan had to rest his hands and head against the cupboard in an attempt to regain control. At no time did it occur to David to resist him or even to stand -he would never think of hurting Sullivan. Six or seven deliberate breaths later, Sullivan slipped to his knees. David braced himself for another punch only to feel his head pulled onto Sullivan's shoulder his hands wrapped around the back of his head. "What do we do know? What do we do know?"

Perhaps half a minute later, Liz climbed into the RV. She too, in her shock, had found it very hard to walk. She glanced numbly at the Corast and at Danjule simply letting her eyes record the facts that she already knew. Sullivan pushed himself away and sat staring at the basin. It occurred to David that he was simply giving her kicking room but the pain from his hand was so intense that he could scarcely care. To his surprise the pain abruptly faded into nothingness. Her doing but the surprising aspect was not the capacity but the sentiment. Kindness and consideration from her were almost non-existent. Which was as it should be -she was juyti and he was lydrinn. He looked blankly up at her. "Shilken petren doas!" she swore fluently, "Sa?"

"Why?" asked David stubbornly echoing her question in English. "Why are we here?" he gestured towards the screens with his broken hand. It would cost him later.

"Ut Corast." She replied unthinkingly: For the Corast. It was easily done, it was the essence of their existence.

"Yes but why was the Corast here? To find out about human weapons and to take that knowledge with him and to use it." he shrugged, "That poor sap today was just the first person to get in the way there would have been more. Maybe hundreds - thousands maybe millions or billions."

"You can't decide that!" she retorted her anger less surprising than her switching to English. "We are dahenro-sat .... dahenro-sat don't ..." The years of living within the strictures of the Corast's knowing had conditioned them so that they could not conceive of a dahenro-sat acting against their Corast. There were no words in the speech for the concept. "How could you though?" Armitage shrugged.

"Human will out." And that earned him a burn. This close and this angry, she could exert pain to compare with the Corast. "That guy today." he forced through clenched teeth and she eased back, afraid of what he might say. "He did it. He was magnificent. Here -in the trailer and outside when he spat at you, in the building. He fought back. I didn't really think it was possible -" Sullivan stood as she sat.

"But you still don't get it you stupid shit!" Sullivan shouted, "He - the Corast-took away everything we had and now you've taken him away. We've got nothing now. We're just freaks again but before we were ..."

"Freaks with a purpose?"

"Yeah. Ut Corast. Ut Corast. Now we've got nothing to live for nothing to make it worthwhile."

"Yes we have."

"What?" They asked in the same uncomprehending instant.

"We've got our own lives." Which earned him Sullivan's despair and another particularly spiteful burn. It was to be the last as, in time, even Liz came to realise that she was something other than juyti and - empty though it was - that there was something other than ut Corast.

The final verdict on James Arthur was suicide despite the numerous contradictions and inconsistencies. The second most inexplicable aspect of the case was as to why Arthur should write his suicide message on the chest of a sixty-two year old business man and witness. The most inexplicable was as to why he should have written: "Remember the angel."

They buried Danjule and the Corast several miles away in a field of maize. Nine years later a single body was discovered after the field had been turned over for development.

Part 3:

The Return of the Greenman.

CHAPTER 26

Confessions on Saturday after six O'clock mass had surely been conceived with one intention in mind - nobody turning up. Father David thought about his homily which had fallen flat. Saturday's often did - it was a real in-and-out mass and half of the congregation was not, mentally, really there. It might work tomorrow. He thought about his hair - which needed cutting - and the plasterwork, which was crumbling, then tried frantically to concentrate as he heard the sound of shuffling outside. The door to the confessional opened. Contemplation - peace - patience. The door closed then had to be closed again. The hasp needed bending out again - no! Contemplation - peace - understanding - patience. The kneeler on the other side of the partition creaked gently. "In the name of the Father..." Oh Christ. Miss Whelan. He would have to put that reaction before God himself but the last thing that he needed was Miss Whelan exposing her lustful thoughts and failings to him. "Forgive me Father.." her muffled south-side drone began.

Miss Whelan had provided one of the early difficulties in his time at St Hereward's her confessions being far too directed at the young Assistant priest. After broaching a hypothetical situation with Father Matt' he had confronted her with the point that if she was truly sorry that she ought not to be deriving a twisted kind of pleasure from trying to shock innocent, young David. She had denied it and complained to Father Matt'. However, she still kept coming to whichever priest was taking the sacrament on Saturday and the last few times had been fine. As was tonight. She did not conceal anything but confessed in general terms to the thoughts that plagued her forty-four year old mind and there were no actions to recount. It had been a good week or, as society at large would have it, a bad week. Penance was nominal and trod down the well-worn path to liking oneself. He felt, even enjoyed, the feelings of relief at absolution and Miss Whelan passed out into society, at least to a degree, grateful, cleansed and refreshed.

Father David settled back feeling far more contemplative and waited. Problem number two entered on sensibly heeled shoes. Julie Luard was in her early twenties, living at home having just finished her degree. She was from an Irish-Spanish Catholic family - which made her just about as Catholic as anybody could be without being a candidate for the papacy. Like almost all of the people that he had encountered within the parish she was an exceptional, wonderful, human being without an ounce of awareness of her own inner beauty and therein lay the problem. Being of mixed race her external beauty was something of a problem too.

They rattled through the formulas and her list of sins whilst Father David struggled to remember his place. Not one of her sins were of any significance other than as evidence which she held against herself in the big debate as to whether she was or was not a good person in her terms, a downright gorgeous one in his. He told her about the sins, his view of her he kept to himself.

The last time, he had made that mistake although that had not been the first mistake. The first mistake had been, as things had gone so well, to make it a face-to-face confession. The second mistake had been in perfectly good faith and, as was appropriate to the substance of the rite of reconciliation, to point out not that she was gorgeous but a few of her key good qualities as a human being. He had had to stop abruptly as the whole male-female attraction thing caught him by the throat. He had been warned about it, damned near had written essays about it and had walked right into it. Thankfully she had crossed no lines. She had still only thought of him as the nice young priest with the emphasis on priest and not on his niceness.

He had blushingly retreated behind a feeble excuse about a migraine and suspected - hoped - that she had not realised.

Her penance was that she look in the mirror each day and smile at what she saw. The formality of absolution came as a welcome retreat to both of them. He gave the final blessing and there was an unseemly silence from the other side of the partition. "Was there anything else?" he asked. In his admittedly limited experience to date, this was when the big missiles were fired. She hesitated. His intellect hoped that she would go whilst all physically connected parts of his body screamed at her to stay awhile.

"No. Goodnight, Father."

"Goodnight." She left. Her scent following shortly thereafter. He adored that scent even whilst knowing intellectually that if it was the smell of pickled haddock's knickers that he would feel the same because of the connections and not the odour. He had a big problem.

The seconds stretched into minutes. In all of his years of training it had not been a problem and yet the first parish after his final vows and here it was written very, very large. He considered seeking a transfer but that would be foolish having had no other cause to and having not faced down this problem. It would not reflect well on Father Matt' and he did not want that.

So how did he become a priest?

That was not quite the best question to resolve the problem but it touched upon something else that did. Was he a priest? He had committed a mortal sin. When he had gone to a priest and the Monsignor to confess and reveal what he was, everything had fallen into place too easily. They forgave what was not their's to forgive, they persuaded themselves to keep his revelation secret, they smoothed his path into the priesthood. Eight years on he could look back and see that he had still been within the cloud of knowing and that whilst his influence was small, they had no protection, and had too easily believed what they wanted to believe.

So what was the mortal sin? Why had he killed the child, of course? It was not a question that he needed to ask himself. Nor, eight years on, was there any reason to put the thought out for inspection rather than to just let it slide below the perceptible surface. He grew very cold and mentally still.

The confessional door opened, closed and a heavier pair of knees settled on the leader. "In the name of the Father and of the Son and of the Holy Spirit." A male voice intoned. "Forgive me Father for I have sinned, " a pause, "but my sins are nothing as to your sins!" A fist burst through the canvas grille grabbed him by the throat and pulled him down onto the collapsing partition.

The partition broke the grip and he found himself prostate staring up at a dark-haired, light skinned man wearing a dark green suit who was as angry as hell.

CHAPTER 27

David came back into awareness on the floor of presbytery reception room. There were numerous sore points where he had been punched and kicked, his face was wet and sticky. If he thought about it he could remember coming into the presbytery, he could remember leaving the church, he could remember the kicking that he had received in the confessional. The memory was there, his tormentor had just switched off his self-awareness so that he did not interfere with what he had wanted to do.

His assailant sat several yards away sucking on Cuban cigars. There was blood on his trousers and he still looked as mad as hell. "Hendy," David muttered.

"No - Marilyn Monroe." He sent the mother of all migraines across the room let it settle in for a minute or two then banished it. David checked his trousers. At least he had been spared that indignity which the Corast, in his contempt for him, had not been above. Not when he was out of doors anyway. "I want to know what happened. Start talking." For a moment David was confused.

"What?"

"Out with it."

"Can't you just reach in and take it?"

"No," Hendy muttered with the nearest thing to humility that David had seen in him. "Not unless you think it *real* loud. Now tell me what happened."

David had never had much contact with Hendy. Initially it was Sullivan who had met with him and then the Corast whilst his lydrinn watched out for hostiles. Sullivan had very strong opinions about Hendy which he had managed to summarise into the two words: "arrogant" and "bastard." It was no surprise given that he had the power to make anybody do what he wanted and had little contact with his own master. He had been the Corast's agent in the world.

Another crippling pain behind the eyes. "Tell me now!" He had been too slow in answering, it was not the unflattering recollection of Sullivan's opinion that had caused Hendy to hurt him and there was a satisfying degree of consolation in that. David took two, three careful breaths.

"It's very simple, I shot him. I killed the Corast." He saw Hendy's fists bunch, he sensed the pain that he could inflict being drawn back, ready to strike again then relaxed.

"Go on." David sat up on the carpet, he wiped his face: fingers bloodying his forehead as he paused for thought. For a moment he considered lying but a moments further reflection identified that as simply an instinctive urge to resist his assailant's bullying.

"Do you know who James Arthur was?" David said, at length. Hendy shook his head. "He was some poor sap that Liz took a liking to in a bar or something. Anyway he trailed us for months maybe half a year. The first time the Corast let us get away with just warning him but when he came back the order was to kill him." He paused, choking back the emotion. Even after several years the pain of it could still jump out at him. Hendy stared at him interested, unsympathetic.

"Go on."

"Well we screwed up but he ended up dead and whilst Liz and the Corast were clearing up the mess, I thought to myself -this can't go on. All that mutant bloody alien wants to do is to find out everything there is to know about killing people and then it's hey-ho back to Mars. Then either there or here thousands - millions of people are going to be killed. So I came to this conclusion all of a sudden - no -I'd known it for years. We all did, we just fooled ourselves that we were maybe doing something that might be for the good and we didn't think that we could do anything about it but we could and did."

"How?" Hendy asked and David knew that he was not interested in the details of the killing. It was the concept of resistance that had surprised him.

"The man - James Arthur - he fought back. When you've got somebody inside your head like the Corast, knowing your every thought, making you do whatever he wants. You don't think you can fight it but you can. James Arthur, was nothing - just a human but he could resist him and when I saw that it could be done, I pulled the gun and did it. I don't know what I am or how he made me but I know that there's a lot of human in me. Resistance was possible." The implications of what he was saying caused them both to pause. The reception room seemed very cold and very dark. Hendy's eyes skirted away from David's for a fraction of a second. Both realised in that instant that for the first time since Hendy's power had appeared that he was faced with somebody who was aware that he was being acted upon and who could resist him. Hendy's reaction was immediate and painful. David tried to push himself back from the pain and found himself faced by a flippant response which flew straight back to the death of the Corast: pull the pistol.

It is possible to put your hand into a fire. Bodily reactions will pull it out immediately but it is possible to switch off such faculties as good sense and to simply perform the action for an instant not that it ever becomes a good idea. Resisting Hendy was on a par with grasping fire. David stood uncertainly as Hendy, in shock allowed the pain in David's mind to lessen. He took several steps towards Hendy who was on the verge of panicking then David paused, leaning on the table, pulled out a chair and sat upon it.

The pain stopped abruptly. Hendy was a pusher not a listener, he had rarely spent more than a few minutes in the cloud of knowing that had surrounded the Corast and Liz. He was not adept at the form of telepathy that David had spent five years of his life sharing. Nevertheless such was his emotion, or expression, that David had no difficulty at all in reading his fear, relief, astonishment and latterly anger. "That's better," said David swallowing blood, "you don't want me down there and you up here. I don't believe in these control things do you?" Hendy jumped to his feet.

"You son of a bitch!" Blankness, blackness.

David awoke again feeling utterly drained. This time there were no memories to call upon. Hendy had knocked him completely, cleanly unconscious. The trouser situation was good. He had probably only been out for a minute or two. "Don't you ever try that again! You son of a bitch!" David rubbed his temples and gave a weak wave of acknowledgement. Hendy's face was composed, his voice was steady if angry but his actions spoke loudly enough of his fear of resistance.

"Message received."

"Good." Almost apologetically. "Now wash yourself up and get your coat we are going."

"Where?"

"Just do it!" For all that he felt utterly wrecked, David could not resist resisting.

"Don't you find that this little 'edge' that you have over others impinges on your relationships?"

"I do all right." Hendy jabbed his finger angrily towards him. "I have the pick of beautiful women." David had not intended it in that way but welcomed the opportunity that had appeared

"I bet you do but is there really any choice there? Do they really choose you?" Moments before Hendy would have hurt him very badly but now it was there in his glance at the tabletop, it was there in his apparent indifference. David had pushed him as no other had been able to and Hendy did not want to find out to what extent David could resist him. It was there in his words.

"Wash yourself - hurry down." Unsteadily, wearily David complied.

Most of the blood had come from a blow to his nose which was spectacular but not significant. Otherwise his face was not too damaged and whilst he could feel the pain of several deep body blows there were no broken bones. David collected his coat, returned to the small basin in his room and considered his options.

He could squeeze through a window and avoid Hendy fairly easily - he was quite sure that Hendy's ability to sense him was very poor compared to Liz' or the Corast's. Run and hide or go downstairs and face him? It had taken Hendy eight years to find him even with all of the resources that he could call upon but he had found him. Even if he did escape, David had no wish to hide, to lose contact with his family again, to give up his vocation. Perhaps he ought to do that but not for this. The face in the mirror shook and turned away. He delved into the back of his wardrobe pulling out a soft, leather pool-stick case. For an instant he hugged the case and looked around the room equally holding the comforting familiarity of it to himself. At length, he opened the door and descended the staircase. He might well be heading for another good beating but he was perversely pleased in his belief that it had not been established as to whom was taking the beating.

Hendy stood at the foot of the stairs, inhaling, the tip of the cigar cupped within his hand. "What's that?" he shifted uneasily and indicated the case.

"My tail wings." David passed it over for his inspection. "I can't fly well without this strapped to my feet." Hendy flicked it open, looked, closed it and passed it back.

"What's that - plastic?" David nodded. "Can I assume that you are going to co-operate?"

"Perhaps."

"It would make sense - things could be to our mutual advantage." A smile almost flickered about his mouth. David shrugged,

"How long have you had your talent?"

"Seventeen years. Why?"

"'Mutual advantage' - I guess that if you spend the best part of twenty years controlling people and moving them about to do your will that you start seeing everybody in terms of advantage and not in terms of liking - loving. Maybe I will co-operate with you because I like you." Hendy's face was a picture of fleeting incomprehension.

"Drop it. You've no liking for me."

"Why not? Nobody else in the world knows about your amazing evil mental powers. I know. Isn't it a good thing that I know and could like you despite it?"

"But you don't. Why should you?"

"Why not?" he shrugged, "We're both victims." He could sense Hendy focussing pain. "As it happens, no I don't like you."

"Well at last we're getting through the bullshit." The pain fell away.

"OK." David met his gaze and held it for a few moments, calculating. "What do you want with me then? Was it just the Corast you were after?"

"Yeah." He ran his hand through his impeccably, expensively cut hair. "No. I had to figure that something had happened to him."

"So - did you just come here to punish me for killing him or was there anything else?"

"Yeah - " he grinned. "Don't you think it was a dumb ass thing keeping your real name? I should have found you years ago. It was just too stupid a thing to do to believe in and what's with this priest thing? What's that all about?"

David sank onto his bottom, four steps up, pausing to gather his much-recalled and reflected upon thoughts. "I did a very bad thing, I felt drawn to do a good thing." Hendy sucked impatiently on the cigar, smoking but not enjoying.

"Since when did they make child-killers into priests? You're no priest."

"You're right but not for the reasons that you think. I made my vows with good intentions but..." David stared blankly at the glowing end of the cigar. All of the reasoning and the justifications had appeared to have been completed many years ago but Hendy's abrupt arrival had lit a match to the whole structure. "I knew that I needed to accept obedience," he said to himself whilst looking at Hendy, "but I couldn't. I've just been waiting for this day. But it's not been a waste. I have done good things.” Hendy stubbed the cigar out on the oak tabletop that he and Father Matt had kept the mail on.

“Shut the fuck up,” he growled. David cupped a hand to his ear.

“But hark - my real world calls!” Hendy mentally pulled him to his feet and down the stairs. David only resisted hard enough for Hendy to know that he was resisting.

“Do you want cut out the smart crap?” He did not give David time to respond. "I'm here because I want to find the others. Can you take me to them?" David considered for a time, wondering as to whether he should risk their exposure but he concluded with a fair degree of confidence that, if needs be, he could resist Hendy.

"Yes, I can," David answered. "Sullivan anyway and he could take us to Liz. Not Danjule though - he's dead too. Not any naughtiness of mine. He just stopped when the Corast died there was nothing to support him." Hendy nibbled at his upper lip, calculating. "I can take you but I need to know why." Hendy perched on the edge of the table. The hair received another rake. He was not somebody who ever had to explain his thinking or motivations to anybody.

"Very well." he said, at length. "I want to see them, and you, because I have finished the Corast's work here. I'd have been finished seven years earlier if you hadn't been so bloody stupid."

"What have you finished?" David asked, unthinkingly. Realising that he had regained the position of power, Hendy smiled.

"I have made a doorway back to where the Lord came from." David reached over and placed his hand on Hendy's face. It was always easier to touch another's mind when there was physical contact and without the Corast, without Liz and many years out of the cloud he needed all of the help that he could get.

"Is that true?" he asked. Hendy brushed his hand angrily away.

"Don't touch me." It had been long enough. What he had said was fundamentally true although there was a further truth behind it. The truth concerned his reasons for acting and behind them there was yet another truth, his real reasons for acting. What they were David was not skilled enough to pick up other than that his nominal reasons were suspicious. "Well? Are you going to take me?" David nodded.

"Where do we go to then?"

"Cleveland." Hendy darted towards the front door, impatient to be gone David hesitated. He wanted to write a note to Father Matt' but how could he explain the blood and the confessional?

"Come on!" It would have to wait, Father Matt would not be back from hospital until the morning and had opted for early Mass.

"Come on!" It was not an argument that was worth fighting at this time. I could call later, thought David, though as he followed the green-suited man. The heaviness in the pit of his stomach told him with a bitter finality that he was not coming back.

CHAPTER 28

The car outside the presbytery was a dark green, highly polished, highly expensive limousine. A large, Hispanic driver wearing the type of hat that servants have to wear in order to look inferior held the door open for them. Hendy ducked inside leaving David to follow. The inside reeked of extravagance. There was a telephone, television and an eight foot pool table... probably...hiding in the carpet somewhere. David sat uncomfortably on the back seat away from Hendy. The vehicle began to move silently forward.

Hendy thumbed an intercom button to the driver instructing him to drive to the station. David thought, idly, that the necessity for the intercom was the distance between the driver and the driven rather than the glass partition. Several minutes passed in uncomfortable silence. David wondered how his companion would take the suggestion of a game of table tennis deciding that not-very-well would be the most probable response.

"You will find things a lot easier if you continue to co-operate instead of fighting me," said Hendy.

"Will I?"

"Yes," Hendy answered completely missing the sarcasm and seemingly embarrassed about even asking, "the language for example. The Corast would only speak it with you and the others. Teach me the language." David considered, decided that he wanted to fight Hendy but only for his own amusement and, therefore, spoke.

"No harm in that but a lot of it cannot be translated. All that you can do is to give the nearest equivalent to the concept." Hendy nodded attempting to signal his understanding whilst scarcely concealing his impatience. "Take language. It isn't a language. The word means speech, to talk. What does that tell you?" Hendy had not even anticipated there being a question. It occurred then to David that Hendy was far from being the sharpest tool in the box. Perhaps that was a little unfair to him. It was fairer to say that he did not think ahead or think consequences through which, with his power, was understandable and, David mused, not disadvantageous. "Wherever the Corast comes from they don't have the concept of there being languages. There is only one language - spoken by all and unchanging." Hendy shrugged.

"What I want is for you to teach me some of the words."

"All right. How about Corast? Let's start with what you know."

"It means Lord."

"Sort of. Only in so far as there are other Lords. If there were no other Lords it would mean God." Hendy looked confused which David could appreciate. It was a concept that for him still remained in the area of knowledge and not of understanding. "Ut Corast. That's all that you need to know- 'for the Lord'. That's what we are. That's why we are. Our whole purpose is to serve the

Lord. You and I are Dahenro-sat. Have you any idea what that means? It's a big one." Hendy did not bother to respond. "Servants is way too big for it so you'd think that Slaves would do but it does not. Dahenro-sat means: to be thrown away. That's what we are. Take away the Corast and we are nothing."

"Which is exactly what you did."

"Yeah, I'd noticed too." There was neither threat nor challenge from Hendy. "This gateway that you have - you want to know the language so that you can find out about the place behind it." A statement rather than a question. Hendy met it with a slow deliberate nod. "Dahenro-sat then. You are -were - without the Corast you are nothing. You were hub - a pusher."

"Pusher?" Hendy was amused.

"You were Dahenro-sat but one of the more useful Dahenro-sat. Not the most useful. Mest were the highest."

"What were they?"

"Like Robert -it means storage place. If you want to know about the Corast then remember that the most highly valued of Dahenro-din were those who did not have a shred of individuality or personality and that you don't matter anything next to mest. "Liz would be next in the Corast's evil little eyes. She was what you would call juyti - listener."

"What are you then?"

"Lydrinn - me and Sullivan. There is no real distinction just lydrinn-that-fly and lydrinn-that-run." David paused trying unsuccessfully to remember the words in the speech for 'that-run' and 'that-fly'.

"Is that all? Are there any other sorts of people?"

"No. Yes. We're not people. The Corast is a person. We are Dahenro-sat but there are other --" There was no concept for them in the speech. "There are other types of people but they are not Dahenro-sat. They are... objects? Improper nouns?"

"What are they? How many more sorts are there?"

"Two. Brood-mares and crop-growers. Ecil and culd. The lowest of the low -" Meaningfully, David indicated the tinted outline of the driver. "The Corast always called them culd. He called humans culd except they weren't human. There are too many associations with the word human too many concepts like dignity that just don't fit."

"You're not being very clear."

"What's the point of a culd that does not grow crops?"

"What?"

"A joke then. What's brown and sticky? - a stick. It's not just words. The concepts are everything. Crop grower. To the Corast we don't even merit names. We are what we do."

"So what are lydrinn?"

"Soldiers. Are we human, Hendy?" Desperately, despairingly, he needed to know. Hendy shrugged. "Do you know how we came to be here? Tell me about the gateway."

"No." He gestured outside to the station. "Later when it's quiet."

David preceeded Hendy out of the car. It had rained which seemed to have cleared the road outside of people.

Hendy hesitated leading David to turn to him questioningly. "Walk on," he said - commanded. David's feet began before his mind could question. His upper body turned comically whilst his lower continued heedlessly on. There was a street light halfway to the station, he stuck out his left arm and hooked it around. He turned which seemed to be enough to break the compulsion.

Hendy was talking to the driver still within David's hearing. "Keep the phone close but otherwise you can just relax. Enjoy your rest. I don't know when I'll be back in touch."

The question, "Or if?" seemed to David to hang expectantly between them. Of a sudden, David knew that Hendy did not *push* his driver, he was his little experiment within the safe confines of an employee-employer relationship. Hendy raised his hand, "Take care of yourself." The driver smiled and shook Hendy's hand.

"You too, sir." David was not sure if it counted as a success. Hendy gave nothing away in his expression except, perhaps, for annoyance at his continued resistance.

"Follow me," he said as he walked past. The command almost followed - his use of the power being virtually automatic.

There was no queue at the Tickets hatch. "We want to go to Cleveland as soon as possible, as well as possible." The forty-something woman behind the glass partition lurched into a much repeated monologue. David did not think that she was being pushed. If Hendy was directing his will at her there was nothing spinning out to the side that David could detect. She finished with the price for two.

"Paid," said Hendy, "fix it." He hurried off towards the platforms. "Come on!" he snapped, "It's due to go in two minutes." David followed reluctantly.

"But you didn't pay her."

"So?"

"So - she could get into trouble over that, she could lose her job." Hendy wisely, and untypically, anticipated the response that another 'so' would provoke.

"She thinks that we've paid her."

"What are you telling me? That this is some sin thing? She could still lose her job. If it is only a knowing thing that just tells me that you are the one who has sinned."

"Well, I think we've both worked that one out don't you?" It was the nearest thing to humour that David had seen in him. "Forget it." Another flight of stairs. "It does not matter."

"Why not?" This close to the trains David had to dodge people to keep up. "Why not?"

"Because .." Hendy had begun to slow as they reached the platform. He deflected a guard almost subconsciously. When it became apparent that he was not going to finish the sentence, David persisted.

"Because what? Because they don't count? What are they - Dahenro-sat to us?" The impact of the statement was cushioned by the sudden distance that grew between them as Hendy strode purposefully towards the front of the train and David instinctively made for the cheaper seats towards the back. He hurried to catch up. "Is it that?"

"What?" Hendy threw over his shoulder whilst stepping on to the train.

"Why doesn't it matter about her job? Why doesn't she matter?" He tried to keep chipping away at Hendy's arrogant disregard for others but his own thoughts kept getting in the way. "Are we human?" Hendy stopped in the narrow passageway and fixed him with a curious stare.

"Mostly."

"What d-do you mean mostly? How much?"

"For you?" Hendy shrugged, "Probably just not the feathered parts." He held up a restraining hand. "Talking to you is making my head hurt. I am going to freshen up for ten minutes or so. You go ahead to the restaurant carriage and I'll meet up with you there." Before David could respond he had turned and gone. David hesitated then began to move forward following a faint cooking smell.

The train jolted into motion tipping him against a sleeping compartment, he gripped the walls, lowered his head and allowed the emotions that he had been holding back to leap forward and grab him by the throat. Tears flowed suddenly freely. He gasped for breath scarcely controlling the sob, his thoughts running uncontrolled to the time, eight years before, when he had returned to face his mother.

They had faced each other in the doorway of his home unable to move or speak for an endless moment then she had held him, pulled his face down to hers, cried, kissed the face of her lost son and wet it with her own tears. "What happened to you?" She had asked then and the memories of that afternoon blurred.

He could remember the story that he given her of the cult (which it was) that he had fallen into and of how he had done something terrible to end it. Of how he had hurt somebody to escape. She had taken a long hard look at him then slowly, deliberately, so that both knew that she was not talking purely emotionally, "I hope to God you killed him then," she had said. Shock number one. "Because if he took my child away from me then he has taken your life, my life, your father's life. If he's dead then I'm glad."

"Dad?"

Then she had told him of how his father had died. Shock number two. And of how he had given up his job when David had left to be with her. Ashamed, he had listened as, defiantly, she had spoken about the best of his father and of how they had re-discovered their marriage in the two years after David's leaving and before his father's sudden death.

As his mother, she loved him but she had also been twice bereaved and then, and in the years that followed, there was always the hard, questioning edge. She was entitled to question just so long as he held the truth back from her and throughout it all he had held back. His mother, the brother who could not remember him, his sister, her family and above all Terri. Each had provided unique and traumatic emotional demands but in each one he had maintained a wall of unspoken deception about himself. It had been founded and facilitated on his belief that he was different, that he was a monster. The possibility that he was human - admittedly a human to whom something monstrous had happened - pulled away every cornerstone of the walls.

And after a time he recovered and made his way into the dining car. Ten minutes passed. A waiter appeared with a menu but no Hendy. Another ten minutes and he felt obliged to order the cheapest offering from the exorbitant menu. The waiter disappeared seeming somewhat doubtful. Hendy appeared at David's shoulder with a waft of chill air and cologne. "Right." He announced to the five or six other diners, "All of you have had enough. Get out and don't come back for at least an hour. Forget that I said this think of it as your idea." They had listened in silent, devout attention. They left abruptly, chattering to each other as they put the flesh of rationalisation on to the bones of his compulsion. David sensed the flare of his anger somewhere way back beyond his consciousness and veneer of self-control.

"You had no right to do that." he said quietly as Hendy sat facing him.

"Say what?" He picked up the menu.

"You shouldn't have done that. You've no right."

"I thought that we had agreed not to fight."

"Yes but you didn't understand what that means. It doesn't mean that I'm not going to oppose you. It means that you have to stop acting like such a swine."

"Yeah?" Quietly. "Don't 'oppose' me. I can hurt you more than you could imagine."

"Your hurting is nothing to what the Corast could do." He had not meant to say it. Had he thought for a moment then he would not have spoken because the uncomfortable truth of their relationship lay bare before them. For the first time in his adult life Hendy was faced with a threat. He thought about responding, to his credit, he did not let his gaze drop from David's until the moment of his choosing.

"Yeah." he said nothing better having come to mind, and looked at the menu. "Boy!" he bellowed down the corridor not commanding insofar as David could tell. The waiter arrived immediately and Hendy ordered a meal and wine from the upper echelons of the menu. "Do you want anything?" he asked, consciously non-committal.

"I've ordered a meal but some water would be welcome - if you are paying?" Hendy shrugged,

"Why not? I've got a roll of it." The waiter scuttled away. Hendy tapped the menu significantly. "These bullet trains aren't far behind 'planes for speed now and the food is far better." David nodded not knowing what to say as his income had never allowed him to sit, let alone eat, in this part of the train. Small talk being a skill that he had never needed, Hendy lost interest and began to stare at the blurring landscape beyond the window.

"The gateway - " interrupted David, pulling his attention back in. "Tell me about it." Hendy shrugged.

"What is there to tell? Top-secret government project. There are plenty of bogus stories about secret projects. They help to confuse things. This one is for real and nobody suspects it. It's what the Corast had me working on -putting together the scientists, getting the military clout. You would not believe how highly I rank in the military not that I have ever had to do any of that fatigues BS. A lot of super-intelligent people know a little bit about it. I'm basically the only guy who can pull it all together. They are just the left and right hands, I'm the one that sees and knows."

"So what is it?" Hendy smiled, habitually pleased to be in the position of power.

"It's a doorway into the Corast's world."

"Have you been through it?"

"Christ no, we have lab' rats for that. Nobody has been through it, it has only just been put together."

"Can you see through it?"

"Yeah - mountains. Hot dusty mountains sometimes something like people way off. No sign of technology."

"Where is it?" A stray thought occurred to him from his experience of flying. "When is it? Is it the future?" Hendy looked embarrassed.

"Christ I don't know which it is, it's just there."

"But you were the one in charge of the project."

"My job was to get the job done. I had to get the brains who could do the thinking. The Corast gave me the information, I did what he wanted." he sneered accusingly, "It seems to me that you've a powerful interest in the details for the guy who tried to stop it happening."

"Did - did we come through the doorway?"

"No. - No. Have you got a hearing problem, I told you that it has only just been finished."

"Yes but could we have come through a doorway from the other side to here."

"No. - Yes. The power demands are enormous."

"So how did we come to be here?"

"Oh - the big question." Hendy smiled fleetingly, sympathetically. "As near as I can tell, they must have sent just a few, programmed cells through every six months or so. These cells found you and me and infected us. We changed into what we are and as they got better, they did not send so much as cells but imperatives." David leaned back in his chair momentarily speechless.

"So we were infected," he said at length. "We are not aliens."

"No. I guess that you are just human with some extra bits." He indicated his head. "Me I don't know about ...there is so much mush up there. Who knows?" He had not hired any scientists to do his thinking on that particular point.

"I -" the words caught in David's throat, "I'm human then."

"I guess - maybe that was how you could kill the Corast." Significantly, Hendy's comment was a simple observation with no anger or other emotion behind it. "Listen - trade. I've made it possible for the doorway to be made. I've told you about it. Now how about some information from you?"

"All right."

"Right so tell me. I know the how it is made, what I don't know is why - what is it for?"

David thought deeply, remembering, letting all of the clues that a worthless lyddrin could pick up fall into place. At length, he said, "It's like I said before, it was just a way back for the Corast. It would be his way home."

"And then?"

"And then nothing. I don't think that he was going to lead any invading armies back through it. He had no interest in this world."

"So why did he come here? I'm not buying any exile story. Everything was too calculated - there's too much power needed - it just does not make sense."

"He came here to find out about weapons. That was all that Robert ever did - research and record weaponry and how to create it from the absolute beginnings."

"That does not make sense either. Wherever he came from they must have had the most unbelievably sophisticated biological technology. It makes no sense that they haven't discovered weapons."

"I was with him for years and I was never worth hiding anything from. I think that the only thing that matters to a Corast is trying to defeat all of the other Corasts. I'm sure that he only came here to steal our weapons technology. It makes sense to me that he was going to take it back and make himself the One Corast. Maybe he would come back after that but I doubt it. We were of no interest to him. There are no Corasts here. Nobody here matters."

The waiter re-appeared with David's meal and Hendy's starter. It provided them both with a fortunate silence to think within.

"So what is this world like?" Hendy asked when they were alone again.

"Corasts and then their mests, their armies probably fighting constantly. What the society was like I don't know. Not like ours I guess and he had no interest at all in the differences. Weapons - that was all that he wanted."

"You had to speak the language though."

"Yes ..." David could sense that Hendy's change of direction was significant but he was unsure as to where it was going. He did not have to wait long.

"You had to know the language. Do you think that he was going to take you back?" A memory surfaced of the few occasions when the Corast had shown interest, even pride towards David and Sullivan and then it was not the wings or what Sullivan could change into but the fact that they could change. They were weapons and their advantage to the Corast lay in their ability to conceal their nature.

"Yes, I think that he would take us back."

"But not me - I never had the language. Do you think that it was his intention to leave me here to act for him on this world. Maybe even just as a kind of escape route?"

"Maybe ... maybe that's right." Hendy did not hear David's hesitation and he was far to unschooled in knowing thoughts to be aware of David's true understanding. Sullivan and he would have been taken if only, as David suspected, because the Corast could have bred some valuable lyddrin out of them. Robert would have gone - he was the true prize but as for Hendy and Liz .... They were tools that the Corast was not prepared to do without on this world but they were not worth taking back with him. After all, they had not spent their whole lives in the Corast's service and some part of them was inferior human. Ecil and culd.

"So that was the plan." Hendy spoke slowly to himself, summarising his discovery. "He came here to find out about our weapons and was going back to wipe out all of his enemies back on his own world. And now we could go back."

"But he is dead."

"But he is dead and there is no mast."

"Mest," David corrected automatically. "We have to make a choice don't we?" Hendy nodded. "That's why we are going to see the others isn't it?" Another slight nod, so brief that Hendy may not have been aware of it himself.

"Now eat your food. I'm going to enjoy this meal and think about what you've said. I don't want to be interrupted." He reached into his jacket and produced a handful of hundred dollar bills. "If it bothers you, you can go and compensate the other diners after you've eaten and then you can teach me some more of the language."

Patiently David accepted Hendy's peace.

CHAPTER 29

The few hours that the train took to reach Cleveland passed relatively quickly. It had been years since David had thought in the speech and he enjoyed trying to teach Hendy the few thousand words that he knew. The concepts behind them he frequently ignored. He had little doubt that Hendy's wish to learn had no good motivation but he had little faith in his ability to do any great harm and leaving him ignorant of the meaning left him as unskilled as if he had no words.

Hendy learned well, even intelligently. Processing information was well within his abilities and had he ever had the need, David was sure, that he could have developed the capacity to draw his own conclusions.

They were approaching the point where David's knowledge was becoming exhausted well before Hendy's capacity to repeat and memorise. On reflection, David did not have anything more than the most basic grasp of the language. Just enough to think in it, just enough not to have to dirty the Corast's cloud of knowing with human words.

They pulled into Cleveland several hours after midnight. "Enough." Hendy commanded a flicker of apology pulling his glance away. "Where are the others now?"

"Sullivan is very close. He lives near to the line just a mile short of the station."

"Good."

David should have anticipated that he would stop the train before the station and that they would have to cross the lines whilst the driver persuaded himself that the signals were red. Thankfully it started off again before any other trains ploughed into it. They could have had another mental battle over it. It could have been a good fight to lose to him.

It was dark and wet in the industrial wasteland near to the line. They soon crossed onto roads near to the heart of the city though there was no sign of other people. Sullivan had chosen knowingly.

They turned a corner coming into sight of the forlorn block where Sullivan lived. Thirty, forty yards and Sullivan appeared at the top of the fire escape. He lowered the bottom section to the ground and waited, watching, still. Neither he nor David had any real telepathic capabilities of their own but they had both lived in the cloud for years and together for a couple of years before that. David had ordinarily visited him every two or three months and each time, when they were close enough, they had known.

It did not even occur to Hendy that he might not go up first. Sullivan met him with a blank expression and a curt nod. His expression, sensed but not shown, was warmer towards David. He took him by the elbow and examined his bruised, cut face with concern. "Come in. I'd better see to that," he said.

Sullivan's apartment had a lived in grubby look. Sullivan, had a lived in grubby look. A solitary cup and bowl lay within reach of the armchair. Everywhere but for his habitual pathways was covered with weeks of accumulated clutter. As he seemed to be every time he had visited, David was struck again with how Sullivan had nothing to live for. He had lived because of the Corast and not for the Corast. His real reason for living had gone when the alien cells had infected him and he had been forced to run away from his wife and daughters for fear of what he was becoming.

The room smelled. To David, it was the smell of Sullivan whom he had lived with for the best part of ten years. He was sure that Sullivan too would recognise David’s personal smell as something uncommonly familiar and welcome it for all of that. To Hendy, however faint, it was the lingering smell of another man's body and he had probably had people commit themselves for less. He stood with an air of offended hesitation whilst Sullivan fetched a wet cloth for David's face. After some consideration he collected the newspapers and magazine from the couch into a pile so that he could sit.

Sullivan deliberately kept his back to Hendy whilst he wiped David's face and applied the wet compress. David instinctively raised his hands and as quickly let them fall. There was always a certain amount of adjustment to be made when he met Sullivan. It was inevitable moving as he did from a priest's isolated world to one where another would unthinkingly grab his face to give it a wash and would expect the same. There was no ego between them, even the concept of self was blurred. David had lost a great deal when he had killed the Corast.

At length, Sullivan sat on a little-used folding chair and faced Hendy. "I'd like to say that it is nice to see you again after all these years but somehow I expect that it's not going to be," he said. "How did you find us?" David could sense the question and the fear behind it. *Who are you working for?* He did not know if Hendy could too, certainly the atmosphere of subliminal knowing was dramatically stronger with the three of them there than when it was just the two of them. Hendy gave a disingenuous smile,

"Our priest, here, was in the telephone book." He did not attempt any further social pleasantries. "I am here because I have completed the Corast's work. I have opened a gateway into the world that the Corast came from." There was probably nobody in the world other than David who would have seen and recognised the look of terror that flicked across Sullivan's face.

"Has anybody come through?"

"No. Nor will they. It's one way. It's for us to pass through into the Corast's world." Sullivan's head turned unconsciously towards David. They looked at each other in mute concentration. Sullivan's arm twitched barely perceptibly beneath his shirt, his eyes narrowed in denial. Hendy had not even noticed but David had. It was the big secret about the big secret. For the past two years Sullivan's ability to change had become increasingly involuntary. The fusion of human cells and whatever else it was had begun to break down. Over the past year David had also found that, at times, he too had to exercise increasing effort in controlling his wings, stopping them from filling.

"You'll be wanting to bring Liz in then."

"That's the general picture," muttered Hendy unknowingly patronising.

"She lives about five miles north of here. I could drive, you'll never get a cab around here at this time of night."

"No. Let flying boy collect her. It's raining and if anybody sees him I'll make them think that it was a crow or something. I want you to stay here so that I can bring you up to speed on what has happened." Sullivan and David exchanged another frank glance. David considered defying the dismissal if only to annoy Hendy. He knew how Sullivan would react. It could as easily be his own mother that he was leaving to defend his interests.

CHAPTER 30

"Head north along the freight lines until you see a large, artificial lake to the West. Cross that and you will come to some very expensive residences," (Homes was altogether too humble a word), "I could give you a name and number but you will not need it."

In all his years of visiting Sullivan he had never known where she had lived nor would he have been welcome. The few drops of rain in the air and the cool of the lake were not enough to touch him, the reunion with Liz was sure to.

Sullivan had been justifiably confident that he would not need an address. There was only one house that was lit up in the dark of that night. He saw her from above waiting outside. She wore a dark, burgundy housecoat her arms folded in the cold and, as Sullivan had before, she waited, still, aware of him. He glided down landing in a half-trot and saw himself through her eyes. Saw the wings fold, the glistening muscles on his spare, uncovered chest.

The communication that he had with Sullivan was like hearing a whisper across a quiet room, near to her it was a megaphone barking in his ear. Perhaps ninety-eight percent of what he had with Sullivan was body language, familiarity and inflexion. There was no true comparison with what she could do. It was not until she felt his shock that she pulled back and the disorientating self-image disappeared. "Hello Liz." he said. She indicated the open, white-lit doorway. He walked in and through a second door into the warmth of a beautifully - expensively - furnished lounge. At her beckoning, he fell into a couch. The first after-flight shakes were beginning, a few minutes recovery time would have been very welcome. He began to let the blood flow out of his wings.

"No keep them up," she said. That always freaked me out, she thought unguardedly.

"OK" He took his first real look at her. As a young woman she had been very pretty, it was no longer an appropriate description. She had grown into her looks. Now she was beautiful. "Damned fine house, Liz," he said hurriedly knowing better than to leave thoughts like that floating around on the surface of consciousness. "It has been a long time. Thanks for not shooting me straight off. I appreciate the stay of execution."

Why should I? She asked / thought.

"Because of the Corast - remember. It was not an insignificant event."

"That's gone. He deserved to die," she said completely stopping his flow of self-protective trivia. When David had killed the Corast, Sullivan had not known what to do except to hit out. It was she who had wanted to kill him. Far more than Hendy had wanted to earlier that night. Before he had time to adjust to her shocking reversal she continued, "What do you want with me now?" and, not waiting, she dived into his mind. Twenty seconds later she was out again contemplating the knowledge that she now shared with him.

"God - damn it!" he cursed despite himself. "Don't do that! Don't you ever bloody ask or knock or something?"

"No, I don't suppose that I do." she muttered far more interested in her discovery than in his offended sensibilities.

"That's my bloody head. My thoughts. I don't want you swan-diving in there and ripping out all of my innermost fantasies. All of that stuff about nurses and whipped cream is private."

"There wasn't - " he had her attention again. Waves of confusion, annoyance flowed over him. He could not, momentarily, recall how many years it was since they had been in the cloud together but he was immediately back into skimming distracting annoyances across to her. Throwing the stuff of male sexual fantasies at her might well give her reason to back off but it had not been right. There were alternatives.

"Liz -"

"What?"

"Could you just - " he consciously sent the image of his hand flicking from his forehead towards her, " could you just lay off a bit? I'm finding it a bit overpowering after all these years." There was an abrupt, mental quiet. A woman faced him across the room. He could not tell whether she was offended or not.

"All right," she said at length, "I'm not used to it either. I seem able to ..," hesitation, the word 'touch' passed between them before she decided that, despite the intimacy of it, it was correct, " touch you more than I can the humans."

"We're humans too," he added forgetting that she had reached in and taken the facts of it already.

"I know, I know from the Corast. You'll find that it's not that much of a consolation."

"Well ..." he felt the need to tell her what had happened but stopped himself. "So what do you want to do?"

She stared at him, through him and looked around at the beautiful home that she had created. "So what's with you being a priest?"

"I'm not," he muttered somewhat bemused, "I just fooled a number of people that I was - including myself." Slowly, an understanding of her sudden changes of direction began to unfold in his mind. "Strange as it might seem I felt that I was called to do something good for others." She was not confident that he could not read her just as she could read him. Therefore she was throwing out these trivial words in the hope that he would not sense the truly important decisions that she was contemplating. Almost by way of confirmation she stood and said,

"I don't think that this is anything that any of us can walk away from." There was no need to explain what it was. "We'll meet with the others and take it from there. I'm going to pack some stuff." She swept her hand towards the staircase. "You can come up too." And, mentally, she opened a door or two letting David become aware of the presence above.

Initially, he thought that it was a child a presumption that remained until she switched on a low wattage light in their bedroom. A dishevelled sheet could barely conceal the perfectly muscled back and the perfectly - he had to use the word – chiselled features. "Who is he?" David whispered.

"You don't have to be quiet, he won't wake." She began to throw clothes into a suitcase, throw being the appropriate word. "He is my husband. Mr Liz Hastings - and I choose my words carefully."

"Well done Liz," he commented passing over her meaning entirely, "it looks like you were the only one of us who got yourself a life." She immediately stopped packing and stared at him, hands on hips.

"No it was not 'well done'. That's the whole point. He used to be somebody, he was a person until I decided that I'd have him for myself." She shook her head. "It was easily done, a little push here a suggestion there. In sex, I'd like you to do just this just now." She did not notice David's cheeks redden. "Little by little, I ate him up and there's nothing to him now. I'd wake him up for you but there's no point I can tell you now what I'd make him say." She sat heavily on the edge of the bed and stroked the sleeping man's shoulders. Her hair fell across her eyes. "What's your advice Pastor Armitage?"

"Father Armitage - advice on what?"

"On him. ... This is something that it's best to walk away from isn't it?" Their eyes met and held, David considered the question knowing what her feelings were, knowing what she wanted him to say because it was the right thing to do.

"You said it." She kicked the suitcase shut.

"I'm not taking that. You can fly me over."

"I don't know that -"

"You'll manage." She pulled several items of clothing out of her drawers and wardrobes and disappeared into the neighbouring room.

Whilst she was out David settled back and contemplated the sleeping man. Being so near to her in her current emotional state still partially unguarded from years of solitude it was relatively easy to pick up her thoughts and feelings about the essence of the man that she had chosen to love. When she returned newly clothed into the bedroom David knew with some confidence, respect and a great deal of satisfaction that whilst her husband looked nothing like him, inside there was, or had been, something that made him in his essential being very much like James Arthur. "Would you wait downstairs while I say goodbye?" Obligingly he rose and left. It hit him halfway down the stairs. David was not listening; it was simply the most powerful communication that she had ever sent. I love you. I am sorry. I am going. You are free. The kiss that followed was even more powerful. It must have stirred even the immediate neighbours in their sleep. Pleasant dreams.

David had no recollection of completing his descent nor of sitting again. His consciousness did not seem to kick back into action until she appeared before him pulling on a leather coat. She began to fill her pockets with credit cards and the other contents of her bag. "Is that all that you are taking?" David asked, she nodded then deliberately placed her wedding ring onto the table. She began to pull on a pair of leather trousers. "Were there any children?"

"No - its not that I can't. I just didn't want to risk passing on my -" Curse? Abomination? She thought struggling to dress the ideas up with less clumsy words.

"Sod that..." His years in the seminary and his own carefully formed opinions kicked his mouth into gear. "Would you not have a child if you were disabled? Or if you were deaf? There's a very good argument for deaf parents choosing for their children to be deaf. You can't think like that - what makes you different is what makes you who you are. God made us all different because he loves variety." He was stopped by the stillness of her expression rather than any mental sending.

"An evil little dwarf made me different not God."

"Well - we are the sum of our experiences and of the people that God created us to be."

"Do you believe all of this crap?"

"I believe that you should have had children." Her tears were a surprise. Her expression did not change and her mind retained its impassive impenetrability but then the real Liz Hastings was somewhere well back of there. "Sorry."

"For what?" He was not sure how to express himself but a long buried instinct re-asserted itself and his flimsy mental barriers dropped inviting her in. The image of a puppy baring its throat floated unwelcomely to the front of his consciousness. He did not have to think back very far to find an alternative answer.

"I'm sorry about throwing male sexuality at you. Not fair that." Her smile was even more unexpected. The image that followed was like a blow to the throat. He saw / sensed her next to him the clothes slipping from her. The smell of her, the curve of her breasts and stomach, the darkness. His reaction was immediate and instinctive. "Christ no!" He jumped back mentally if not physically and she was back, out of his mind, calm, impassive. "I'm sorry - it's nothing personal. It's just that when you have spent so long, so close to somebody - - it's like - it would be like having sex with your sister. It's not that you are unattractive - no you are really beautiful - quite the- " She smiled flicking him into silence with a gesture of her hand.

"I don't need you to define how I feel about myself. There's not a day that I live through when I don't see every sick fantasy that men have about me."

"So what are we doing here?" David asked, bemused. "Fighting?"

"No," she shrugged. "I was just looking. I've had a relationship with a man and it hasn't worked for years. Part of me was thinking that maybe I could find what I want with somebody who really knows what I am." He did not want to ask the question, he was afraid to ask the question but he had to ask.

"Were you being serious?" To their mutual relief, she smiled.

"With you? No." Smiling again, she sent him the memory of his feet carrying him unbidden across the hall floor back to Terri. "You haven't the good sense to be afraid." As gently as she could, she was reminding him of their fundamental incompatibility. She was somebody who needed walls. He was somebody who needed to jump off cliffs.

"There is that." She moved towards the door.

"Come on."

"Where to?"

"Fly me to the city."

CHAPTER 31

It needed two goes before he could pick her up. David would not like to say which of them had ducked out the first time. He had carried Sullivan on a few occasions and had never managed more than a minute or so. The journey back to Sullivan's would be perhaps nine real-time minutes. Sullivan massed significantly more than her, the question was as to whether he weighed eight minutes more.

The second time he rose almost vertically above her then spread his wings and making no effort to beat them he began a long, downward loop. Time had slowed as always when he flew but at the instant that he caught her there was a sickening, uncontrolled flurry of movement before he rose sharply again hastily regaining lost height and velocity. By the time that he had acquired comfort in both she was all over and in him. He was inordinately aware of her body in his arms of the familiar, but exhilaratingly new to her, feel of the wind and the cold. He was not simply aware of her feelings, so close, touching and in unguarded moments he felt what she felt. Her excitement, her fear, her joy.

Through two sets of eyes he saw the light lines into the city, the treetops and the darkened silver of the lake. She breathed in then the double vision left him as she twisted panicking him until he felt her arms reach around his shoulders and her face rose up centimetres from his. “I understand now.” Her words were almost carried away. I know why you live, she thought at him. All those years of being nothing, of being lydrrin, and yet you had this. You had reason to live. I understand your madness now - there is nothing as real as this. I understand how you could kill him – he couldn’t own you. He could feel her breath in his face, her warm, moist breath. It was not there – the wind whipped it away but she wanted him to feel it. Her legs took a new grip around his pulling them even closer. She wanted him again but the initial thrill of her sensuality was dangerously like Hendy's. She wanted him and there was no consultation about it but, David thought, why not? Her self-interested sexuality was not fundamentally in the way of a good screw. After all she was the only woman that he could ever have. She smiled, he smiled. She tugged at his lower lip with her teeth. He shook his head away and looked beyond her to where he could now see the dim line of the freight tracks. All these things the little head tells the big head to do. It was not just her, he wanted it too but the fact that she was urging him from inside was the biggest no that there could be. She twisted again looking away.

They had been up for some minutes by then and he became dimly aware of his own warmth. Heat far greater than that produced by his normal flight exertions. He was burning up but his mind had been closed to the pain of it. Land on the train, she thought. Her mind pointed him further along the line to where a slow, empty freight train stretched out before them. He took a cushioned dive adjusting easily to the time-slowed rear carriage. Her suggestion was not timed coincidentally, she had not wanted him to think the thought that he had been heading towards: that much more of her air-borne pleasure would have killed him. It was a failed attempt, however, some things just crept in as knowledge. David put her down and braced himself in the corner waiting for the inevitable after-effects. She let his body do what it had to but kept his mind clear of the pain. He appreciated but knew that her disapproval of his judging was more responsible for the kindness than empathy.

"You're not walking a straight path," gasped David, his lungs objecting to the unnecessary effort. She kept her face and shoulders still but shrugged.

"I know but I'm walking my way you're walking yours."

No – he pushed out. It was easier to think than to talk and she was willing to just read his surface thoughts. If I am not responsible for you then nobody is. We are responsible to each other.

"Maybe."

What's the problem is it a lydrrin thing?

"No – don't pull that you're the one judging from an elevated position."

I just fly up there don't I?

"Yes, so cut it out. I've tried to live a good life since you did it."

Even with the husband? David knew almost as he asked, that she had had good intentions. She turned away moving warily to the front of the juddering carriage. There was not long to go now. He moved forward equally cautiously until he was next to her. "Liz."

"What?" She did not look at him.

"There's something I need to know. I want to believe that you are trying to live right but there's something that bothers me. I think that we should clear this before we reach the others.

"Go ahead," head bowed.

"Your parents – I sent messages to you through Sullivan. How come you never contacted them." Her head dropped until she could feel the cold metal of the carriage's front on her forehead.

"I am a monster." She said looking him full in the face. It was a human touch unnecessary within the cloud but it went back further than they did, further than the cloud. At length, finding no condemnation, she looked away and continued. "No - being normal was too precious I couldn't go there being what I am. I couldn't let this monster into my childhood." He placed his hand on the back of her head, she almost inclined her head towards him before catching herself. It seemed perfectly plausible but he was not convinced or at least that was what he found in the touch.

She looked away, closed to him. The flickering lights of the street silhouetted her face and David began to understand how alone she was. She dared not return to her parents for fear of truly knowing them and of finding them to be the same flawed people whose unwelcome thoughts she read every day. The man that she had taken for her husband must have been a prince of noble thinkers and yet she had been forced to deny him all independent thought. She could not let herself be truly loved because those who love us sometimes hate us as strongly as they love us and nobody sees us as we see ourselves. It had to be even worse for Hendy who could never be sure of what others where thinking. Hendy could make others be in love with him but never make them love him. To be open to another person was to truly risk letting them get under our skin which, with their powers, neither ego or self-respect could survive. "Shut it down," she muttered, "I don't want to hear it. Don't judge me."

"Absolutely, no right at all. On the other hand..." She turned to face him, it took no intelligence at all to sense the danger that he was now facing. Nevertheless. "I've met your parents, Liz. They are good people."

"I said drop it, lydrrin. I couldn't do it."

"No – I understand that but why is easing your pain more important than easing theirs?" It was not her area of expertise but she was marshalling a life-ending burn for him.

"Don't preach at me," she spoke when he expected pain. "I'm going to spell this out clearly for you. I am an adult woman. I have chosen my life, I have made my decisions. I might not like myself for some of it but it is my choice and you do not choose for me." Agreed, David sent.

"It's your choice and your life – that's why it took you all of a minute to walk away from it." Her eyes narrowed, she was closed again and he expected to be on the floor with blood pouring from every orifice. "I know that I've no right to judge you but why not? I know you – for the record, I happen to think that you are a beautiful person who got screwed. So did we all. I know you through and through – I know how good you are. Everybody that I've ever truly known – my family, you, Sullivan – I've loved. It's in the nature of the human beast, Liz, he is magnificent." Again, she stared back at him, seemingly coldly but he sensed at an intuitive level that the danger had passed.

"There is a flaw in your argument – you lived with the Corast but you did not love him."

"Nope," David shrugged, "I couldn't take to the evil little dwarf as my actions subsequently proved but he wasn't human anyway." She looked forward again and shivered in the wind buffeting the train. I never could get your logic, she thought at him. You love people for their human failings, you love flying despite the risk, despite the pain and the sheer madness of it. You've got no life. You're lydrrin. You're a bloody dirty freak. "Oh yes, life is just grand." Well don't expect anything from me, she retorted. You will not judge me, you will not control me and you might say you love me but you'll have nothing physical from me. "Absolutely. One hundred percent. Believe me, when you've hit thirty as a virgin and with a pair of wings sprouting out the back you have genuinely accepted that some doors are closed."

"You don't love me," she spoke out loud, "you've just known me for a long time."

"There's a difference?" Cold, damp and rattling they neared their journey's end.

It took her two attempts to urge the driver to stop. It was dark, she could neither see nor touch him and it was not her talent but they both knew how upset she must have been. She let him recover on the bank next to the rail tracks. They did not speak then nor as they walked on and ascended the fire escape. David had wanted to say again that he could respect her, that he knew the sweet, violated, woman that she had been and that he understood that her hostility was just a wall that she needed to protect herself with. He could have said it but did not, the words would have just filled space in and, besides, some things just crept in at the level of knowledge.

Hendy still sat in the room as if he was reluctant to touch the chair. Liz had cleared a pile of twine-bound papers onto the floor and had occupied the bench that they had rested upon. Sullivan closed the door behind David and moved, slowly to stand beside him. Both lydrinn waited cautiously sensing that the dam was about to collapse. "Long time..." said Hendy. David found it difficult but not impossible to believe that Hendy could not feel the tension. He had to feel it, why else would the words catch in his throat? After perhaps a minute of strained, unnerving silence. Liz leant backwards.

"All right," she said, "I've heard the words. Now let's hear the truth of it." And triggered the cloud. In an instant of sickening recollection she dived into their minds. Sullivan and David immediately, automatically, tried to hide in an awareness of self, to stream out each other's thoughts and in the moment or so that they needed to re-adjust both realised that she had scarcely touched them. She had gone for Hendy and he had been completely taken.

"God almighty!" he screamed then he fired back at her with a massive, blunt thrust of anger and compulsion. She deflected it. Both Sullivan and David turned to watch it as, seemingly it hit the wall between them. It had no direction or substance of course and there was no hole in the wall as they had both unconsciously expected. They looked from the wall to each other, David laughed out loud at the silliness of it all. Grinning, both turned their attention back to the conflict. Visual images could do nothing to describe what was invisible and without substance yet still the two lydrinn mentally grasped at images to picture what they could feel was happening in the room. Hendy had changed his attack to sharp, spiked compulsions which tried to dive around her deflections. He was having no success at all.

"This is great," muttered Sullivan after a minute, tired of the perceived dangers of deflections. Hendy's attack stopped instantly. There was utter peace. Liz had not even bothered to send anything back at him.

"You're not allowed," finished Hendy, lamely. "You keep out of my head." He looked about in the awful silence. There was no feeling of embarrassment that could be hidden in the cloud. David and Sullivan settled companionably onto the sofa. "Look. Let's just respect each other's heads. OK?"

"OK." Agreed Liz and she withdrew though David doubted that she could ever withdraw to the point where they could not know each others stronger and more focussed thoughts. "OK." She repeated. "We know where it is, we know what its for the only question is what to do with the Corast's gateway."

David sensed Hendy's resistance growing, his need to regain control and, as had happened before in the cloud when Sullivan felt the same, Sullivan spoke David's words before David could. "Don't go trying anything Mr Green suit. You won't leave this room alive if you try to force it." Hendy met his gaze.

"Pushy scum."

No, this from Liz, but calm. No games.

"Fair enough," said David, knowing that Sullivan agreed. "You two must have had a pleasant time while I went to fetch juyti."

"No games so then we go for reason." Sullivan continued. "You don't try to force us because we all know that you were playing us for saps. We all know that you were telling yourself that you wanted us to go through the gateway while you stay here in the expectation of using us to pick up some sort of Corast technology which would make you Lord and master of all the earth. But that was just a room full of crap that you told yourself because you know that a compliant woman and a compliant chef are all that you really need to be Lord and Master. Messing with a Corast is the only damned way to risk your not being Lord and master of this damned world.

"So you try to use us because you are fooling yourself into not believing that you've got some screwed up God complex and need a Corast to tell you what to do. The proof of which is here in this room because you came back for us because now you want us to make your decisions for you." David felt the need to broadcast the sound of a grandfather clock ticking away to emphasise the silence and the fact that Hendy could not put up an argument.

"Jesus," muttered Hendy, "I thought that she was the dangerous one." Sometimes, thought David, I could almost like him.

"OK," said the juyti, "this is the plan. I think that we should all go and take a look at it then we make our minds up and whilst we are going we keep out of each other's heads."

"What's this a democracy thing?" asked Sullivan.

As near as you are going to get. We go, we see, we decide.

They sat for several, respectfully quiet moments whilst Sullivan gathered a bag together and David deflated then dressed. David was ready by the time that Sullivan returned from his bedroom. The three of them rose, ready to leave. "No." snarled Sullivan dropping the bag and sitting again.

"What?" asked the juyti.

"We're not going."

"Why not?"

"Because – do we do this respecting each other's heads thing or not?"

"I'm staying out. You know that."

"Not you – him." He pointed at David. Hendy and Liz followed his finger with surprise.

"He's not in anybody's head. He can't." Persisted the woman. Sullivan folded his arms across his chest.

"You still know nada about anything." Smiling, unresisting David sat again. Reluctantly the other two followed suit. "Just ask yourself what we are doing here. Why should we go there? – Hendy, what have you to gain? Nothing and you could lose everything. Liz? Where are you going? You're on the fast track to subservience. Do you really want that? Why should you want to go there? And yet here we are, all going to take a look-see. And why? Because you two swell-headed bastards dived into his head and found a little bomb waiting there and because it was what he believed you took it as gospel and swallowed it whole."

"I don't go for bible consumption," Hendy muttered. "Continue. What little bomb was this?"

"Hope. He wanted you to think that this gateway could be the solution to all of our problems and you both took it." There was perhaps a minute of silent comprehension in which they all turned to look at the gently smiling accused.

"He's right, isn't he?" asked Liz and the fact that she chose to speak was pleasingly considerate.

"Probably," said David. "All though I guess it was unconscious – I wasn't really aware that I had done that." He spread his arms wide. "My apologies. You three decide for yourself." He swallowed then acknowledged yet another subconscious decision. "I want to go through it but you three do what you will." Another silence, another pleasing absence of pain.

"I still want to see," conceded Liz. "My decision – I want to go. Sullivan?"

"Oh yes. I know that I have it in me to kill a corast."

"Hendy?" He shrugged.

"Let's go and see – on the way I'll figure out to what extent these two no-account powerless lydrrin have been playing me for a sap." There was a fair degree of annoyance in his words, but cold. He respected heads.

Epilogue

Afterward

CHAPTER 32

Lieutenant Sami Jowett had a rare, empty shift and a lottery routine that was going to net her a fortune. The evening security monitoring shift at USAF base 1842 normally allowed her the time and the opportunity to test out his system using low-time computer memory. None of her routines had produced any results that were out of the ordinary but this one might just be the one. She hoped not. Even if she won she did not seriously want to give up her position. She had worked very dutifully and very hard to achieve her rank and her, apparently, do-nothing job on an isolated, desert base. The lottery routine was more for the intellectual exercise that it involved.

It was something of a relief then, when she noticed the four by four approaching the out perimeter post. She adjusted the cameras whilst half listening to the exchange between the point, Frister, and the vehicle's occupants. There were four people inside: a woman and three men. She had excellent CCTV frames of them when they were unexpectedly passed through and drove on to the inner perimeter post. Jowett thumbed the communication button to Frister. "Frister – Security monitoring here. You have a negative swipe on three of the occupants. Please confirm pass details."

There was a momentary pause during which Jowett watched the vehicle accelerating out of the bend towards post two.

"Frister here, pass details are confirmed. Four occupants Colonel D.M. Hendy and three authorised civilian aides A. Schmidt, B. Tanner and C. Devlin. I confirm that authorisation pass details are correct at my terminal."

"I'm sorry Frister. I still have no confirm on the other three. Please check your net connections I am doing so at this end." Two mouse clicking minutes later and the connections were fine at Jowett's end. The vehicle had reached point two, its occupants climbed out and point two began their security checks.

"Frister here, possible net connection problem here. I am investigating. Frister out." Something about the names had begun to gnaw at the back of Jowett's mind.

"Security Monitoring here, Rossman," she said to the inner point two guard on a closed connection, "please confirm your details from perimeter one." The first man had passed through the security cubicle without triggering any alarms, the woman followed.

"Rossman here, security, I only have one confirmed swipe from perimeter one."

"Confirmed Rossman please check your net connections to central and to perimeter one."

"Acknowledged." The woman was through and the second man had entered. Jowett accessed the Perimeter One camera recall systems. It was probably nothing but she had just realised that Frister had a daughter called Devlin. The second man was through by the time that she had found what he was looking for and had doubtfully replayed it three times.

"Rossman – make sure you get nice clean swipes off them. – Frister?" Another pause as if Frister had been scrabbling about under his console.

"Frister here."

"Frister, I have no footage of four swipes. Only one passcard was swiped through your system."

"Negative central all four cards were swiped. I have confirmation on my system and there's just no way that I would have let them pass." Jowett clicked Perimeter One out of hearing. "Rossman, did you hear that?"

"Acknowledged." The four were being led towards point two by three armed guards whilst their vehicle was being driven away for further security scans. "Net connections to central and perimeter one check out 100%"

"Good." He began to type furiously calling out Platoon One to Point Two on "active silent" alert.

The four passed into and rapidly through Point Two. "Rossman – what the fuck is going on? You have only one confirmed swipe."

"Negative central, all four swipes check out."

"Check your god-damned system – confirm immediately." Sh watched with an impending sense of powerlessness as the four and their obliging guard headed towards the inner base and their inevitable interception by Platoon One. "MF2," - she sent to the platoon leader which meant in plain terms: safeties off and bullets in the breech. "Rossman confirm details."

"Rossman acknowledging."

"Do your systems show what my systems show – only one swipe confirmed?"

"Security details are fine all four check out."

"What is this? What does Maxwell say?"

"Maxwell confirms everything fine. They are absolutely OK." Jowett had Rossman's screen and the single swipe before him now.

"Rossman – I want some immediate security protocols now."

"Everything is just fine." Jowett could hear Rossman humming distractedly to himself. He threw the picture of Point Two up on to the large screen. Both Rossman and Maxwell gave every appearance of having nothing whatsoever to distract them. Maxwell was filling in some T31s whilst Rossman played idly with an elastic band.

"Rossman – are you going to do anything?"

"No." Jowett could see the blankness of his expression a metre and a half wide before him. "Nothing to do, everything's fine." On the smaller screen Platoon One had intercepted them. Jowett watched fascinated, waiting for explosions or gunfire.

"Rossman....." They were beyond any microphone but he could see them and what was rapidly developing into an apparently inconsequential conversation. "What were the names please?"

"Rossman here the names were D.M. Hendy and his army liaison aides Starsky, Hutch and Goofy."

"Starsky, Hutch and Goofy?"

"Acknowledged." On the main screen Rossman had now taken out a tub of paper clips and was sorting them by size. Jowett placed the image of the four strangers and the platoon on to the main screen. She watched disbelievingly as the platoon and the armed guard marched away leaving the four to enter the main building. Jowett could feel herself redden with embarrassment as the sweat, damp and cold, clung to her body. It was happening on her shift. A moment's indecision gave way to frantic action as she keyed a message out to Base 1841 – although there was every chance that the four had been through their and that they too were busy sorting paper clips. She also summoned the base commander and his personal back-up neither of whom were likely to appear for at least ten minutes, and triggered orange alert. The four had entered the main building past another compliant guard. Jowett hit the seals trapping them in the outer defences. At least the mechanical defences had worked and, if they were to be believed, the four were not carrying anything dangerous. Jowett thumbed another button, "Onslow confirm that your detachment is heading for the outer defences."

"Onslow here, my detachment will be there in seconds. Please describe situation, Central."

"I will do but first make sure that there is no communication at all between you and the four intruders."

"Onslow here. We have reached the outer defences they appear to be secure and if they want to try some Morse code through six inches of sealed steel I shall ignore them as per your request." She pushed her chair back thanking God for steady, stoical Onslow and an end to the nonsense. All that she had to do now was to fill in her back-up when he arrived and hope that it had all been worth interrupting the base commander's meal for.

The sirens abruptly died. Hands shaking with fear, Jowett replayed the previous few seconds on the outer defence's cameras. She saw Onslow releasing the seal, the four emerging and Onslow clearing all of the defences. The strangers were now only a few minutes uninterrupted walk from Pandora's Box and Onslow had a higher security clearance than Jowett. There was no way that she could trap or kill them mechanically from Security Central. Onslow was in with them, everybody was - apart from her. She could wait for back-up and the commander but the four would have reached Pandora's box before then and there was no guarantee that the other two officers would not simply turn on her too. Pausing only to open a few other controls, Jowett headed out of Security Control.

Jowett's first stop was at an arms locker, she threw a bandoleer of grenades over her shoulder, and grabbed a semi-automatic rifle and two clips to go with her regulation pistol. If she ran, she would just reach them before they reached the box.

Two doors, running, hardly even breathing hard and she burst into the inner foyer which led off to Pandora's Box. There was no sign of the four but Onslow and two of his detachment were spaced evenly around the far doors. They held their weapons casually, ready. Jowett dived for the safety of the main pillar which was three metres further into the room. She flattened against it at the same instant that their bullets splattered on the wall behind her. Jowett knew that if they were going to outflank her, she was done for. If they held their position she had a chance. Training took over – she would have to take the initiative before they did. There was no advantage in shooting it out with them – the grenade, almost unconsciously, was in her hand. She pulled the pin.

It was then that it struck her that she had never knowingly killed another human being. There had been the time undercover, in the South when she had fired with intent but she had never known the outcome. These were fellow Americans – more – workmates. Onslow was a friend. Jowett could not believe that he was a traitor...there had to be something at work here. She could call out – delay the inevitable. She threw the grenade short giving them time and space to dive.

The detonation hardly seemed to be in the same room as far as the noise went. The smell and the air-borne debris, however, were instantly upon her as she rose and headed for the inner door. There was no sign of the others or of blood. Something moved near to the outer doors, she fired high and ducked into the inner door. Manually, she shut the door behind her. The far door, the one leading into Pandora's Box was also closed. She raced down to the access box whose door was hanging open. If she was lucky Onslow's men would be expecting her to have rigged the first door with a grenade, if she was lucky they would be alive enough to think. The inner door had a failsafe. She could open it and more. Excitedly she looked over the other options. Jowett had no idea as to what was within the room. For virtually every member of the base staff it was on a strict, "You don't want to know basis." The specifications for the intelligent particulate were, happily, at her fingertips when he needed them. She could send everybody within the room to sleep. The confirm button flashed, she pressed it and turned covering the far door.

One minute – two. By the third minute it struck her with a leaden, nauseating certainty that the detachment through the door would be patrolling unaware of her presence and if not patrolling then at least filing paper clips. Either that or dead.

Three – four – five. She released the seal and pushed the door through. Part of her wanted them to be still conscious, for them to attack him even to kill hEr. Anything, in that moment, rather than to have to face what she had done. No bullets, no noise. She slammed the access box door too, scrambling it and waved her hand in the doorway. Nothing. She stood in the doorway, then walked into "Pandora's Box" and pushed the door too. It had a simple release lock from the inside.

Colonel Hendy lay on the floor near to a control panel, his swipe card still in its slot. Apart from the panel and a camera aimed at the dimpled grey wall opposite there was nothing within the room that Jowett could see to justify its security rating. No sign whatsoever of the nuclear research that she had always assumed. The woman lay curled in a foetal position within a nest of clothing. The second man twitched on the floor, Jowett looked then jumped back in unconscious terror. The man's face and arm were not just moving but changing uncontrollably. After a few seconds, she relaxed her aim lowering the point of his rifle when it became apparent that the man was as unconscious as the other two. Cautiously, she moved over to Hendy then pulled him towards the door wall. Straightening up she aimed at the second man. When they began to revive, Jowett thought, she would probably have to shoot the other two before they brought to bear whatever it was that they had used outside – she did not believe that a simple hostage situation would have gotten them all the way through. He looked again at the man's arm watched it stretching and transforming. Unbidden, acid rose to the back of her mouth. It was not human, for that reason alone Jowett was ready to kill it in the instant. Her arms tensed ready to fire. There were three bodies when there should have been four.

What followed was seemingly too sudden for thought to intervene but, nevertheless, before she pulled the trigger, Jowett cursed herself for being an in-numerate fool and managed to glance upwards as the body fell driving the rifle out of her hands and to the floor. A flurry of black, pink and grey then hands were upon her reaching for her waist. She managed to land a solid cross-elbow to the man's chest which forced them apart and gave her enough reverse momentum to reach the wall. The rifle was kicked away, sliding towards the far wall. Jowett took in the slender bare-chested man, wondered for an instant why, if he was going to wear costume wings, the man should choose grey ones rather than white and then attempted, pointlessly, to back even further into the wall in fright. She had seen the wings moving and reflexively reached for the absent gun in his holster. "Jesus it's alive!" voicing her thoughts to her own sense of, army-trained, embarrassment. The man raised the pistol uncertainly pointing it at her.

Breathe! Thought Jowett, this is just a situation, deal with it. All the while she watched the wings transfixed by how real they looked. It was as if they were part of the man, they moved and reacted as his shoulders might. Then, with a sickening hollowness in her stomach she remembered the twitcher on the floor. The winged man was on one knee checking the pulses of the others. Last of all he checked the woman. "How long will they be out for?" he asked in an unreasonably calm voice.

"Another hour yet." Jowett lied. The man indicated her bandoleer.

"Over there." She nodded towards the rifle Jowett complied, removing it and slinging it on top of the other weapon. Grenades were not yet an option that she wanted to take whilst both her instincts and training urged her to concede the first point of conflict. The winged man placed his hand on the woman's forehead. "How long will they be out for?" he repeated.

"An hour at least." The man shook his head slightly then advanced on Jowett. Suddenly she reached down, grabbing her shin in the gap between her fatigues and boots. "How long will they be out for?" he repeated yet again. Jowett did not answer but made a circular kick connecting with the winged man's forehead. The intruder fell to his left dropping the gun which he immediately kicked towards the far wall rather than let Jowett reclaim it.

Jowett stood hands ready, feet braced. If it was a race to the far wall then she had the clear advantage. The man stood, blood dribbling from his cut temple. There was something about the way that he moved to stand between Jowett and the weapons that lead Jowett to pause. Jowett was a good judge of movement and of expression but it would have been apparent to anybody that the winged man had no intention of racing him to the weapons. Jowett took another step towards him. There was no reaction at all. His stance was terrible, hands were nowhere ready and his eyes were looking anywhere but where they should be, the man was no fighter. Jowett took another two rapid, balanced steps.

A fraction of a second later and the intruder lay in a crumpled heap to Jowett's right. Three good blows, two of which should have resulted in serious damage but Jowett, sensed that they had not. There was something wrong about how he took a punch; he did not seem to be as heavy as he ought to be. Half turning to cover another attack from the man Jowett retrieved his pistol. The man was still struggling to orientate himself but he was clearly attempting to rise. Jowett strode over, aimed and slipped the safety off. She could read movement, she was pretty good at reading people – the man was beaten. "Open your mouth again and it'll be the last word you ever speak," Jowett barked. Blinking through blood, his captive nodded his agreement.

What to do now? A bullet was the quick end to his difficulties. Three bullets and Colonel Hendy could pick up the pieces when he recovered. Pull his finger a quarter of an inch in and she would have won, she would have protected the base, She would have done her job. Finish this inhuman creature and the other two. Jowett had no real idea what was happening but he could be sure that, whatever in hell they were, a couple of bullets would certainly be doing what was right for Mother America and her fellow man. She wanted to shoot the vomit-inducing freak. It was an adrenaline-fuelled reaction, she knew that, she just wanted to be sure that it was also a justifiable response to the situation.

The winged man stood up. "I'm sorry," he said, "it's nothing personal and I certainly don't dispute that you have control of the situation. It's just that if I am going to die then I don't choose to die cowering in a corner. And if I am going to die then I refuse to die in silence because you have told me to." Jowett corrected his aim and forced herself to breathe. More than when She had seen the transforming man, more than when she had seen the wings for what they were, Jowett was shocked. Wide, open grey eyes held Jowett's brown. Unblinking seconds crept by. The goddamned freak has called my bluff, she thought, I have to kill him now. I can not lose control here. Jowett wished that the pistol had a hammer to cock – something to give him that extra second to take in the fact of his defiance. The man was beaten, the man was dead and yet still he stood up. Eyes, breath held for desperate seconds. He was not even angry, Jowett realised. Yes, some guys would have stood up again – mad as hell – but this was beyond understanding. "Of course, in an ideal world I would prefer you not to shoot me, anyway," he added, calmly, politely. He had a Canadian accent,

Jowett realised, which, to her, seemed to explain a lot. Self-effacing, overly polite bunch of bastards every last one of them.

The woman stirred slightly in her unconscious state.

She had to act soon but what to do? The Canadian was pushing him not in his manner or demeanour but in his actions. She should shoot him but that would mess up the feathers – Christ, in the territories, he'd probably be considered something of a catch. Wings probably were not that rare amongst that bunch of in-breeds. She indicated the wings with a flick of the weapon. "We went down some strange gene-mutated road when we did that to you."

"You didn't do it to me – not the US government," commented the man, the speed of his response leading Jowett to questioning his own assertion. Jowett's eyes widened and she took two steps back renewing her aim and the tension in her grip.

"No." Jowett muttered. "That wasn't my thought – that stuff about wings and in-breeds. I didn't think that – I know how you got past everybody. You've got some sort of autosuggestion thing. I'm right aren't I?" Their eyes met again, held again. A fresh trickle of blood trickled down the man's chin and still he did not answer. "What is it then?"

"I just want to be clear on something here. Either you shoot me or I explain. Either you try to understand or you just follow orders. Maybe its something you don't want to know about because of orders, maybe you are not cleared and could be in danger if I talk to you." A further, drawn out silence. Both knew that Jowett would end it with either words or a bullet. The challenge was from the

Canadian but the decision was hers. Sh was not helped by the inescapable feeling that, in the openness of their look, she had a rare connection, a near-complete understanding of what the man was thinking.

"Those are options A and B," said Jowett, "I'm going to go for option C: you explain to me and then I shoot you." The moment had passed, both knew that the bullet was no longer the immediate choice. "Start with how you got in here – how did you make everybody turn crazy?"

"It's an auto-suggestion sort of thing. But look, why don't you lower the gun – we both know that you don't need it to whip me."

"That is correct." She did not lower the pistol an inch.

"Understood. OK – my name is David by the way."

"Fine – now cut the terrorist negotiation tactics and answer the question." Jowett smiled what she hoped was a cold, insincere smile.

"OK. Autosuggestion. We do have something like that." Time to buy a little trust with a little truth. "But not me – if I had it I'd have used it. What I've got is wings – as you might guess."

"No – so who has it?" David did not make to answer but both of their gazes flicked in a moment of mutual understanding to the prone woman. "She has it – so there's not one of you that is normal then." Jowett stepped back to the far wall and allowed herself to slip down against it. She let the pistol drop on to her knee and whilst she told herself that she was simply allowing himself to put the semi-automatic within reach, she knew that the adrenaline was deserting her system.

“I am normal,” muttered the winged man, “I’m just a different normal.” The soldier ignored her.

“I knew it – when she moved she was not far off coming around. That’s when I started to think wrong. So when she comes to – she’ll make me think what she wants me to. So – I’ll need to shoot her before she comes to fully. It's not an hour it's just a few minutes of unconsciousness. I lied about that."

“A long time before that’s necessary.” Then denying the lie that they were both clinging to, he walked forward and crouched between Jowett and the woman. “Come the hour, of course, I can’t let you do that. You’ll have to come through me to get to her.” It was at that moment that Jowett truly lost the will to kill them. She was unsure as to what the correct thing to do was but she was certain that the winged man was, in sacrificing himself, doing something that had to be right.

“No problem – I’ll make it quick for you.” Jowett might still kill them – no discipline, no army – but she would regret it. “What is going on here then?”

“Nothing that is a threat. We’ve every right to be here. This is Hendy’s project and he brought us here.”

“You didn’t kidnap him?”

“No – it’s his project – you’ve never seen anybody higher up than him here, have you?”

“No,” Jowett admitted, “and of course if you *say* you’re supposed to be here well then it must be all right.” Jowett thought momentarily and came to a decision. “So what is this? What is Pandora’s Box? Is it something to do with gene manipulation?”

David shrugged and indicated the wall that Jowett was leaning against.

"No. It's a gateway to somewhere else. Hendy was one key press away from showing us. If you will let me, I can show you."

"Don't press anything."

"Why not? If I was going to hurt you I would have shot you before when I had the gun." Jowett became uncomfortably aware of what it meant for her to be holding an unused gun.

"Wait," he picked up and carried the weapons as he moved to the opposite wall. "Go on then." David rose, pressed a single key on the control pad by Hendy and then interposed himself between the soldier and his companions. The far wall began to flicker and then to, apparently, melt and transform. In time it grew lighter and clearer. After a time both of them relaxed. Jowett carefully put the safety on the pistol back on despite having no wish to do so. Without looking, she knew that the unconscious woman had now woken and was staring at her. "That is one hell of a screen."

"It's not a screen. It's real."

"I'm telling you that there is nothing but solid rock behind that wall."

"Like I said, it's a gateway to somewhere else."

"Where to? California? China? The Sun is too high there for it to be here. Where is it?"

"It's somewhere else. – It's where we came from and it's where we are going to. We mean no harm to anybody here – we just came here to go home."

"I'll bet your wings that it's just a projection." Jowett muttered aware of the implications in her choice of words for its probability. Carefully, she placed the pistol in his holster. "It's just as well that you mean no harm to anybody – take it from a professional – you haven't got the moves for it. .... Can you really fly?"

"Yes"

"Is that how you got up there above the spray?" David nodded. Jowett slouched against the wall. "She's awake isn't she? That's why the gun's gone - that's why I'm thinking so sleepy and peaceable." The winged man inclined his head slightly. "Eh, Canadian?"

"What?"

"I might not have shot you, anyway." Dull-eyed she watched the woman as she turned on to her side. She coughed lightly and crawled over to them. Hazel eyes held the marble of the winged man. She cupped his chin and kissed the unbloodied side of his face softly, warmly.

"Thanks," she murmured, "she meant to kill us. You've saved our lives – again." She brushed his forehead and the ghost of a smile touched her lips. "Why you take such risks is beyond me – but I'm grateful." She crawled towards the soldier her body slowly becoming freer.

"Are the others all right?" asked David. She nodded.

"They'll be around soon, they must have breathed in more." She touched Jowett's unresisting up-turned face. "I want you to understand." A few moments passed thus with both touching each other's minds. She stopped and turned stiffly towards the winged man. "She's a good one," she stated.

"I know, she nearly killed us all."

"No – I meant that she is a good human – but even the best of them are scared of us. You are very, very lucky that she was strong enough to stop herself from killing." She pushed herself into a more upright position and looked across to the other world. The two other men began to splutter and wake. "Is that where we will go?" The Canadian gave a nod, a nod that she did not see but knew. A drop of congealing blood fell from his forehead to her knee. "Maybe we should go – they've no love for us here. We have to face ourselves to love ourselves."

"And it's important that we love ourselves if we want to be happy?" Surprised hazel eyes turned to him again. "That's a crock of psycho-babble. Come on Liz – think about people who love themselves. What are they? Arrogant. Conceited. Self-centred – these are not good qualities. You should be content with yourself – that's different. That's just a case of learning to play the cards that you've been dealt. We should play the cards and be thankful for being alive."

"I told you not to preach at me." She lowered her voice as the other two began to stand.

"But Liz, I spent seven years training. I've got the bit of paper." The woman reached without looking to touch Jowett. The soldier, who had listened with increasing awareness, smiled heavy-lidded and slipped into unconsciousness. The woman stood and unexpectedly embraced the Canadian. Her fingers drifted through his feathers. “I’m glad that she didn’t kill you.” A hint of a smile touched her lips. “Honestly David, it would be like losing not so much a part of me, more a favoured pet.” She turned to face the other two.

“Tell us what happened,” growled Hendy. Obligingly, Liz replayed David’s most recent memories.

“Bloody lucky,” commented Sullivan. He swept his hand across the bright scene which somehow still failed to illuminate the room that they were in. “Time to decide children. Hendy – empty your pocket.” Hendy nodded and pulled out a small, dark cylinder. He thumbed a switch then pulled a strip of metallic material which divided into two. With a flick they formed two sides of a triangular prism one side being a solar panel and the other making a flat screen. A second strip became a touchpad-keyboard.

“There’s everything that you could want to know about how to build this place and ..almost anything else that you might want to know about anything.” Hendy tailed off under Sullivan’s gaze.

“So we go through for you. Set up a trade route and you act as Mr Import-export?”

“Don’t sneer. They must have technology that’s way beyond ours. If we don’t trade and compete they’ll come back here and wipe us out.”

“If their technology is so great, how is it that Robert was taking crossbow technology in?” asked David.

“OK Hendy –that’s good top-of-the-head reasoning.” Sullivan interrupted. You can fool yourself but we know that it’s just your slave mentality kicking in. It's just that you haven't the nerve to go through yourself."

"You believe what you want – my reasons are my concern."

"Not in the cloud they're not," muttered David. "So what's the decision Sullivan?"

"I'm going through," he gnawed on his lower lip and continued with his needlessly spoken justification, "they destroyed my life and I'm going to give some back."

"Revenge is no reason to do it."

"Oh yes," Sullivan arched a disbelieving eyebrow. "What are you going there for?"

"It has to be a wrong society. It has to be changed." Sullivan gave him a slow, critical look.

"Don't go laying that top of the head nonsense on us too." The younger man began to reply, hesitated then continued.

"Out with it then."

"You're a god-damned liar. You want to take that world apart. You say that you killed the Corast because he would have killed maybe millions of others. But that was not why you killed him – that came afterwards. You had an instant to act. If you had thought that thought he would have given you a terminal burn. You killed him by acting on an emotional impulse that was too deep for him to read. You killed him because you wanted to – you'd had enough of him – you were not going to take him commanding you." David raised an objecting finger.

"On the other hand ---," he frowned, "OK – yes that's true but so is the top of the head stuff and I'm not going to kill anybody this time."

"So you are going to destroy a society but you won't dirty your hands by killing an individual."

"Something like that."

"Well, I'm sure that we can find some common ground." He turned and took two steps towards the wall. The winged man stood beside him. "Liz?" Neither of them turned to look at her, neither needed to.

"You are a pair of lydrrin. You've forgotten what they are like. They'll destroy you in an instant."

"If you are offering to come you're very welcome. If you're not – fine, we're going."

"They'll destroy you."

"Maybe," conceded David. "Maybe not. Their thoughts are too narrow. They rely on your sort too much. One of them tried to destroy us – we killed him." She appeared at his side, her arms firmly crossed.

"That's top of the head stuff," she said. He nodded and looked away from the bright horizon.

"Yes but this isn't: we will infect them and we will destroy them."

"How?"

"James Arthur. We're human –"

"We've got some of him in each of us." She finished the sentence for him then took his hand and turned to face the wall. At the touch, his smile set as rapidly as it had risen. I killed him, she thought. Through the closed connection of their touch he could sense her tears, her pain. He was trying to save us and I killed him. Momentarily he did not know what to say, which was for the best. He squeezed her hand.

"He did save us," unconsciously, David spoke out loud, "now we've got to save the others."

"Set the slaves free," the words caught in her throat, "Carry the flag? Make his death meaningful?" She looked at him for the first time, hazel eyes darkening. "It hurts David." The winged man thought then of the child that he had been and the man who had died in his arms. It had been a good death.

"Yes," he agreed quietly, "no reason to stop though."

"James Arthur," Sullivan smiled as he echoed their words. "We finish it then. Goodbye Hendy you spineless nothing. You stay here with your money and your sycophants who'll never have a good feeling for you that you don't make them feel." He did not look away even when Hendy moved to stand beside him.

"You're not forcing me," said Hendy quietly, "You wouldn't have had those things to say if I didn't let you see them." As one they smiled and, remembering James Arthur, they stepped towards the gateway. The lights dimmed and failed across half the state as the gateway flowed out to envelop them.

Printed in Poland
by Amazon Fulfillment
Poland Sp. z o.o., Wrocław